Praise for t...
DO...

"Loaded with subtle emotions, sizzling chemistry, and
s... on the real choices [Grant's]
cl... ake as they choose their loves
fo... —*RT Book Reviews* (4 stars)

"... ils, and enchanting characters
gu... nd [don't] let go."
—*Night Owl Reviews* (Top Pick)

Praise for the Dark Warrior novels

MIDNIGHT'S KISS

5 Stars TOP PICK! "[Grant] blends ancient gods, love,
desire, and evil-doers into a world you will want to
revisit over and over again."   —*Night Owl Reviews*

5 Blue Ribbons! "This story is one you will remember
long after the last page is read. A definite keeper!"
—*Romance Junkies*

4 Stars! "The world of the Immortal Warriors is a thoroughly engaging one, blending powerful ancient gods,
fiery desire, and touchingly human love, which readers
will surely want to revisit."   —*RT Book Reviews*

4 Feathers! "*Midnight's Kiss* is a game changer—one
that will set the rest of the series in motion."
—*Under the Covers*

MIDNIGHT'S CAPTIVE

5 Blue Ribbons! "Packed with originality, imagination, humor, Scotland, Highlanders, magic, surprising plot twists, intrigue, sizzling sensuality, suspense, tender romance, and true love, this story has something for everyone."   —*Romance Junkies*

4 1/2 Stars! "Grant has crafted a chemistry between her wounded alpha and surprisingly capable heroine that will, no doubt, enthrall series fans and newcomers alike."
—*RT Book Reviews*

MIDNIGHT'S WARRIOR

4 Stars! "Super storyteller Grant returns with.... A rich variety of previous protagonists adds a wonderful familiarity to the books"   —*RT Books Reviews*

5 Stars! "Ms. Grant brings together two people who are afraid to fall in love and then ignites sparks between them."   —*Single Title Reviews*

MIDNIGHT'S SEDUCTION

"Sizzling love scenes and engaging characters fill the pages of this fast-paced and immersive novel."
—*Publishers Weekly*

4 Stars! "Grant again proves that she is a stellar writer and a force to be reckoned with." —*RT Book Reviews*

5 Blue Ribbons! "A deliciously sexy, adventuresome paranormal romance that will keep you glued to the pages . . ."   —*Romance Junkies*

MIDNIGHT'S LOVER

NIGHT'S BLAZE

DONNA GRANT

St. Martin's Paperbacks

This is a work of fiction. All of the characters, organizations, and events portrayed in this novel are either products of the author's imagination or are used fictitiously.

NIGHT'S BLAZE

Copyright © 2015 by Donna Grant.
Excerpt from *Soul Scorched* copyright © 2015 by Donna Grant.

For information address St. Martin's Press, 175 Fifth Avenue, New York, NY 10010.

ISBN: 978-1-250-06073-0

Printed in the United States of America

St. Martin's Paperbacks edition / April 2015

St. Martin's Paperbacks are published by St. Martin's Press, 175 Fifth Avenue, New York, NY 10010.

10 9 8 7 6 5 4 3 2 1

The adventure continues . . .

ACKNOWLEDGMENTS

I cannot thank my wonderful editor, Monique Patterson, enough. You're the bomb! To everyone at SMP who was involved in getting this book ready. Y'all rock!

To my agent, Natanya Wheeler, thanks for loving dragons!

A special thanks to my family for the never-ending support.

And to my husband, Steve. I love you, Sexy!

CHAPTER ONE

Dreagan
September

"Lily."

Rhys closed his eyes and stood atop the mountain listening to the wind whisper her name.

She walked in his dreams, teasing him with her black eyes and curtain of onyx hair. Awake, he never stopped thinking of her, longing for her.

Yearning for her.

Their all-too-brief kiss haunted him. He could still taste her, could still feel her in his arms weeks later. Lily had no idea of the feelings she stirred within him. She was gentle and shy. She lit up a room just by entering, and he ached to have her close.

He recalled the party weeks ago where he found her standing outside watching everyone through a window. She looked . . . lonely. And it prompted him out of the shadows as nothing else could.

Then, her closeness and the way her eyes lit up when

she saw him took away the last of his defenses. He'd had to hold her, kiss her. Taste her.

Rhys took in a shuddering breath. That one simple kiss slayed him as nothing in his very, very long life had ever done. It physically hurt him to release her and turn his back to everything she offered, but it was for the best.

"Well . . . at least you picked a pretty spot."

His eyes flew open when he heard Rhi's voice beside him. He turned his head to the Light Fae to see her standing next to him surveying the land just as he had a moment before. Was it really her? Or was she a figment of his imagination? No one had seen Rhi since Ulrik carried her out of Balladyn's dungeons weeks ago.

"Rhi? What are you doing here?"

She turned her head to him and raised a black brow. "I'm here for you, idiot."

Rhys frowned. Perhaps it was Rhi's smartass quips or her saucy attitude, but they had become friends quickly. She had been there whenever he had needed her, and he made sure to do the same for her. But there was nothing she could do now. Surely she knew that. "You've wasted your time then."

"You're still a Dragon King, handsome," she said with a saucy wink.

Not even her teasing could break the hold of desolation that gripped him. Only Lily could do that. Nor could he hold back his sarcasm as he said, "Am I? I can no longer shift into a dragon. That puts a crimp on things."

Her face softened as she put a hand on his arm. "You're still a Dragon King, shifting or not. You have your dragon magic, right?"

"Aye, but for how long?" Rhys ran a hand down his face and let out a long breath. "Everything I am, everything I ever will be, is a dragon. Do you have any idea how it feels to watch the others from afar, wishing I could be with them?"

"Yes."

Her reply was soft, barely above a whisper, and it held such sadness that he physically winced.

Rhys felt like the biggest ass. Of everyone, Rhi came the closest to knowing how he felt. She wasn't a dragon, but a Light Fae who happened to be in love with a Dragon King. The love between her and her King had flared quick and strong, until the King ended it out of the blue. Now, eons later, Rhi still carried a torch for her King. Theirs was a love of the ages, a love that would never diminish.

If only the fool would realize it and claim Rhi as his own again. But the King wouldn't.

"It's not the same though," Rhi said with a flip of her long hair over her shoulders as if she hadn't delved into dark memories that scarred her soul. "Your wings were taken. Someone mixed dragon magic with that of the Dark to do this to you."

"Ulrik." As if Rhys had to guess who had condemned him to such a life. "To think I pitied that son of a bitch no' so long ago. I would've thought he might do this to Con, no' me."

Rhi crossed her arms over her chest and nodded. For the first time Rhys noted Rhi's attire. She wore a shirt that molded to her body in a black-and-white geometrical pattern. A white belt encircled the waist of her black pants, and black sandals with four-inch heels encased her feet.

His gaze lowered to her nails that were divided by a glittery gold line diagonally across the nail with one half white and the other black.

"Finished with your perusal?" she asked, no heat in her words as she wiggled her fingers before his face. "Unfortunately, the black is simply called Black Onyx. They could've done better, I think. The white, however, I couldn't resist. It's called Funny Bunny."

Rhys met her silver Fae eyes. "You wear your mood on your nails."

"Ah," she said and dropped her arm as she looked down at her hand while straightening her fingers. "What do you think this means?"

"I think you're still trying to work things out, which is why you continue to wear white and black."

Her smile was wide when she looked up at him. "So perceptive. Tell me, why aren't you as insightful in your own life, stud?"

"You mean, why did I no' know Ulrik would do this to me?" Rhys asked. He looked to the craggy peaks around him. "I remember flying these same mountains beside Ulrik. He was born to lead, just as Con was. It's part of who they are. The difference came in that Con wanted to be King of Kings. Ulrik was happy leading his Silvers."

"I know," Rhi said, her voice barely above a whisper.

"For some Dragon Kings, it was an easy decision to stand with Con when Ulrik began the war with the humans."

Rhi snorted. "He didn't start the war, Rhys. The humans did when Ulrik's woman tried to betray him."

"War is war," Rhys said in a flat tone. "We were meant to protect humans. From everyone," he said and looked pointedly at Rhi.

She rolled her eyes. "I know this story well, remember? I know all the Kings cornered Ulrik's woman and killed her. I know he found out about it later, and felt betrayed by his brothers. I know his betrayal cut both ways. He wanted, needed to lash out, and he did it to the only people he could—the humans."

"If he had only stopped the killing when Con asked," Rhys said. "Then Con wouldna had to exile Ulrik from

Dreagan, taking his ability to shift into a dragon, and forcing Ulrik to walk this earth for eternity immortal."

"I think the ultimate blow came when the Silvers were caught," Rhi said with a twist of her lips. "How would you feel knowing the last dragons on this realm are being held beneath a mountain in an eternal sleep by your mortal enemy?"

"I'd do whatever it took to get to them."

Rhi cocked her head to the side. "Every Dragon King here would, and yet Con wants to kill Ulrik for doing exactly as Con would do himself."

"Look at me!" Rhys shouted angrily and held out his hands as he faced her. "Look at what Ulrik has done to me! How can I remain at Dreagan? I can do nothing to help the other Kings in this war. We've enemies battering us on every side."

Rhi put her hand on his face and looked deep into his eyes. "I didn't let you die when you were stuck trying to shift back into your human form. Do you think I would stand aside now and not help?"

Rhys dropped his arms and stepped away from her. "What can you do? You told Con you've done all you could."

"I can talk to Ulrik."

Now that Rhys hadn't expected. "Why would you?"

"You're my friend."

He shook his head, knowing there was more. With Rhi he had to be careful about gaining information she wasn't willing to share. "I can no' let you do this. Ulrik is dangerous. You can never forget that, despite his helping you."

"You think he wants something from me?"

"I do."

She shrugged nonchalantly, the wind tugging at the long strands of her black hair. "You're probably right. It's fitting since I want something from him."

"You love to push the boundaries."

She cocked her head to the side and looked intently at him. "I also want something from you."

Rhys was instantly wary. There was no telling what Rhi wanted, and though he would gladly help her any way he could, he knew better than to agree before he heard her out. "What is it you want?"

"You to return to Dreagan."

"Nay."

She sighed and spread her arms as she looked around her. "What can these mountains give you? Will you hide like some of the Kings in your mountain? That's not the Rhys I know. The Rhys I know would never run from anything," she said and poked him in the chest with a finger. "Even a woman. He would face it head-on, laughing as he took the advantage."

Damn. He should've known Rhi would know about his feelings for Lily. Rhi always knew the very things he wanted kept private.

"Return to her," Rhi pressed in a soft tone, her gaze beseeching.

"I can no' protect her."

"Even unable to shift, there isn't a single being on this realm who could protect Lily as you can."

Rhys considered her words. He yearned to return to Dreagan to see Lily, to hear her voice. If he was close to her again, he wouldn't be able to stay away. She was in his blood now, a part of his being. He craved her like he yearned to take to the skies again.

"I willna drag her into this shite we've gotten ourselves into."

"She works for Dreagan, Rhys," Rhi said in a dry tone. "She's already in the middle of it whether she knows it or not."

He hadn't thought of it that way. Double damn. Now he

was really in a corner. Rhi was right in that no one could watch over Lily like he could. He was the only one who knew how special she was, the only one who watched the sun rise knowing the day was going to be extraordinary because she was in it.

"When did you fall in love with her?" Rhi asked gently.

Rhys dropped his chin to his chest. It never entered his mind to lie. "Somewhere between the time I first saw her at Dreagan and today."

"Don't be a stupid asshat and push her away."

He looked over to Rhi when he heard the catch in her voice, but she had turned her face away. "I doona push Lily away to be mean. I keep my distance because I doona deserve her."

"You do deserve her," Rhi said and faced him, her silver eyes bright with unshed tears. "Love is rare, Rhys. You found it without even trying. I had that kind of love. It's a gift, a type of magic all its own."

"I can talk to him," Rhys offered. "He needs to know you still love him."

"No," Rhi said loudly, her face once more a mask of indifference.

Rhys bowed his head in acceptance. It was the same answer each time he'd asked through the centuries. "As you wish."

"Now," Rhi said and cleared her throat. "I'm going to go see Ulrik and figure out why he targeted you."

Rhys wanted to know that as well. Out of all the Dragon Kings, why had Ulrik chosen him? Unless it was because Rhys was always butting heads with Con. He recalled Shara's words about how the Dark would try to divide the Kings until they were fighting each other. It would make the Kings weak, make them easy to overpower.

Rhys turned to look at Dreagan. "Aye. I need to return home."

"Good," Rhi said and put her hand on his arm.

In the next blink, Rhys was standing in his room at Dreagan Manor. "What the hell?" he asked and jerked away from Rhi. "Dammit, Rhi."

She put her hand to her lips. "Shh."

"You did that easier than before."

"I suppose," she said with a shrug.

"Rhi," he said, concern filling him. He wasn't sure she understood just how much had happened to her while Balladyn held her prisoner with the Chains of Mordare. "How much magic do you have within you?"

"Apparently quite a bit." She glanced away. "Balladyn unleashed it."

Rhys shook his head back and forth. "Nay. You released it when you broke the Chains of Mordare. Those chains were unbreakable."

"You say that as if I didn't have them weighing me down, filling me with pain each time I tried to use my magic. I know exactly what I had on my wrists."

"What set you off? What was the final straw that made you break the chains?"

She turned away to look out the window. She didn't respond, because she couldn't lie without feeling great pain.

But her aloofness said it all. Balladyn had spoken about her lover, and whatever he said brought about a surge of fury within Rhi that shattered the indestructible Chains of Mordare and leveled the ten-story compound.

"If anyone finds out about how much more magic you have now they'll do anything to get you on their side," Rhys cautioned.

Rhi took interest in something outside the window. "Don't worry about me, handsome. You should be more concerned with things closer to home."

Rhys walked to her side and looked out the window.

That's when he spotted Lily walking with Denae around the back of the shop. The manor was far enough away from the rest of the distillery that Lily would never see him, but Rhys's eyesight had no trouble soaking in every detail of Lily's too-large red sweater and ankle-length black skirt.

"Do you wonder why she wears those clothes?" Rhi asked.

As if Rhys paid attention to Lily's clothes. "Nay."

He expected Rhi to make another comment. A few minutes later he looked over to find her gone. Rhys turned back to Lily. She lifted her face to the sun and closed her eyes.

Her wealth of midnight hair lay straight and thick down her back. The sun seemed to shine a spotlight on Lily, highlighting her skin as soft as down. Her large eyes fluttered open, her long lashes and gently arching brows accentuating her eyes. She had wide, full lips that enticed, invited.

Seduced.

Did she have any idea how he fought not to go to her? How it went against everything he was not to take her and make her his?

He spent his many years bedding woman after woman with no other thought than his immediate needs and pleasure. The women were forgotten, their faces fading instantly. How many times had Lily seen him with those women? Too many to count. Though that wasn't what made his heart clutch in fear.

No, that was reserved for his greatest terror—that Lily would only want him for one night.

CHAPTER
TWO

Lily loved her job. It was an odd thing, especially since she grew up with money. Neither she nor her siblings had ever wanted for anything. Yet, there was something fulfilling in doing a job to earn an income. Even when those jobs were terrible or dirty.

As soon as she arrived at Dreagan months ago, she knew it was a special place. Its beauty was unrivaled, and the people were unlike any she had ever come across. Perhaps that's why she liked going into work every day. While at Dreagan, she learned to forget the past a little every day. She also realized that she was the only one affected by what she couldn't let go of or face.

Lily walked out the back of the shop and stacked the crates that workers would pick up to refill with bottles of the world-famous Scotch. She lifted her face to the sun and closed her eyes. It was a perfect day. Her life was on track, and she was slowly gaining back her confidence. The only thing that could make it better would be Rhys.

Rhys with his charming smile and tantalizing body. She wanted to run her fingers along his hard jaw, square chin, and lean cheeks and feel the bristle of the dark stubble from his five o'clock shadow.

She wanted to trace his nose and his straight brows a shade lighter than his dark brown hair. She would then sink her fingers into the cool length of his long hair that hung to his shoulders. All the while looking into his aqua-ringed dark blue eyes, wondering when she would feel the soft touch of his lips again.

Ah, his lips. A man shouldn't have such a mouth. His smile could melt hearts, but his kiss could reduce anyone to ash. It was his bottom lip, fuller than the top, that made his mouth so irresistible.

She sighed and opened her eyes as she lowered her face. Who was she kidding? The women Rhys preferred were the exact opposite of her—tall, leggy, blonde, and big chested. Those women exuded sexuality, and she could barely muster a smile in Rhys's presence she was so nervous.

But she could still dream.

No one could touch her dreams. No one could take them away.

Lily looked down at her sweater and skirt. It was one of several outfits she had left over from a time she yearned to forget. Dennis had been a jealous boyfriend. He hated when anyone looked at her, and most times when it happened, he would get into a fight.

She sought to divert some of his anger by asking him what he wanted her to wear. Soon, her closet was full of loose, baggy clothes that were meant for someone six sizes larger than her. The clothes became a habit, but she hated them. She had changed her fate. It was time to do the same with her meager wardrobe.

Lily turned to retrace her steps, but halted when she caught sight of Dreagan Manor through the tall hedgerow.

All she had ever seen was a glimpse of the manor, but she knew it had to be impressive, like everything else on Dreagan.

It was also where Rhys lived.

She discovered that fact by accident when she overheard a conversation between Cassie and Jane. Lily felt awful for eavesdropping, but how could she not once she heard Rhys's name? Knowing that tidbit was like holding a special secret.

Then again, everything about Dreagan was unique.

Not just because they were selective about who they allowed to sell their whisky, but because they kept the distillery small instead of growing it, which kept the staff intimate. In her first week of work, she learned she was the newest hire in over two years. That didn't count any of the Dreagan wives, as she called them.

The wives were a close group, closer than was normal. They were also careful never to talk too much about their lives in front of others. They were kind, giving, friendly, and welcoming, and yet Lily knew they were hiding something.

It wasn't obvious to most, but her time with them made her see what others did not. Curious since childhood, Lily had gotten out of that habit quick enough with Dennis. She didn't need to know the Dreagan wives' secret. It was enough that she was part of Dreagan in her very small way. The people had no idea how they helped to change her. The land healed her with its simple and wild splendor.

All she needed was a little bit more time to find the girl she had once been. Then, she would gather her courage and return to her family.

Lily pivoted and walked back into the shop since Cassie and Jane were gone to lunch. She smiled as she looked at the walls lined with whisky that brought in scores of people each day. The distillery wasn't open for tours all year round, but the shop rarely closed. It allowed the people of the nearby villages to buy the whisky.

She made her way to the shelves nearest the door. The two sections of shelving six feet wide and seven feet high were the only portion of the shop that didn't have whisky.

Lily ran her hand down the spine of a book titled *Dreagan Whisky: How it All Came to Be*. She straightened the book with the others of the same title. It was one of the most popular sellers. Everyone wanted to know Dreagan's secret so they could repeat it. As if Dreagan would tell anyone their secret.

She moved to the next set of books, which contained pictures of Dreagan from the distillery to the sheep and cattle. She knew every picture by heart since she looked at the book often enough.

There were several other sets of books, all about Dreagan in some way, shape, or form. What wasn't in any of them? Anyone associated with Dreagan. Constantine's name was mentioned, but there was no photograph of him. The books—all of them—focused on the whisky.

Next, Lily straightened the stickers. Dragons were apparently popular. They sold dozens of stickers every day. Then again, the Dreagan logo of the double dragons back-to-back was beautifully done. All anyone had to see were those double dragons, and they knew it was Dreagan. It was smart marketing.

Just another way Dreagan cornered the market where others failed.

Lily walked to the back to get another box, this one holding the whisky glasses that sold as well as the whisky itself. The glasses were short and wide with the double dragon logo etched into the glass. She was stocking the shelf with more of the glasses when the chime over the door dinged, letting her know someone had entered.

"Welcome to Dreagan," Lily said over her shoulder. "I'll be right with you."

"Take your time."

She froze. That voice, gravelly and a little whiny, sounded just like Dennis. She gave an inward shake of her head. Once again she was letting her past intrude upon her new life. She hated that Dennis was back in her thoughts again. Ever since her flat was broken into, she kept thinking she was seeing him everywhere.

Except she didn't really see him, just caught a glimpse of ginger hair that turned out to belong to someone else. Or heard a laugh that made her heart clutch until she realized it wasn't him.

It didn't happen every day. Just when she had convinced herself it was all her imagination, she would think she saw or heard him again, and it would start a vicious cycle she feared wouldn't break.

Last night had been the worst. She was picking up her favorite ale and a sandwich from the co-op when she heard the whistling. It was a tune she hadn't heard before—or since—Dennis, and yet it filled the tiny store.

The ale had slipped from her fingers to shatter on the floor, soaking her boots in the alcohol, but she hadn't noticed. Her gaze was pinned to the end of the aisle as she waited for Dennis to round the corner. Just as suddenly as the whistling began, it ended. No one turned the corner, nor did she see Dennis.

It was everything Lily could do to stay calm now. She reminded herself that she was at Dreagan, and that Dennis had no control over her anymore. She set the glass on the shelf and forced her fingers to release it. Then she turned to the customer, half expecting to see Dennis leaning on the counter with his ginger hair and cocky smile.

Instead, she found an elderly man with thick white hair and a warm smile. Lily was so relieved her knees couldn't hold her. The man was instantly at her side helping to keep her standing.

"Are you all right?" he asked with concern in his faded gray eyes.

Lily nodded, a hand on her chest. She could feel her own heart pounding from the scare. "Yes. Thank you for your help. I guess it's been a long day."

"Lass, it's more than that," he admonished gently while walking her to the counter.

Lily was grateful for his assistance, but hoped Cassie or the others didn't see her. She needed the job for more than just the money. The last thing she wanted was for them to think she wasn't up to working.

"What can I get for you today?" she asked the man.

He handed her a piece of paper listing the whisky he wanted. With the fright behind her, Lily took a deep breath and let the past fade again. She began to gather the bottles of whisky while the man talked to her about his day of fly-fishing.

Thirty minutes later, she checked him out and waved while he departed the store. She shook her head with a chuckle at the stories he'd told her, which she imagined had all been made up. Still, they made her laugh and forget for a time.

Lily suddenly stilled. A prickle on the back of her neck began, her body beginning to warm at her jaw and going lower down her neck.

Rhys.

She was a mess of stuttering words and bumbling idiocy when it came to him. He had a habit of coming up silently behind her, and then talking, his rich voice sending chills racing over her. It had been weeks since she saw him. She searched for a glimpse of him every day, hoping to catch sight of him.

She spun about, a smile upon her lips, eager to hear his

voice. It was rich with a hint of cynicism and a large dose of carnality. It made her envision long nights of loving, moans of pleasure, and boneless abandon.

But there was no one standing in the back hallway, no towering figure with long dark hair and aqua-ringed dark blue eyes staring at her.

Her disappointment was almost as great as her earlier fear. Lily glanced at her watch and walked to the door of the shop, which she locked. It was time to close things up. It was one of her favorite times of the day. She normally had the shop to herself.

It allowed her to feel as if she weren't just a visitor to Dreagan, but part of it.

Rhys flattened himself against the wall as he listened to Lily walk around the shop. He'd known it was folly to venture into the store, but he'd need a closer look at her.

His concern grew after witnessing her reaction to the last customer. It was the man's voice that set her on edge. Rhys stood in the shadows of the back hallway and watched as she set her shoulders and faced the man.

The utter relief when she saw the man had been palpable. Her knees even gave out. Rhys was about to go to her when the old man stepped in. Even now, Rhys could feel the fury slide through him that someone made Lily feel such fear.

She bounced back quickly. The smile on her face, and the easy way she spoke to the customer all indicated that she had moved past the episode. Rhys, however, hadn't.

He stalked from the store back to the manor. His hand was on the dragon-head banister when he looked up and saw Cassie and Hal coming down the stairs. "What do you know of Lily's past?" Rhys demanded of Cassie.

Hal paused, surprise on his face and in his moonlight blue eyes. "Rhys. It's good to have you back."

He gave a nod to Hal. "Cassie, tell me what you know of Lily?"

Cassie shook her brunette head, her dark brown eyes glancing at Hal before she said in her American accent, "I don't know much. None of us do. She rarely talks of the past."

She was keeping something from him, Rhys was sure of it. "Tell me," he stated through clenched teeth.

Hal immediately stepped between Cassie and Rhys. "What's this about?" he asked Rhys.

"A suspicion."

"Of what?" Hal pressed, his face going hard.

Rhys glanced away, remembering the look of dread that flashed in Lily's black eyes. "She's scared of someone. A man. I want to know who it is and what he did to her."

Cassie put her hand on Hal's shoulder and moved a step down so that she was even with her husband. She looked at Rhys, indecision warring. "I want your word, Rhys, that you won't confront her with what I tell you."

"You have it," Rhys answered.

Cassie threaded her fingers with Hal's. "I saw something weeks ago. It was by accident. Lily was embarrassed by it, which is why I never brought it up again. She has a scar on her left shoulder. I don't know how far down it goes, but the scar tissue itself is thick."

"Damn," Hal mumbled.

Rhys tightened his grip on the banister, unmindful of the wood cracking beneath his hand. "What did you think made the scar?"

"It looked like a burn. But I just had a glimpse," Cassie hurried to say. "It could've been anything."

Hal looked at her then. "What does your gut tell you?"

"That she was hurt on purpose." Cassie's shoulders slumped. "I know she's had a few broken bones."

Blood pounded in Rhys's ears. He was taking in

everything Cassie said, absorbing it, gathering it. Because he was going to find the fucker and make him pay.

"I know the signs," Cassie continued. "I had a friend who was physically and mentally abused by her husband. I could never convince her to leave, and the ass eventually killed her."

Rhys spun around and walked off. It was worse than he feared. So much about Lily made sense now. Then he'd gone and acted like a brute by kissing her as if she were his. Now he had a mission. He didn't need to be able to shift into a dragon to handle a wanker who beat on women. This was something he would relish.

Rhys was at the door when someone called his name. He didn't want to stop, didn't want to be deterred from his task, but Con's voice still halted him in his tracks.

Rhys closed the door and slowly turned around to face Constantine, expecting to be lectured for being gone so long.

"It's about damn time you came home," Con said while turning the gold dragon-head cuff link at the wrist of his French-cuffed dress shirt. He motioned Rhys to follow. "I need your help."

CHAPTER THREE

"You have seconds to explain yourself," Taraeth, king of the Dark Fae stated from his black throne, his voice laced with cold fury.

Balladyn looked into the red eyes of his king and fought the urge to plunge his sword into Taraeth's heart. After all he had done for the Darks, after all he had become for Taraeth, the king now admonished him.

But they weren't alone. There were six guards, one posted on either side of the door and the other four placed throughout the narrow throne room.

"Do you have nothing to say for yourself?" Taraeth demanded with a sneer. "The great Balladyn brought low by a Light."

"Rhi is no mere Light Fae," Balladyn said.

"That she isn't. In your quest for revenge, you lost me another Dragon King!" Taraeth bellowed.

Balladyn watched as Taraeth shifted his left shoulder and touched the nub that was left after a human female, now mated to the Dragon King Kellan, cut it off.

"Rhi will be ours," Balladyn replied.

Taraeth snorted. He gazed at Balladyn icily. "For months you've been unable to find her. She eludes you at every turn. I thought you said you knew her."

"I do," Balladyn said between clenched teeth.

"Apparently not. You thought you could turn her Dark. Since she's not here with us, you obviously failed."

"I doubt that. You didn't see her."

"She leveled your compound!" Taraeth exploded, his Irish accent thick with his fury. "By herself, no less. What aren't you telling me about her?"

As if Balladyn would divulge such information. "Nothing, sire. I pushed Rhi to the brink, and her rage took over."

"While she wore the Chains of Mordare? Do you think me a fool?" Taraeth's red eyes blazed as he leaned forward on his throne. "Tread carefully, Balladyn. You might be my favorite, but I've had many before you."

Balladyn watched as Taraeth ran a hand through his long hair that was more silver than black. The more evil a Dark committed, the more silver threaded through their black hair.

The strength of Rhi's magic was no one's business, most especially Taraeth's. The king wouldn't appreciate knowing Balladyn was conspiring against him. Then again, not even Rhi knew her full potential. Balladyn, however, did. He'd glimpsed it within her while torturing her. Once she was fully Dark, the two of them would be unstoppable.

Not even the love she held within her for that imbecile of a Dragon King would survive once she was Dark.

Balladyn could hardly wait. Nothing had gone to plan, but he knew with a surety of his black soul that Rhi would be his. When she returned, she would come to him. She was always meant to be his.

"I removed the Chains of Mordare from Rhi," Balladyn lied. "I wanted to see how the rage changed her."

Taraeth sat back slowly. Ever the one to consider all sides, he asked, "Did she exceed your expectations?"

"Unequivocally. She's a Fae we should pursue wholeheartedly."

"And this has nothing to do with the fact that she left you on the battlefield for me to find and turn Dark?"

Balladyn was used to telling this lie, so he didn't hesitate to shake his head. "I was meant to be Dark. I've known that since I let it inside me. I thank her for leaving me to you."

"Is that so?"

How many more times would Balladyn have to kiss Taraeth's ass? It was becoming a chore that enraged him each time. "Of course."

"And your promise to hand me a Dragon King?"

"I've not forgotten that promise, my king. It's one I intend to carry through at all costs."

Taraeth chuckled. "My, how you hate them. I think you despise the Kings more than I do."

"I do," Balladyn replied in a low voice.

"Kiril was in our midst for months in Ireland. Most recently, we learned of the hidden doorway for us to get onto Dreagan undetected and find the weapon that will end the Dragon Kings. Yet we can't even get near the doorway. How is it we keep failing? We have to have that weapon!"

Balladyn bowed his head. "We'll have it."

"Just as I'd hoped you would say."

That's when Balladyn realized he'd stepped right into whatever it was Taraeth wanted him to do. He fisted his hands at his sides as he thought of the precious time spent away from his search for Rhi.

"Aren't you curious?" Taraeth asked with narrowed eyes.

"I'm merely waiting for your instructions."

Taraeth stood, the sleeve of his left arm hanging loose

with nothing to fill it. "There's a meeting I need you to attend in Inverness."

"So close to Dreagan?"

The king shrugged. "Take as many Dark as you wish. There will be those from MI5 there as well as our . . . friend."

Balladyn scrunched up his nose. "He's not a friend."

"Nor is he an enemy. For now. He's the one giving us information on Dreagan. Without him, we'd never have known the location of the secret doorway to get onto Dreagan."

"The Dragon Kings have now secured that doorway. We can't get near it thanks to Iona Campbell taking over as guardian of the Campbell land. Not to mention she's mated to Laith."

"I don't need to be reminded of the humans binding themselves with the Dragon Kings," Taraeth said tersely as he came down the four steps to stand in front of Balladyn. "The enemy of our enemy is our friend. Remember that during this meeting."

Taraeth walked around him before striding away. Balladyn turned to watch the thirty-foot double doors open of their own accord as Taraeth neared.

Balladyn spread his fingers after Taraeth was out of sight. The last thing he wanted to do was go to this meeting. Then again, there might be something useful he could glean from the mortals—and even his enemy.

Because, regardless of the fact that the "other" was an enemy of the Dragon Kings, it didn't make him a friend of Balladyn's. Ever.

The first chance Balladyn got, he was going to kill the bastard.

CHAPTER
FOUR

Rhys followed Con into his office and found Kellan, War-rick, Banan, and Kiril already there. Rhys locked his gaze on Con. There was always a reason for whatever Con did. Usually Rhys could piece it out, but this time he couldn't.

"Glad you're back," Warrick told Rhys.

Rhys nodded, feeling Kiril's shamrock green eyes on him. Finally Rhys turned his gaze to Kiril. The Dragon Kings were close, but Rhys and Kiril's friendship went stronger, deeper. They were brothers by choice.

"When did you return?" Kiril asked.

Rhys didn't want to lie, but he wouldn't tell them about Rhi's new ability. "About thirty minutes ago."

Con moved behind his desk and sat. With all the other seats occupied, Rhys stood near the closed door. His mind was on Lily, on who could have hurt her and why. It took him a moment to realize Con wasn't talking. Rhys nar-rowed his gaze when he discovered Con staring at him.

"Are you with us?" Con asked.

Rhys crossed his arms over his chest and leaned back against the wall. "Of course."

"Good, because you appeared to be anywhere but this room."

"Why am I here?" Rhys asked. "It's no' as if I can be of any true help."

Con leaned back in his chair and steepled his fingers. "Doona let any of the females hear you say such words. They'll take offense."

Rhys shot Con a hard look. "Involving me in whatever is going on willna keep me here."

"You think I want to force you to stay?" Con gave a shake of his head of blond hair, his black eyes penetrating. "In case you've no' been paying attention, we're being attacked by multiple enemies."

"How could I have forgotten?" Rhys knew his anger was ruling him, but he knew better than anyone about their enemies. "If Ulrik can do this to me, what's stopping him from doing it to every other Dragon King?"

"Me," Con stated.

Rhys blew out a hard breath. "I've suffered no' being able to shift for only a few weeks, and it's making me crazy. At least I have my magic still. If this is a fraction of what Ulrik feels, then I completely understand his hatred."

"I willna reverse what was done to Ulrik," Con stated.

Warrick crossed an ankle over his knee. "No' that it would do any good if we did give Ulrik back his power. Do you think his hatred for humans has waned?"

"Doubtful," Rhys answered.

"We'll find another way to ensure you can shift into a dragon, Rhys," Kiril said.

Rhys wasn't so sure. He gave a nod to Kiril, appreciating his words. "Ulrik is another matter. What's going on now?"

"Actually, it's about Ulrik," Banan said and ran a hand through his short, dark brown hair.

Rhys met Banan's gray eyes. "What about him?"

"He's set up a meeting between MI5, himself, and the Dark Fae," Kellan answered.

Con laced his fingers together and let his hands rest over his flat stomach. "Henry North is using his skills to become one of the traitors of MI5. He's going to this meeting Ulrik set up."

"Does he know it's Ulrik?" Rhys asked.

Banan's lips flattened. "Nay. But regardless, he knows every player is dangerous."

Rhys liked Henry. The human had stuck his neck out for them numerous times, but this time was different. "If Ulrik or the Dark discover he's a spy, they'll kill him."

"Henry is too good at his job," Banan said.

Warrick was just as unconvinced as Rhys if the look on his face was any indication. "I doona know Henry like the rest of you, but asking any human to become involved with the likes of Ulrik or the Dark, much less them united, is folly."

"Let's no' forget Ulrik has magic now," Kiril said, glancing at Rhys.

Banan rose and began to pace the office. "I didna know Henry planned this, or I would've talked him out of it. He's been undercover with the traitorous faction of MI5 for weeks. I got his coded message this morning about the meeting."

"Do we know where it's being held?" Rhys asked.

Banan shook his head. "Do you no' think I'd be there if I did? Henry is my friend."

Rhys could tell Banan was upset. To them, Henry already knew too much, and that put him in danger. To Henry, he didn't know near enough. What little he did know could be enough to get him killed.

"If Henry gets out of this alive, we need to tell him everything," Kellan said.

Con nodded slowly. "I agree."

That caused Rhys to look at him in shock. Con was the King of Kings, the one dragon that had more magic and power than any other. Though they were charged with protecting humans, it wasn't like Con to be willing to bring one into the fold so easily.

Con gave Rhys a droll look. "I'm no' insensitive, nor have I forgotten how Henry helped Banan find Jane when she was taken in London, or how Henry helped get Denae free of MI5, or how he's kept track of the Dark Fae for us. If we'd known he infiltrated the group of MI5 that is loyal to Ulrik, I would've demanded he know every detail."

"When is the meeting?" Rhys asked.

Banan glanced at his watch. "Today. I doona know a time."

"We've no idea how long these things last," Warrick said.

Kellan turned his head, his long caramel-colored hair held back in a queue. "I doona imagine any of the two groups want to be near Ulrik too long."

"I doona think a human would want to be near the Dark at all," Kiril stated.

Con rested his arms on his desk as he sat forward. "Good point. You saw the Dark as none of us have. We've fought them, but you lived among them for a few months."

"It was hell," Kiril said softly.

There was so much more to Kiril's words than that short sentence. Rhys hadn't been in Ireland with Kiril, but he'd spoken to him often. Rhys didn't think he could've done what Kiril had. He would've killed every Dark Fae he encountered instead of gathering information.

"How long are we going to wait to hear from Henry?" Rhys asked.

Banan shrugged. "I doona know. They could be anywhere."

"They're in Scotland."

Every eye turned to Rhys. He dropped his arms and hooked his thumbs in the belt loops of his jeans. "The Dark wouldna call a meeting. Neither would MI5. Ulrik called the meeting, and he will stay on Scottish soil."

"He's right," Con said.

Kellan sat forward, leaning to the side so his forearm rested on the arm of the leather chair. "They willna meet in a city or anywhere someone could see them."

"They could be in any glen," Warrick pointed out. "Any of them, and there are hundreds."

Con rose to his feet. "Banan, you let us know as soon as you hear from Henry. If you doona hear from him by this evening, we'll know something went wrong."

No one mentioned that it would probably be too late by then. They held onto their hope, because that's all they had.

Rhys wasn't listening as Con began to talk about patrols and who would be flying what sector of Dreagan since it didn't pertain to him.

When the meeting wrapped, Rhys was on his way out when Con stopped him. Rhys waited while Warrick, Banan, and Kellan walked from the room. Kellan closed the door behind him, and Rhys faced Con and Kiril.

"We wondered if you would ever return to the manor," Kiril said into the silence.

Rhys shrugged absently. "I didna think I would."

"What brought you home?" Con asked.

Rhys wasn't ready to tell them about Lily or his infatuation. "Rhi." He was watching Con, but the King of Kings didn't so much as blink at her name.

Kiril, on the other hand, widened his eyes in surprise. "Rhi was here?"

"She found me," Rhys admitted.

Con adjusted the sleeve of his burnt orange dress shirt. "What did she want?"

"To talk, I guess. She didna say much other than to tell me I should return here."

Kiril's dark blond eyebrows rose. "I'm glad she told you that and doubly glad you listened."

Rhys wondered what they would think if they discovered he hadn't come back for them, but for Lily. He didn't imagine either of them would be particularly overjoyed. Oh, Kiril would be happy to know Rhys had found someone he was interested in for more than one night, especially since Kiril had suspected for a while now.

As for Con, Rhys wasn't sure. Sometimes he welcomed the women and other times he didn't. It was like Con was fighting with himself over how to feel about the Dragon Kings mating.

"You said you can still use your dragon magic," Con said.

Rhys shrugged one shoulder. "Whatever has prevented me from shifting doesna seem to have affected my magic. Perhaps that's what Ulrik plans next."

"He'll be dead before then." Con's words were spoken low, hard.

Rhys met Con's black gaze. "I want to be with you. After what he's done to me, I want the bastard dead once and for all."

"Deal."

Rhys turned and stalked from the office. He paused when he reached the stairs and decided to go up another level to the computer room where Ryder was stationed. The door was open, and Rhys poked his head around the door in time to see Ryder stuff a donut in his mouth with one hand and reach for another with his other.

Ryder looked up and motioned him inside with his hand holding the jelly-filled donut. Rhys walked into the room and stood at the row of thirty-two-inch monitors facing Ryder.

"You look into anyone's past that works here, right?"

Ryder nodded and swallowed the bite. "Each and every one. Who do you want to know about?"

"Lily Ross."

"Ah," Ryder said with a grin. He set aside the donut and leaned forward to type on one keyboard. "She is quite the stunner, even with those awful clothes she wears. I think it's her long dark hair. Or it could be those black eyes of hers."

Rhys gripped the table to keep himself from reaching over the computers and punching Ryder. It wasn't as if Ryder was saying it to get a rise out of him. Ryder didn't even know of his interest in Lily.

"What do you want to know?" Ryder asked.

Rhys desired every detail. But he just wanted it to come from Lily herself, not a computer. Rhys pushed away from the table. "Never mind."

"What made you crave to know about her?"

Rhys looked into Ryder's hazel eyes and shrugged. "I think she's hiding something about her past."

"Most people do. I can tell you—"

"Doona!" Rhys yelled and held up a hand. "Doona tell me anything."

Ryder's forehead furrowed. "I thought you wished to know."

"I do, but how would you feel if someone looked into your past instead of asking you?"

"Then I suppose you better ask her, though she probably willna tell you."

Rhys knew Ryder was right, but he also knew he couldn't stand the look Lily would give him when she discovered he'd delved into her past—because she would find out. People always did.

He ran a hand down his face in frustration. "Is there anything that tells you about her past lovers?"

"No. Lily is clean, Rhys. Whatever she's hiding is personal and has no bearing on Dreagan."

"Thanks," Rhys said as he walked from the room, more determined than ever to hunt down whoever hurt Lily.

The more mundane her activity, the more Lily found herself daydreaming. It was becoming quite the problem, if she considered thinking about the gorgeous, aloof Rhys a problem.

She bent and grabbed two round canisters of Dreagan's ten-year-old single-malt Scotch to set on the shelf as she thought back to the annual party Dreagan hosted. Lily had been outside looking into the warehouse full of people when Rhys came up behind her and spoke. The sound of his deep, stirring voice made her stomach do flips. Hell, who was she kidding? Just thinking of him made her feel the same.

Lily put the last of the canisters in place and walked to the back to set aside the box. Cassie was manning one of the two registers while Jane was talking to a small group just coming off a tour. After a look to make sure all the customers were being taken care of, Lily headed to the bathroom. She shut the door and then let out a long sigh as she looked in the mirror.

Her parents called her pretty, but then again, parents were biased when it came to their children. Why was it easier to believe Dennis's words than her parents? Lily put a hand to the mirror to hide her face from view. It had happened again last night. She thought she saw Dennis while driving home. Why couldn't she get the arse out of her head? Why did he still have some kind of hold on her?

"I'm going insane," Lily told herself as she turned away from the mirror. "It's finally happening. My mind has broken."

She took a deep breath and slowly let it out. A soft knock made her jump and jerk her head to the door.

"Lily?" Denae asked from the other side of the door in her Texas accent. "Are you all right?"

"I'm fine," she quickly replied and then flushed the toilet she hadn't used and opened the door, a smile in place.

Denae stepped back, her copper brown hair down and loose about her shoulders. Denae's whisky-colored eyes were smiling. "I'm heading into town to The Fox & The Hound to grab some lunch. Want to come?"

Lily liked all of the women of Dreagan, as she dubbed them. But seeing them with their men made her heartsick for what she knew could never be—regardless of the kiss Rhys had given her over a month ago.

Afterward, Rhys disappeared for a week. She got a glimpse of him, and then he vanished again. As far as she knew, Rhys had yet to return to Dreagan.

"Please," Denae said with a grin. "I hate eating by myself, and Kellan is in a meeting."

"How can I refuse that?" Lily asked. "Let me grab my purse."

Denae followed her out to the front and talked to Jane while Lily made her way to Cassie.

"I see Denae roped you into lunch," Cassie said with a grin, her American accent coming out strong.

Denae and Cassie weren't the only Americans at Dreagan. There were also Elena and Jane who hailed from the States. Lily had only worked there for a few months, but she was the lone one from England. Most of the workers hailed from Scotland, though there was also Shara, who was from Ireland.

"She did," Lily said as she slung her purse strap over her shoulder. "Want to come?"

Cassie turned her head to the door as it opened and her

husband Hal walked in. His moonlight blue eyes saw only Cassie, and by the way Cassie lit up when he walked into the room, everyone disappeared for her as well.

Lily turned away with a grin and joined Denae and Jane who were watching the other couple with interest.

"Those two," Jane said with a smile and a shake of her head.

Denae gaped at her. "As if you have room to talk. I'm going to video you when Banan walks in, then you won't be able to say anything."

"You're no different with Kellan," Jane said with a laugh.

Denae merely smiled. "Oh, I know exactly how Kellan makes me feel. I can't think, much less form words. The first couple of times he tried to talk to me, I'm pretty sure it was gibberish that came out instead of actual words."

Lily joined in with the laughter, because it was difficult not to. Then, Denae looped her arm in hers and steered Lily toward the door.

"I'm sure he's okay," Denae said as they walked to her car.

Lily looked at her, frowning. "Who? Kellan?"

"Rhys," she said with a wide grin.

"Oh." What else was Lily supposed to say? She thought she kept her feelings tightly under wraps, but apparently they were so clear everyone saw them.

Denae unlocked the black Range Rover and got in. Once Lily was seated, she asked, "Does that mean Rhys is in some kind of trouble?"

"Not at all," Denae said too quickly as she backed up the SUV and put it in drive. "Rhys just needs time to himself."

Lily touched her lips, remembering how firm his hand had been on her back as he held her, how gentle and steady his hold. She recalled how he'd kissed her with such abandon, with such skill that it left her reeling, grasping for anything to hold onto.

She clung to him, as if he were the breath that filled her lungs, the light that guided her way. The kiss had ended much too quickly. Like a fool, she had been unable to find words as he pulled away and sank back into the darkness. If only she had known what to say to keep him with her.

If only . . .

There were times she thought she dreamt the entire thing. Then her lips would tingle, reminding her she knew Rhys's taste, knew his touch. Knew the strength of his arms and the power of his embrace.

She blinked and focused, realizing Denae was pulling into the pub. At least Denae wasn't looking at her oddly, which meant Lily didn't have to come up with a lie to explain why she had been daydreaming again.

Or who she was daydreaming about.

Denae found a parking space and shut off the SUV. Then she looked at Lily. "You sure you don't want to talk?"

"Why do you ask that?"

"For one, you've been staring out the window for the last ten minutes. But it's more than that. You watch the world as if you aren't part of it."

Lily briefly closed her eyes and clutched her purse in her hands. "A habit."

"It's just . . . well, I want you to know that we're your friends here. If you ever need someone to talk to, please don't hesitate to come to me or any one of us."

"Thank you. That means a lot." It was the truth. If only Denae knew what Lily had endured before.

"Now that that's out of the way, let's eat," Denae said with a smile.

They got out of the Range Rover and made their way inside the pub where Sammi, Jane's half-sister, was working alongside Laith, the owner.

Both Sammi and Laith waved as they entered. Lily followed Denae to a table and sat down. She put her purse on one of the extra chairs and noted Iona sitting in the back booth with her camera and computer.

Laith walked up with a grin. "If she knew you were here, she'd be over, but my Iona doesna even see me when she's involved with her work."

"Oh, she sees you," Denae said with a laugh. "It's all right. We know she's busy."

Lily didn't know Iona very well, but it was common knowledge around the distillery that she and Laith were in love. Just one more couple. Lily sighed. Once, she'd thought she was lucky enough to find love. How very wrong she had been.

"What about you, Lily?" Laith asked, turning his gunmetal gaze on her.

"Oh," she said, belatedly realizing Denae had already ordered. "I'll have the shepherd's pie and tea."

Once Laith walked off, Lily sat back and looked at Denae. "Thanks for asking me to join you. I forgot to pack a sandwich this morning."

"Did you not sleep well?"

Sleep? It had been weeks since she'd slept properly, and it was beginning to take its toll. "Not really."

"I remember when my sister drowned. I didn't sleep for days, and even after that I could only sleep for a few hours at a time."

Lily's heart clutched for Denae. "I didn't know about your sister. I'm sorry."

"It was ages ago, though I still miss her," she replied with a sad smile. Denae posed an expectant look on her face toward Lily.

"I've not lost anyone," Lily said.

Denae gave a nod of thanks as a Coke was set in front of her. She took a drink and nodded. "Ah. Your past then."

Lily was so shocked at her words that she sat there with her tea halfway to her lips.

"I'm sorry," Denae said with a grimace. "I didn't mean for that to come out like it did. It's *my* past coming out there. It's none of my business."

Lily set her tea down and folded her hands in her lap. "You're right. It is my past."

After the words were out, Lily looked around waiting for Dennis to show up. When he didn't, she let out a small laugh that she quickly covered with her hand. For three years she had pretended that she lived a happy life, and for the last year, she was pretending those years hadn't happened.

Denae leaned forward and lowered her voice. "I'm gathering that you've never told anyone that?"

Lily shook her head, unable to find more words.

"It's all right," Denae assured her. "Your secret is safe with me. Is there anything I can help with?"

Lily lowered her hand from her mouth. "I must deal with this on my own."

There was that heat on her neck again. This time Lily didn't hurriedly look for Rhys. He was gone from Dreagan, and though she wished she could see him, she knew it wasn't him. She rubbed her neck as the heat spread down her chest.

She looked past Denae to the kitchen doorway and saw Rhys as excitement rushed through her. Their gazes locked, held for a moment. He gave her a nod, and then disappeared. Lily hadn't even had time to call his name he was gone so quickly.

A smile pulled at her lips. She hadn't just seen Rhys. He had been looking at her. The day certainly was looking up.

"So, I have a confession," Denae said with a bright tone. Lily wasn't fooled. Denae might have changed the subject, but Denae would never forget her words. It was a look in Denae's eyes, eyes that saw minute details of everyone's lives. "What?"

"I have an unnatural thing for shoes. I love shoes. I have so many, but with the distributor party next week that Kellan and I are attending, I don't have a single pair that will go with the dress I bought. Kellan is no help, and the other girls all have something going on over the next few days. How are you with shoes?"

Lily loved shoes. She loved shopping. A memory of her past surfaced of walking into Harrods in London with her mother. Perhaps it was time to revisit the past. "A woman can never have too many shoes."

"Oh, thank God," Denae said with a clap of her hands. "Are you free tomorrow to go into Edinburgh?"

"As a matter of fact, I am."

CHAPTER
FIVE

Inverness

Henry North stood with the other MI5 agents in a small field. None of the other agents knew of his connection to Dreagan, or that he was helping the Dragon Kings. If he were lucky, none of them would ever know anything.

It was risky, his being at the meeting place. With the help of Denae, he discovered the agents at MI5 who had joined forces with the Dark Fae. Most of those dumbasses had been retired from MI5—in one form or another.

Henry himself was responsible for three of the retirements, and he didn't lose sleep over his part in it. The Dark were like a virus. Once they infected someone, there was no going back.

Henry had been working tirelessly to locate the Dark. The Dragon Kings thought they kept to Ireland, but he discovered the Dark Fae were slowly and surely making their way across every confinement. The only place they weren't so wide spread was the UK.

In other words, they were surrounding the Kings.

That's when Henry used his skills as a spy to infiltrate

the small band of MI5 betrayers. It had taken little effort, which was a red flag. Remaining in their confidences had proven more difficult, and yet here he was at the meeting.

He stood in his black suit with his arms clasped behind his back. The wind gusted, sending the hem of his jacket ruffling.

Suddenly, a group of Dark Fae stood opposite them led by a hulking Dark with red eyes that filled with disgust when he spotted them. His long black and silver hair was pulled away from his face by several small rows of braids and gathered behind his head to fall with the rest of his hair down his back.

"That's Balladyn," the man next to him muttered, a thread of fear in his voice.

Henry knew all about the infamous Dark Fae. At one time, Balladyn had been the fiercest warrior of the Light, but the Dark captured him and then turned him. Since then, Balladyn crushed anyone and anything in his path. Most recently, his attention had been on Rhi.

A smile threatened. It happened every time Henry thought of the Light Fae with her silver eyes and black hair. Her beauty was beyond compare. She was forever out of his reach, but that was all right. Henry was content to just look at her on the rare occasions she appeared.

His gaze turned hard as he looked at Balladyn in his black pants and silk shirt. Balladyn had dared to kidnap Rhi, then attempted to turn her Dark. Fortunately, Rhi managed to escape. If only Henry could see her and know she was as fine as Banan promised she was.

"Get ready," the guy on the other side of Henry whispered.

Henry pulled his gaze away from Balladyn and saw a lone figure walking down the slopes toward them. The man wore a charcoal gray trench coat that hung open to reveal a dove gray suit beneath.

Conversation from the agents around him drew Henry's attention.

"Don't look at him."

"He's trouble."

"Nearly as much as the Dark."

"We'll be lucky to get out of this meeting alive."

The man in charge of the contingency of MI5 agents, Daniel Petrie, turned and gave them all a withering glare. Daniel stood at the front with only ten feet separating him and Balladyn.

It didn't take long for the lone man to reach them. He had thick black hair that skimmed his shoulders. Even though he wore a confident smile, his gold eyes appeared to see everything.

He finally reached them and stopped a few paces from Daniel and Balladyn. "Well, gentlemen," he stated in as fine of a cultured British accent as Henry had ever heard. "It seems we're all here."

"Why?" Balladyn demanded.

The man paused and slowly turned to look at Balladyn for a long period. "We all want the same thing—to bring Dreagan down and expose the Dragon Kings."

Henry imagined that was about all they had in common. Each group had its own agenda once the Kings were toppled, and allies would quickly become enemies. The world would become a shell of what it once was if any of the three groups standing before him got control. Not that MI5—or any human for that matter—stood a chance against magic. Henry didn't understand why no one at MI5 realized that yet.

He felt the weight of every human's existence resting upon his shoulders, and he staggered beneath the burden. This was his first foray into protecting not just the UK, but the world, and it left him feeling a bit . . . stressed.

The Dragon Kings had been doing it since the beginning

of time, and yet they didn't discount any threat to humans or Earth. They faced the evil each time.

If only the humans knew what the Dragon Kings had done for them. Perhaps then they wouldn't be so eager to see them exposed.

Somehow, in his dealings with the Kings, he came to realize he was naïve and green. The Kings opened his eyes to an entire new world, a world that involved them, regardless if they were hiding in it or not.

Nothing good could come out of letting the world see a Dragon King. MI5 were fools if they expected the Kings to roll over and do whatever mortals wanted. Henry had seen the Kings in battle. He'd witnessed their power, their raw fury. Anyone who went up against the Kings was an idiot, because the Dragon Kings couldn't be killed.

His gaze rested on the new arrival. The man looked human, but the way both MI5 and the Dark were a bit wary of him told Henry the man was much more.

How could the Dragon Kings defeat three enemies at once? The Kings would have to decide to protect mankind as they always had, or themselves. No matter their decision, they would lose in the end.

The truth of it all hit Henry right in the chest. He was sick with it, and though he wanted to kill everyone around him, he remained standing, his eyes on the man in the trench coat.

The man raised a brow at Balladyn. "Am I right? Dreagan is our common ground. We've worked together before, and it'll be to our benefit to continue."

"We don't have the weapon," Balladyn said, his words thick with his Irish accent.

The man shrugged. "I gave you the location of the doorway."

Henry seethed. So this was the son of a bitch who had deceived Iona for years and killed her father. No wonder Laith wanted to kill the man.

"A doorway," the man continued, "that would've been impossible to find without me."

Daniel glanced up at the clouds gathering above them. "Why weren't my men involved in this?"

"As if," Balladyn said with a sneer. "All you and your men are good for is dealing with humans. Leave the Kings to someone who knows how to take them on."

"Which would be me," the man said before Daniel could reply. He looked from Daniel to Balladyn. "The fact is, gentlemen, we have two issues to deal with."

Daniel smirked as he rocked back on his heels. "So now you need me."

"Definitely," the man said.

Balladyn crossed his arms over his chest. "Unless you found another way to get us the weapon, the Dark won't help you."

The man walked a slow circle around Balladyn. "I know Taraeth would disagree with you. There's no need to bring this to his attention, however. He sent you in good faith. I also hear you aren't in good favor with him right now."

Balladyn's red eyes glowed with hatred, but he didn't respond.

The man rubbed his jaw as he looked Balladyn over. "The Dark want the weapon, and I told Taraeth I would find him a way in. I did, but the Kings—and a human—outsmarted you."

"Are you trying to get me to kill you?" Balladyn asked between clenched teeth.

With a shrug, the man said, "You can try. Now, I've found us something else to use to hurt the Kings and get the weapon."

Henry perked up, as did the Dark. He wished he were closer to the three so he could hear every detail.

"There's a woman working for Dreagan, a human," the man said. "She's weak and broken. The man who broke her works for me. He'll use her to get inside Dreagan."

"A human hiding from the Kings?" Balladyn threw his head back and laughed. "It'll never happen."

The man's gold eyes sharpened, hardened. "There isn't a play I've made that hasn't moved our goals forward. Only a fraction of my plans haven't worked out perfectly, but I'm steps ahead of the Kings. They'll never see what I have coming."

Daniel glanced back at his agents. "And what do you want with MI5?"

"You're going to take her family as incentive to get her to do what we want."

"Hold them?" Daniel asked. "How am I supposed to do that?"

"You're MI5," the man said menacingly. "You and your comrades told me MI5 would be of benefit. Most of your colleagues are dead. Are you now telling me as high rank-ing as you are within MI5 that you can't find a place to hold one family?"

"Give them to me," Balladyn said.

The man considered Balladyn as he shifted his focus to the Dark Fae. "They would certainly be contained, as well as soulless in a matter of hours."

"Isn't that what needs to happen?" Balladyn asked.

One side of the man's lips lifted in a half-smile. "Right. Because then I would have leverage to use."

"What about the woman?" Balladyn asked. "She'll need to be disposed of after."

The man blew out a long breath. "Yes, she will. How-ever, I'm going to use MI5 for that."

Balladyn dropped his arms and took a step toward the man. "If the Dark couldn't keep a Dragon King from coming after their women, what makes you think MI5 can hold against them?"

"Bloody hell," Daniel muttered. "We've nothing to stand against a Dragon King."

The man sighed heavily. "Gentlemen, gentlemen. You're not seeing the big picture. This woman I speak of isn't attached to any Dragon King. They might notice she's gone, but they'll just replace her with another worker. No one will be the wiser to where she's gone."

"Then give her to us," Balladyn said tightly. "We deserve some compensation for our losses."

"Your losses?" Daniel asked in disgust.

The man held up his hands. "It's true MI5 has lost men, but the heaviest toll has been on the Dark. There is a reason, Balladyn, that I want the girl with MI5."

Daniel raised a dark brow littered with gray. "And that is?"

"I want the Kings' focus away from the Dark and centered squarely on the humans if they look for the girl."

Henry briefly closed his eyes. Ah, but the man was smart. Little by little he was making the Dragon Kings turn against the humans.

Balladyn gave a nod. "Fine. While the humans have the female, what will we be doing? You don't expect us to wait around while your man gets the weapon?"

"Not at all," the man said. "He's going to find where the weapon is being hidden and bring it to me. Once I have it, I'll turn it over to you."

"You'll turn over the very thing that can kill you as well?" Balladyn asked with a loud snort.

That made Henry frown. He didn't know of a weapon the Kings had, but then they didn't tell him everything.

Obviously, whatever it was could kill the Dragon Kings. Since only another Dragon King can kill a Dragon King, this weapon could turn the tide of the war.

"Our goal is to rid this realm of those pesky Dragon Kings," the man said.

Balladyn took a step back. "You did find us the secret doorway. Let's see if you really can locate the weapon."

The man gave a slight nod to Balladyn. "There are still a few matters to work out on the first issue, but let's move on to the second. Traitors."

Henry saw some men beside him stiffen. He wasn't worried. He was good at his job, and he covered his tracks well. No one there would ever know that he was spying for the Dragon Kings.

"Traitors?" Daniel repeated.

The man nodded and walked among the Dark Fae. "There is one among us, one who would take everything he's learned here and report to our enemy."

Balladyn faced the man. "My men wouldn't betray me."

"No, they wouldn't." The man stopped and looked right at Henry. "But he would."

Chaos erupted as agents were shoved aside as Dark Fae grabbed Henry and he was forced onto his knees. That's when he recalled a conversation when Banan had told him they suspected the man responsible for everything was a Dragon King who had been exiled eons ago—Ulrik.

CHAPTER
SIX

Rhys pressed against the wall, his hands clenched at his sides. Lily was only feet from him—again—and he somehow managed not to go to her. He pressed his lips together and recalled how soft her mouth had been beneath his, how seductive her kiss.

The way she smiled when she saw him made his heart pound and his blood run like fire through his veins. Desire, hot and thick, consumed him. Lily. He wanted to hold her, to simply savor her scent of roses.

He also burned to rip away her baggy clothes and feast his eyes upon her body. He would lay her down and caress and kiss every inch of her, worshipping her. To sink his hands into the long, silky length of her inky hair and hear her sighs of pleasure.

Rhys would go through the pain of trying to shift again if he could hold her for one night. It was a lot to ask since he didn't deserve one minute with her, but Rhys was desperate. His life had been ripped away from him without his being able to fight against it. That was difficult enough, but to know that the one woman that consumed his thoughts day and night, the one woman who captured his attention with a mere smile would never be his . . .

It was beyond cruel.

And yet Rhys had done it to himself.

Lily deserved so much better than a man like him who had a different woman on his arm every night. She should have candlelit dinners, roses, surprise picnics, and long walks among the heather.

He saw the strength in her, the steel in her spine he guessed she hadn't realized yet. How he wanted to be there to see her find it. He also saw the sweetness within her. She was all that was good and right in this world.

She made him forget the travesties the humans had committed against the dragons and the Kings. Lily simply made him forget all the awful things.

He opened his eyes, his jaw clenched. She was the one who had gotten him through the pain after the wound Ulrik inflicted. It was Lily who was his beacon, the light that found him in the darkness.

"Rhys?" Laith said as he came to stand in front of him.

Rhys pushed away from the wall and ran a hand down his face. "Aye."

"I didna know you were back."

"I returned yesterday." Rhys fought against looking back into the pub at Lily. She called to his soul, and he was powerless to ignore her. "I . . . I . . ." He couldn't think of a single excuse to explain his presence.

Then Rhys looked around the corner at Lily. She was smiling at something Denae said, her head nodding. Lily tucked her hair behind her ear, the action bringing attention to her long neck that he yearned to trail kisses down.

Rhys faced Laith and shrugged. "I just wanted a look around."

Laith's lips flattened. "You doona have to lie to me. I

know your affinity for women. Is it the redhead that's caught your interest?"

"No' this time." Rhys only had eyes for Lily. Sure, he had tried to carry on with his ways at first. He thought Lily was just a passing interest that would quickly fade, but the truth was, he compared every woman to her.

And they all came up short.

The ache within Rhys intensified. He regretted so many of his decisions now, because he couldn't face Lily. She knew him, knew his ways.

Laith's look sharpened "Are you all right? You look . . ."

"Lost?" Rhys supplied.

Laith shook his head, his frown deepening. "I was going to say vulnerable."

Ah, but Rhys was vulnerable all because of one black-haired, black-eyed woman who kissed sinfully and touched him like a siren. He saw—and felt—the passion within her longing to break free. What he wouldn't give to be the one to bring it out in her.

Rhys cleared his throat. "Any word on Henry?"

"Nay," Laith said, though his gaze didn't waver. "Do you still have any pain?"

"It stopped with Rhi's help when I was in dragon form."

Laith stepped to the side and peered into the pub. His gaze slid back to Rhys. "You shifted to human form when Lily went missing."

It wasn't a question, and Rhys didn't take it as one. "She's part of Dreagan."

"Aye. And she's important to you."

Rhys opened his mouth to deny it, but the words wouldn't come. "Laith—"

"I willna speak of it to anyone," Laith interrupted. "Now I know why you finally returned."

He took a step closer to Laith. "Forget we had this conversation."

"Why? Why no' go to her? See where this goes?"

"Because I am this," Rhys said tightly and motioned at himself with his hands. "I'm no' worthy of her."

"Because you can no' shift?"

Rhys laughed, the sound devoid of humor. "Because she deserves better than someone who hops from one woman to another."

"You doona give yourself enough credit. I know Kiril would tell you the same thing, my friend. You doona only deserve her, but you deserve happiness."

Rhys was shaking his head before Laith finished. "My duty is to watch over Lily and ensure she's no' touched by the shite we're arse deep in. Other than that, it goes no further."

Laith made a sound at the back of his throat. "You've looked at her three times since we've been talking."

"I've no'," Rhys argued and found himself about to look again. He stopped and clenched his jaw.

"Keep pretending you can watch over her and no' give in to the desire," Laith said with a sardonic smile. "Especially when you realize Lily wants you just as badly. We've all seen how she looks at you. Her feelings are there. You've already gotten too close to back away now."

Was Laith right? Damn. Rhys sidestepped Laith and walked out the back of the kitchen. He had to get away from Lily for a bit and clear his head. She would never leave his thoughts, but he had to get away from Laith and all that he'd said.

Rhys turned the corner of the pub not looking where he was going until he saw a flash of black hair. He looked up a heartbeat before he ran into Lily. Instantly he reached out to grab her. The moment his hands touched her, he was lost.

He found himself tumbling, falling into her black eyes. "Lily," he whispered.

Her lips parted as she looked up at him. Then her eyes crinkled in the corners as a small smile played about her tempting lips. "I didn't know you'd returned. I . . . I mean we, we've been so worried about you."

The warmth of her hand on his chest seeping through his shirt scalded him just as the desire rushing through his blood. He breathed in, loving her fresh, clean scent with just a hint of roses. His dragon magic rose within him, the shadows rising to close around them so he could have Lily all to himself.

It was movement out of the corner of his eye that made him realize they weren't alone. He spotted Laith standing with Denae watching them. Rhys dropped his arms and called his shadows away, but he couldn't take the step back no matter how hard he tried.

Lily's eyes dropped to his chest where her hand was. Slowly, she let it fall. He had to fist his hands not to put her hand back.

"Are you well?" he asked.

Her smile, which slipped, returned. "I'm . . . getting by. And you?"

To his surprise, he found one side of his lips turning up at the corner. "Getting by."

"We're a pair, aren't we?" she asked, glancing at the ground.

"That we are, lass."

She licked her lips nervously. "It's really good to see you, Rhys."

He watched her walk away, waiting until she was in the SUV with Denae before he said, "My day isna complete until I see you, Lily."

Lily was still thinking about her run-in with Rhys at the end of the day. She drove from Dreagan, and just before she pulled out of the parking lot, she looked in her rearview mirror. It was a habit that began after the first day she was hired. All the way to the village where her flat was, she thought about her new life.

Anticipation charged through her at the prospect of shopping with Denae. Nestled inside her wallet between receipts was her credit card that accessed the bank account her parents had given her at eighteen.

When she told them she was leaving with Dennis, they threatened to cut off her money. Dennis hadn't been happy about it, but he had assured her eventually her parents would come around. Lily adjusted to life with Dennis with a steady income working for some rich guy. Sometime in her first year of living with Dennis she had accidentally grabbed the credit card from her parents for the ATM and learned they hadn't cut her off or withdrawn the money.

It was a secret she kept to herself. She'd hidden the card in her wallet in case she ever needed it. After she left Dennis, there had been a few times she almost had to use it, but she always managed to find a way out of those situations.

Not because she didn't want to use the money, but because she wanted—needed—to do it on her own. The temptation of that money, however, was impossible to ignore now that she wanted to go shopping. She had some of her own money saved, and it wasn't like she was going to buy an entire wardrobe.

Lily parked on the street near her flat and started to get out of the car. She was halfway out when she swore she saw Dennis turn the corner in front of her. Her heart accelerated, but she closed her eyes and focused on breathing regularly.

"It's not him. It's not him," she repeated over and over to herself.

Dennis wasn't anywhere near her, nor did he know

where she was. He was intruding upon her new life, and she had to stop him.

When she opened her eyes, she was once more in control of things. Lily closed her car door and walked to her flat. She looked at the new door before she put her key in the lock. After the break-in, she had been more than a little paranoid.

A glance around showed her no one was paying her any mind. She turned the key, unlocking each of the three dead bolts while looking to the right and the corner where she thought she had seen Dennis. Then she pushed open the door and stepped inside.

Lily hastily closed the door behind her, then locked all the dead bolts. She let out a breath, letting her shoulders sag. It wasn't until she was hanging her purse on the coatrack by the door that she realized she wasn't alone.

With her hands still on the strap of her purse, she locked her eyes on the one face she'd prayed never to see again—Dennis.

"Well, well, well. Fancy seeing you here," he said with a smirk from her favorite chair.

Henry kept his eyes closed when he woke. He took quick stock of his body and realized he had at least two broken ribs, three broken fingers, a broken nose, and a deep cut on his lip and left cheek.

But his entire body felt as if he had been soundly thrashed.

Which he had.

How the hell had Ulrik found out? Henry had been more careful than on any of his other jobs. There's no way Ulrik should've known. Hell, Henry hadn't even told Banan. The only ones who knew were in MI5.

Anger simmered. Apparently there was more than the

small faction of traitors in MI5. Since he was part of an elite task force to bring an end to the traitors, the group who knew his moves was small. It wouldn't take too much to go through each of the ten and figure out which one had betrayed him.

If he lived.

Henry's mouth was dry. He longed to swallow, but if he did they would know he was awake. They. He inwardly snorted. He wasn't sure which "they" it was, but it was obvious he was being watched.

He doubted Ulrik or the Dark Fae would've allowed MI5 to take him, which meant he was either with the Dark Fae or with Ulrik. And neither scenario was good news.

Henry pushed such thoughts aside for the moment and concentrated on what was around him. He lay on a soft surface, the smooth feel of leather beneath his hands. A sofa. Not something he expected after being ratted out.

The quiet around him was only broken by the occasional pop of a fire. What the bloody blue blazes was going on? He wasn't in the prison he imagined, or dead as he had fully expected.

Finally, Henry cracked open one eye and saw the lights dimmed around him. He moved his left arm across his abdomen and took as deep of a breath as he could manage without crying out in agony. Then he sat up. The room spun around him, and his breathing grew shallow from the swarms of pain that assaulted him.

"Not such a good move, agent."

Henry recognized the voice. Ulrik. He put his wounded hand with his three broken fingers on the sofa to steady himself and looked to the doorway where Ulrik was standing.

The banished Dragon King wore a navy suit with white pinstripes and a white shirt beneath without a tie. His hands were in the pockets of his pants, pushing his suit jacket open.

"I bet you didn't think you'd wake up here?"

Henry glanced at the dark wood paneling, the large stone fireplace, and the array of artwork hanging on the walls. "I admit I thought I'd be in a prison somewhere."

"There's no reason prisons can't be . . . comfortable," Ulrik said as he sat in a chair to the left of the sofa.

"Why am I not dead?"

Ulrik shrugged. "Oh, I'm sure you will be soon. I wanted to question you myself."

"And you managed to get me away from MI5 and the Dark Fae? All by yourself?"

Ulrik's smile grew, while his gold eyes glittered with humor. "There are those who think me inconsequential. Others don't know what threat I am. Still others would disregard me. They'll all learn soon enough."

"Why tell me this?"

He shrugged. "Why not? I want people to know how powerful I am. What better way to spread the word than through you?"

"So that's why you kept me alive?"

"Oh, I wouldn't say that was the only reason."

Henry refused to look at the tall crystal decanter filled with water on the coffee table in front of him. He leaned back carefully, biting his tongue in pain. "Why use the fake accent? I know you're Scottish."

Ulrik chuckled and rested his arms on the thick rolled arms of the chair. "You pretend to know me?"

"I don't pretend. I know who you are."

"Really?" he asked in mock surprise. "Then enlighten me. Who am I?"

"Ulrik, the banished Dragon King." Henry's announcement didn't have the effect he expected. Ulrik didn't bow his head in agreement or even sputter in outrage.

He simply smiled.

Something wasn't right. Something wasn't right at all.

"Trying to piece it all together?" Ulrik asked. "If you had forty lifetimes you wouldn't be able to. See, Henry, I've been setting all of this up for thousands of years. I've been patient, I've bided my time, accumulated allies and assets, and amassed a fortune."

Only one other time in his career as a spy had Henry felt as if he were thrown to the wolves. He'd nearly lost his life that first time, and he was certain he would this time. It wasn't so much that he was going to die, but the fact that everything he knew—or thought he knew—wasn't the whole story.

All he had to do was look into the gold eyes and know that Ulrik held all the cards in this particular game. No matter what the Dragon Kings did, no matter if MI5 got rid of all the traitors, no matter if the Dark Fae left Earth, Ulrik was going to win it all.

"You look a bit green," Ulrik said as he sat forward. He took the decanter and a crystal glass and filled it with water before handing it to Henry. "You could probably use something stronger, but this will have to do for now."

Henry took the glass with his good hand. As he brought the crystal to his lips, he briefly thought the water might be poisoned, and then he didn't care. He was thirsty, and he was going to die. Did it really matter how it happened?

He downed the first glass quickly. As he set the crystal on the sofa, Ulrik refilled it. Henry drank two more glasses before he shook his head at Ulrik's offer of another refill.

Ulrik put the decanter back in place and sat back in his chair once more. "I like you, Henry. You seem like a smart man. What would make you stand against me? You know I'm going to win."

"Just because you're going to win doesn't mean the rest of us just move aside for you."

Ulrik shook his head and propped his elbow on the arm of the chair before resting his head against his fist. "Isn't it better to live in my world than die in yours?"

"No."

"You say that without even knowing what my world is going to be."

"I do know. If the Dark get this weapon of the Dragon Kings', then the Kings will be wiped out. You'll try to stand against the Dark, but you won't be able to."

Ulrik's smile was gone as he carefully watched him. "The Dark will never get the upper hand on me. Oh, they'll try, but they'll fail. As for the Dragon Kings, what do you know of them?"

Bloody hell. Henry knew better than to talk so freely about the Kings. He was going to have to construct a good lie, not an easy thing when he was in such pain. "How do you think I knew about the group of traitors within MI5? How do you think I knew of the Dark or of you?"

"I'd like to know."

The words were spoken calmly, softly, but Henry didn't miss the menace that underlaid them. "I was asked to join the task force to find the traitors in MI5. When I agreed, my superiors informed me of just what I would be seeing."

"Hmm," Ulrik said. "That's a very plausible explanation. I wonder though, did one of your superiors have any dealings with the Dragon Kings? Because any normal human would want any such magical beings eradicated from this realm posthaste."

"I don't know if he did or not. From the files I read how Dreagan Industries was being targeted. Once we learned those at Dreagan were really dragons, we realized they haven't done any harm to us. It's a human thing to stand up for the ones who are being picked on."

Ulrik laughed and leaned forward so that his forearms rested on his knees. "Trust me when I say the Dragon Kings don't need your help. Besides, Earth will be better off without them."

"Why?"

"Because I was meant to rule."

Henry wished he had some way of getting all of this back to Banan. Thinking of his friend made him realize Banan would likely go looking for him when he didn't check in.

He looked at Ulrik and twisted his lips in a sneer, ignoring the pain when he split open his lip again. "You belong in Bedlam."

"I'm taking what was mine by right. You have a choice here, Henry. You can live or you can die."

Henry snorted derisively. "I suspect it isn't that easy of a decision."

"You pledge yourself to me, then I let you live."

"I could lie."

Ulrik rose. "You could try, but the magic I use will ensure your promise to me is kept."

"So you don't trust me?"

"I don't trust anyone."

"Give me a reason to side with you, Ulrik."

His face contorted with rage for a heartbeat, and then it was gone. "Doona ever call me that again."

Henry didn't comment on Ulrik's slip into his brogue. There had to be a reason he didn't want his name known or for others to know he was Scottish.

"As for why? Henry, I would think your life would be answer enough," Ulrik said, appearing to collect himself, his English accent back in place. "You have until dawn to make your decision."

CHAPTER
SEVEN

Lily's heart pounded, her blood turned to ice, and she was unable to move. Years of being terrorized by Dennis returned in an instant. She began to shake uncontrollably, hating herself for the fear that seized her.

"Aren't you happy to see me?" Dennis asked with a wide grin. He pushed from the chair and stalked toward her with a knowing look in his eyes of just how much she feared him. "I should be angry at you for leaving the way you did."

"You were the one who broke in and wrecked my flat," she accused.

He held up his hands and winked. "Guilty. It's been a lot of fun watching your eyes dart around when you've thought you saw or heard me."

"So it was you." Lily felt a little better knowing she wasn't going insane, but it was negligible compared to having Dennis around again.

"It was me," he confessed and walked around her tiny kitchen. "I've been watching you. You've done quite well despite not having your parents' money. And here I thought you'd go rushing back to them. Still feel guilty about that, don't you?"

How she wanted to scratch that smug smile off his face. Looking at him now, she couldn't fathom what she ever saw in him. He was marginally good looking, but he had an awful temper and little respect for anyone but himself. He used people, just as he'd used her.

Why hadn't she listened to her parents? They saw what he was, but Lily thought she knew better. She had four broken bones, a multitude of scars, and nightmares to prove how wrong she had been.

An image of Rhys flashed in her mind. She tried to hold on to it, to his strength, but Dennis intruded once more.

Dennis moved to stand in front of her, the smile gone. His fingers bit into her arms. "I'm back, Lily. I'm back in your life, so you'd best remember your place quickly. Wipe that look off your face before I remove it for you."

She poured every ounce of hate and loathing through her eyes. Even when she saw his hand coming, she didn't stop.

Lily hit the door, her head slamming against it with the force of his slap. Her feet came out from underneath her, and she slumped to the ground. The only thing keeping her sitting up was the door. She blinked, the room spinning and her ears ringing. She also tasted blooded, proof that her teeth had cut the inside of her cheek.

"You must think I like hitting you," Dennis said with a tsking sound.

She wanted to tell him to go fuck himself, but her cheek was numb.

Dennis laughed and roughly hauled her to her feet. "Well, in truth, Lily, I enjoy it very much. I told you I'd break you. I thought I'd done it, but you were too good of an actress. This time, you'll be broken one way or another."

That last threat wasn't idle. She could hear it in his voice.

Lily tried to fight him as he dragged her to the sofa and

shoved her onto it. She wiped the blood from the corner of her lip and sat up, glaring.

"I'll be happy to beat you until you can't stand. I've done it before, so you know I'm more than capable, but I need you to go into work tomorrow."

Work? Why did he care if she went into work?

"Asshole," she mumbled.

That stopped him as he was turning away. He looked back at her. "What was that?"

"I called you an asshole," she said loudly.

"I'm so much more than that, darling. Shall I tell you?"

She held his gaze, terrified and nauseated at the same time. Dennis had made life a living hell. It took everything she'd had to leave him, and to have him back in her life now? It didn't seem fair.

"It's no accident I'm here," he said as he resumed his seat in her chair. "I've the added benefit of having you again, but that's not the only reason."

"What benefit could I be to you?" she asked scornfully.

He lifted a bottle from the table next to him, showing her the double dragon logo. "This is fine whisky."

Lily touched the cheek he'd hit and felt the heat of it. She looked from the bottle of Dreagan whisky to Dennis. "I only work in the store."

"That's all I need."

"Why? So you can steal whisky?"

Dennis laughed loudly, an evil light coming into his eyes. "You're going to get me onto Dreagan."

"Anyone can come to Dreagan." Lily wasn't sure if he was that simple, or if hitting her head had rattled her mind a bit.

Dennis poured a splash of whisky in a glass and lifted the glass to the light. "I'm going to want to go places the public isn't allowed."

"No." No way would she be a part of something like that. She liked everyone at Dreagan too much, liked her job there.

Dennis sipped the whisky and licked his lips. "So predictable. I knew you'd say no. It's why I've got insurance."

She really was going to throw up, because there was only one thing that could make her agree to do anything—her family.

"I've seen how friendly you are with those at Dreagan, and how they rush to your side when you're in trouble. If you don't do what I say, I'm going to kill one of them. Perhaps one of those who work in the shop with you? What are their names? Cassie, Jane, and Elena?"

As Dennis said the names, the faces of Hal, Banan, and Guy popped in her head. Those men—any at Dreagan, really—would rip Dennis in half for even thinking of harming their wives. All she would have to do is go to them and tell them.

Let Dennis think he was winning and getting what he wanted. Hal, Banan, and Guy would be there waiting for him.

"And when is this supposed to take place?" she asked tightly.

"Tomorrow."

Lily suddenly realized she wasn't as afraid of him as she used to be. She'd left once. She could do it again. She had also survived many of his beatings. She stood and walked to the door where she unlocked every dead bolt and then held it open. "I need time to scout the area."

Dennis drained the rest of the whisky in his glass and set it down on the table before he rose. He walked to her and paused in front of her. "You've got a day."

She let out a sigh when he began to walk through the door. Then he stopped and backed up, carefully shutting the door. He looked at her with a cold, confident smile.

"Let me be very clear," he said with a smirk. "If you think to go to anyone at Dreagan and tell them what's going on, they won't believe you."

She made a sound at the back of her throat. "Of course they'll believe me."

Dennis raised his ginger brows in mock surprise. "How naïve you still are. Do you think anyone has seen me? How do you think it'll sound to them when you tell them you've seen and heard me for weeks, but only just came face-to-face with me tonight? You'll appear touched," he said and pointed a finger at his head.

Lily's stomach rolled. No matter how daft she seemed, she would tell someone at Dreagan so Dennis could be stopped.

"On the off chance they do believe you, I'll do more than kill one of them," Dennis continued. "I've got a backup plan."

She had been waiting for this. He was going to threaten to kill a member of her family. Lily steeled herself, wondering who he would choose. Her father, who Dennis hated with a passion? Her mother, who had made her distaste of Dennis perfectly clear? One of her three sisters, all of whom had told her—in front of Dennis, no less—that she could do better? The only one safe was her brother.

Dennis pulled his mobile phone from his pocket and held it up for her to see the screen. Lily stumbled backward until she ran into the counter of the small bar in the kitchen when she saw her brother's face.

In the four years she had been gone, Kyle had developed into a fine-looking young man. He was her father's pride, the only son of five children, and the baby of the family.

"Kyle is quite funny," Dennis said, a knowing look in his blue eyes. "We've become very close, he and I. It started out innocently enough by telling him I was trying to get you to come back to the family."

Uncontrollable rage welled up inside Lily. For the first time in her life, she wanted to hurt someone. No. She wanted to kill.

Dennis, the charmer who had wooed her so effectively four years ago had now wormed his way into her brother's life. Why? She hadn't even been at Dreagan then. None of it made sense, but it didn't matter.

"Focus that hate, Lily," Dennis said as he closed the distance between them, leaving the screen of the mobile phone up so she couldn't look away from her brother's smiling face. "Use it against Dreagan."

"I will kill you for this."

Dennis chuckled. "You? I doubt that, darling. Kyle is such a clever lad. He wants to make a name for himself, you know. He doesn't want to use the family name to do it either. He wants to prove to your father he can do it alone."

Lily gripped the counter behind her and wished the knives were closer so she could plunge one into Dennis's black heart.

"You hate that Kyle and I have become close, don't you?" Dennis asked. "How do you feel about us spending weekends together? It hasn't been easy explaining your continued absence, but Kyle is so hungry for a companion near his age that he isn't thinking about you as I show him how to do things."

"What things?" she said through clenched teeth.

Dennis's smile was slow, taunting. "It was so easy to lie to you all those years about what I really do. I work for one of the most dangerous men to walk the earth."

"I don't believe you."

"Do you recall that trip to Japan I took? I really went to France. I'm sure if you think back you'll remember reading how a wealthy businessman was killed. That man tried to cheat my boss."

"And you killed the businessman?" Lily's body went

cold, because she did remember reading about a man being murdered in France while Dennis was supposed to be in Japan.

"You accepted every lie I told about where I was going, and why I made the money I did. My boss rewards loyalty, and kills traitors without blinking. He's vicious and unyielding, and he's taken quite an interest in Kyle."

Lily's eyes were fastened on the small screen as Dennis touched the play button and the video began. Kyle was laughing, his dark eyes crinkled. His black hair was cropped short on the sides, and left longer on top. Kyle sat beside Dennis on top of a wooden picnic table, their friendship obvious from how Kyle interacted with him.

Dennis stopped the video and lowered the mobile phone. "If you don't get me onto Dreagan, I'm going to bring Kyle into the fold. He'll disappear, Lily. He'll become a killer, sell drugs, steal, and whatever else our boss tells him to do."

"You took quite a chance befriending my brother on the off chance that I would become useful to you," she said derisively.

Dennis chuckled. "Do you really think you stumbled upon the job at Dreagan accidentally? We pushed you there."

"Liar."

"You did what we wanted, and went where we wanted. If you hadn't gotten that job at Dreagan, we'd have ensured you got another one. I hope this clears up any hope in your mind that you can get out of helping me achieve what I need to do. If not, one of your new friends is going to die, and you'll never see your brother again."

It took Lily a moment to realize Dennis was gone. She glanced at the locks on the door, but didn't bother to turn them. He had gotten in once. Nothing would stop him from getting in a second time.

She walked to her bedroom and sat down on her bed, the entire conversation with Dennis running through her mind. Lily didn't want anyone from Dreagan getting hurt, but not a single one of them mattered as much as her brother.

From the moment Kyle came into the world, he was happy. He brought smiles to everyone's face he encountered. There was a light inside him that burned brighter, a spark that drew others to him.

Because of her, Kyle had been drawn into a world he knew nothing about. A world that would destroy his light in an instant.

Lily had no choice but to help Dennis. The thought left a bad taste in her mouth, but Dennis was sorely mistaken if he thought she would sit back and not retaliate.

She would get her brother away from him, and then she would hunt Dennis down and kill him.

CHAPTER
EIGHT

Rhys walked by Lily's flat four times. He told himself it was just to make sure she was home and safe, that he had no intention of going inside. But every time he got close to her door, he found himself heading right to it.

He finally got tired of fighting it and started toward her door. It suddenly opened, and a man stepped out. Rhys halted in his tracks halfway across the street. Of course someone as beautiful and kind as Lily wouldn't be alone.

Rhys hated the jealousy that rose up, but that was nothing compared to the urge to rip the mortal apart. Lily was his. He knew it to the bottom of his soul that they were meant to be together throughout time.

He stopped his thoughts right there. Lily wasn't his. Lily was only a human who he wanted with every fiber of his being, someone he would watch over until the day of her last breath.

Rhys turned and retraced his steps. He kept hidden until the mortal was gone. Then his gaze went back to Lily's door. It seemed like yesterday that he learned her flat was broken into and she was missing. His mind ran rampant with all the ways she could be hurt, and he wanted to kill whoever had dared to harm her.

He felt the same for the man who scarred her, the man who made her fear. If he couldn't have her for his own, he could make sure that the man responsible never got near her again.

"You'll no' have to fear him again, Lily," Rhys vowed.

He should've felt better. Why then did the ache in his chest intensify?

There was only one way to lessen it. He had to see her. Rhys strode across the street and walked up to her door. His hand was raised to knock when the door opened. As soon as he saw Lily's pale face, concern flared.

"Rhys," she said, her shoulders sagging as if in relief.

He frowned and glanced over her head inside the flat. "Are you all right?"

His worry intensified when he swore he heard her mumble under her breath, "I am now."

"It's just been a long day," she said louder.

"Want to talk about it?"

She shook her head. "I would actually like to take my mind off of it."

"Let me help." Rhys understood all too well about wanting to forget something horrid. He suffered through it every day he couldn't shift.

Her dark gaze met his, visibly relaxing. "I'd like that very much."

"What do you want to do?"

"Anything," she said as she grabbed her purse.

Rhys stepped aside when she walked out of the flat and closed the door behind her. He waited as she locked all three dead bolts, his heart thumping wildly at getting to spend some time alone with her.

He didn't miss how she looked nervously around the

street. Her hands shook when she tried to put her keys in her purse, and they ended up falling to the sidewalk.

Rhys bent and grabbed the keys. He then dropped them into her purse and caught her gaze. "You doona need to fear anything as long as I'm near."

Her head dipped, her breath catching in her throat. She swallowed hard and lifted her face to his. "Thank you."

It took everything he had to step back and not kiss her again. She had no idea how appealing she was, how he hungered to taste her—to claim her. Rhys began to walk, and she fell into step beside him. He shortened his strides to walk with her.

"Where are we going?" she asked.

"For a walk."

"That sounds nice."

Rhys felt the knot in his chest loosen the longer he was with her. He talked of mundane things such as the weather and work, anything to take her mind off whatever was troubling her. How he wished she would confide in him, but it wasn't like he was the best at telling others what bothered him. Which was why he didn't push her. If she wanted to tell him, then she would. Until then, he would take her mind off it.

He took her past the small park to a trail used by hikers and runners. It took them over hills and into the forest as well as past a small loch. Her smile grew, her eyes brightening once more. Rhys hated to admit it was the first time he had done something like this with a woman, but he felt as if time had been waiting for Lily to enter his life.

While she looked at the scenery, he watched her. He loved the way she would pull her long hair over one shoulder when she bent to inspect something, how she gently touched the petals of the flowers. Everything she did was fluid and elegant.

Rhys took every opportunity to touch her. Their hands skimmed on several occasions, as did their bodies. He touched her hair multiple times without her ever knowing it. Each time was burned into his mind and soul—and she sank deeper into his psyche.

"Where did you go when you left Dreagan?" she asked as they walked along the path.

He waited until they reached the top of the summit of the hill to look out over the land. Rhys waited until she stopped beside him before he said, "I was on Dreagan."

"Well, there are sixty thousand acres," she said with a small smile.

His lips softened when he looked at her. "I just needed to get away."

"I did that once."

"How did it turn out?"

She folded her arms together. "I'll let you know. The fact is, Dreagan is an escape for me. I don't know what it is about the land, but I can't wait to get there. And I hate to leave it."

"It's magical to be sure." He sighed. If only she knew just how much magic was there. She was obviously able to feel some of it to have such a strong pull to it.

"You're very lucky to have it as your home." She turned to him then, her gaze searching. "You seem different."

He lifted a shoulder in a shrug. "I guess I am."

"I am too." Lily hastily looked away and rubbed her hands on her arms.

"You're chilled." Rhys could've kicked himself for not having a coat to give her. "You should've told me."

Lily chuckled as she spread her arms to encompass the view. "And miss this? Never."

"I wouldna advise coming in the morning. It's full of runners. I'm surprised there are no' more people up here now," he said and turned her to begin walking again. "The trail makes a loop around the village."

"I know where I'll be coming from now on."

Rhys was about to tell her to watch the root, but her foot hit it before he could. Lily pitched forward. His arms snaked out and grabbed her, yanking her against his chest to keep her from tumbling down the hill.

Her lips were parted, her pulse rapid at the base of her throat. She had her hands fisted in his shirt tightly. Rhys's own heart was pounding at the thought of her hurt in any way. He knew he'd grabbed her roughly, but it was his first reaction. The fact he responded so hastily confirmed how much he loved her.

It didn't matter when he had fallen in love with Lily. It was as if she had always been in his life. She felt . . . right.

Rhys lowered his head, his mouth on hers before he knew what was happening. Her lips moved beneath his, open and eager. He groaned and wound his arms around her. The kiss was ecstasy, bliss—pure rapture.

Desire blazed through him as hot as dragon fire. There was an ache inside him that only Lily could ease, a yearning that only she could relieve.

The sound of someone coming broke them apart. Rhys didn't pay the group of runners any mind. His gaze was locked with Lily's. Her lips were swollen, just as they had been the night of their first kiss. Then, like a fool, he had walked away from her.

There was no way he could do the same now. He might not deserve Lily, but he longed for her desperately. Without even knowing how or when, she was the center of his universe, the one person who could lift him up or destroy him with a simple touch.

One of the runners bumped into Lily hard enough that

she grunted. Rhys jerked his head up, trying to pick out which one had hurt her.

"It's all right," Lily hurried to say. "It was an accident. I'm fine."

Rhys looked back at her, his gaze dropping to her lips. He wanted to kiss her more, to slowly—nay, quickly—yank off her clothes. Then he would slowly make love to her for hours, days even. No one had ever made him feel as she did, and it was . . . unsettling to say the least.

She shivered in his arms. Rhys mentally kicked himself as he rubbed his hands up and down her back. It was time to get her home. Whether he left her there or not was completely up to Lily. He was unsure of her past, but he would go gently with her no matter what.

"Let's get you home so you can warm up," he said and kept an arm around her as they walked the path back to town.

Rhys was lost in his thoughts, reliving the kiss again. He didn't realize until they reached the village that the tension had returned to Lily. She stood stiffly, the smile gone as lines pinched around her lips.

"I didna do a verra good job," Rhys said.

Lily was quiet for long moments. Then she said, "You took me away from my troubles, just as I asked you to do. That means a lot to me. I can't thank you enough."

He stopped them before her flat and turned her to face him. "Is there anything else I can do?"

"If there is, I'll let you know."

Rhys gently touched her face. The lines of strain on her face maddened him. He wanted to know who was causing such stress in her life and why. "I'll see you tomorrow then."

"Good night, Rhys," she said.

He took several steps back while she unlocked her door. Their gazes met once more before she walked into her flat.

Rhys waited for several minutes, hoping she would come back out and ask him inside.

Eventually he returned to Dreagan.

Henry might have been left in the plush sitting room, but a prison was still a prison. As the hours drifted by, his body continued to ache worse and worse. Every breath, however small, only added to the pain of his broken ribs.

He tried to get up and walk and was covered in sweat in seconds from that exertion. All he managed was one loop around the room, but it was enough for him to see there was a single way in and one way out.

In other words, he was royally fucked.

Henry spent the rest of the night weighing his options. By now Banan would know something was wrong, but his friend wouldn't have a clue where to start looking. There was no way Henry would agree to side with Ulrik. The man was a psychopath. But neither was Henry ready to die. That left him little wiggle room.

Henry turned his head to the fireplace and the fire that hadn't died down once nor had the logs burned, and they were real logs. Magic. All his years as a spy when he thought he had seen the worst of what was out in the world, and he hadn't even scraped the surface of the hidden world of magic, Dragon Kings, Fae, and God only knew what else.

He sighed and grimaced at the pain that simple movement caused. If only there was someone he could ask for help. Immediately, an image of Rhi popped into his head. Henry smiled as he thought of the Light Fae. He hadn't seen her since he first discovered there were Fae in the world, but he had tried to join the group going after her.

As a human with no magic or powers, he would've been a liability. Even with all his training, he'd never felt so . . .

weak and inadequate. Banan and the other Kings were right to leave him behind, but it still grated.

At least Rhi had gotten free. He hoped wherever she was, she was happy.

What he wouldn't do to see her unusual silver eyes that seemed to glow on their own, her black-as-pitch hair that hung luxuriously down her back, and her sexy-as-hell smile.

It was no wonder mortals couldn't refuse a Fae. Someone that beautiful couldn't be denied anything. He certainly wouldn't deny Rhi a single thing.

"I hope that smile's for me, sexy," said a sultry voice he immediately recognized.

Henry's gaze jerked to a darkened corner where Rhi stepped from the shadows.

CHAPTER
NINE

Lily didn't realize she had sat up all night until her alarm clock went off. She turned and looked at it, confused as to how she had lost so many hours. The walk with Rhys had done her a world of good, but when Dennis ran into her on the trail with the runners, he ruined everything by reminding her of his visit and what he demanded.

She rose and turned off the alarm before she removed her shoes, skirt, and shirt. Her head was stuck on what had occurred the night before, and she couldn't get herself moving. A shower that normally took her ten minutes, took her twenty. Once she was finished, she stood in front of her closet in a towel with her hair dripping, but she wasn't seeing her clothes. She saw Kyle.

Lily mentally shook herself and quickly grabbed a black long-sleeved shirt and a black skirt. She dressed and dried her hair. As she walked from her room, she caught a glimpse of herself in the mirror. She looked like she was going to a funeral.

Then again, it fit her mood perfectly.

Lily found it difficult to concentrate as she drove to Dreagan. It took her the entire drive before she convinced herself she was saving a life at Dreagan, as well as her brother.

Besides, what was the worst thing Dennis could do? It wasn't like they wouldn't catch him. And if he did get away with stealing whatever he was after, those at Dreagan had enough money to cover it. If it were as valuable as she expected, there would also be insurance for it.

Two lives were worth much more than some piece of art or jewelry.

Lily turned down the long drive to Dreagan. It was the first morning since she started work that she didn't feel the excitement at being on Dreagan. Now she wished she'd never set foot on the land. She parked and turned off the car, but she didn't get out. Instead, she sat in the car and stared out her window. Dennis had given her a day to find an entry point.

The idea that they—whoever the collective "they" were he worked for—pushed her to Dreagan seemed . . . improbable. There was no way anyone could've known where she would end up, especially not Dennis.

"Wanker," she said aloud.

To think that at one time she had loved him. She had given up her family for him, given up herself for him. And for what? What did she have but scars, broken bones, and a fear of him that she wished she could cut out?

Lily might be naïve at times, but she wasn't a fool. If she did this for Dennis, he would return wanting something else. It was one of *many* reasons she had to kill him.

Then she needed to tell her family everything. Lies, even untold lies, were what had put her family in this position. Only truth could set everyone free.

She would need a weapon. Though she longed to plunge a knife into Dennis's heart, he wouldn't let her close enough. It was going to have to be a gun.

As long as she and Dennis had been together, there were

things about her he didn't know. For instance, he had no idea that her father had taken every one of his children hunting. Lily could shoot a handgun with deadly accuracy from fifty feet, and a rifle from 350 yards.

Dennis didn't stand a chance.

Lily grabbed her purse and opened her car door. She would buy a gun after she got off work. Or perhaps during lunch.

She stepped out of the car and faced the store. It was no longer her refuge. Dennis had intruded upon her world once again. After today, she would leave, as hard as it would be to do.

She walked slowly to the store. As usual, the door was already unlocked. Lily stepped inside and heard Jane's voice coming from the back. A moment later, Lily heard Elena's as well. Lily put her purse behind the counter and grabbed the bag of money set aside for her. She opened the cash register and began to set up for the day.

"Morning," Elena called.

Lily glanced up into Elena's sage green eyes. "Morning."

Elena walked toward the back with two bottles of thirty-year-old Scotch in her hands, her dark blond hair in a low ponytail. "I think it's going to rain today."

Lily paused in counting the money and looked down at her right wrist. She was so distracted she didn't even realize it was hurting until Elena said something about the rain. "Yes, it is."

"It is Scotland," Elena said with a laugh as she placed the bottles on the shelf. "It rains almost every day."

Lily forced a smile when Elena turned to her. "True enough. I used to think England got the most rain. Then I came to the Highlands."

"Are you all right?" Elena asked with a frown as she approached.

"I didn't sleep well last night."

Elena's frown deepened. "And the bruise on your cheek?"

"Bruise?" Lily touched the cheek Dennis had hit and winced when her fingers grazed the spot. She forced a chuckle. "I knew after such a spectacular fall that I wouldn't get away without some kind of wound."

"What fall?"

Elena was suspicious, and she had every right to be. Lily, however, was used to telling lies about her bruises. She was, she hated to admit, quite adept at it. "Yesterday when I went to my flat I stepped up on the curb, and my foot got caught in my skirt. I went down. Epically, I might add." She finished it off with an embarrassed smile. "Wouldn't you know there was a group of teenage girls who saw it all?"

Elena cringed. "They didn't laugh, did they?"

"I was laughing," Lily said with a grin.

"I'm just glad you weren't seriously hurt." Elena patted her hand and walked around the counter to the second register.

Lily bent and got her purse. "I didn't realize there was a bruise. I'm going to go see about hiding some of it before I frighten away customers."

Elena smiled and nodded as she counted the money.

Lily hurried to the back and into the bathroom. She turned her head to the side to see the large bruise that was a dark blue and green, with a hint of yellow on the edges. No amount of makeup in the world was going to cover that.

If only she had taken a moment that morning and really looked at herself, she would've seen it and hidden most of the damage. Instead, she hadn't given a second thought to makeup. She normally wore very little of it anyway.

Lily got out her concealer and put some on her finger. She held her hand over the bruise, angry that she was once more lying as well as covering bruises. She had left that world behind. It wasn't fair that it found her again.

For the rest of the day she was going to have to act like she had a one-of-a-kind accident. All she could pray for was that Dennis didn't hit her again, because she couldn't play the klutz card, not with Jane about—who was quite literally a klutz. Not to mention, in the time she had been at Dreagan, she hadn't run into anything, tripped, or done the things Jane did on a daily basis.

Lily began to lightly dab the concealer over the darkest parts of the bruise across her cheekbone. When she finished, she looked at her reflection, and hated what she saw.

The woman staring back at her was the frightened, timid woman she had been before she left Dennis. That woman she left behind, or so she had thought. But how easily Dennis brought her back.

She didn't want to be that woman anymore. She hated that woman, hated the life that went along with it. If she wanted to eradicate that woman from her life, then she needed to make a stand.

Now. Today.

Right this minute.

"I'm not that woman," she whispered to her reflection. "I left her behind."

Then act like it.

Lily took a deep breath. Yes, she had to act like it. Dennis could still hurt her, but so what? There was a possibility he could kill her, but she doubted he would do that. Not when he needed her.

But she no longer cared about him or their relationship. She didn't fear his fists or his temper, because she knew what to expect. Fear bred fear. She had to fight the fear with strength and faith.

"He has no control over me," she said in a stronger voice. Those six words gave her power to take a stand.

Lily glanced at her watch and tossed the concealer in her purse. She had taken too long, and was now behind on her duties. Lily opened the door and hurried out to the main room, only to discover Jane and Elena had covered for her.

"Thank you," she told them.

"It's not a big deal," Jane said with a wink. "Elena told me about your fall. I know something about embarrassing falls."

Lily genuinely smiled at Jane, because Jane was sweet, trusting, and able to trip on a flat surface—barefoot.

"It's a perfect chance for you to buy shorter skirts while you're shopping with Denae later," Elena said.

Lily had completely forgotten about her shopping trip with Denae. She looked from Elena to Jane and closed her eyes with a loud sigh. "It's my day off, isn't it?"

"It is," Jane said. "That fall must have rattled you."

"It did." Much more than they would ever know.

Elena looked at the clock and shrugged. "You're meeting Denae in a bit anyway. You can hang out here if you want. No work required."

Lily's eyes grew moist with unshed tears. She didn't want to lie to her friends, but also didn't want to be responsible for one of their deaths. "I think I might walk around for a bit, if that's all right."

"Um . . ." Elena hedged as she glanced at Jane. "That should be fine."

Lily adjusted the strap of her purse on her shoulder and walked from the store. She didn't look over her shoulder, even as she suspected that they might be watching. It was obvious they weren't keen on her strolling around the land.

There were only a few buildings the public ever saw of Dreagan. The rest was kept behind huge hedgerows. Lily started along the same route as those who took a tour of Dreagan. She walked slowly, stopping at the small bridge and looking at the stream flowing beneath. She ambled from one spot to another, but no one ever stopped her.

Lily walked behind the stilehouse, but didn't go to the hedgerow. She wound her way to the back of the store. There she stopped and leaned back against the white brick.

She had never been the kid who pushed boundaries to see how far she could go. Lily kept well within the rules. If someone said she couldn't go somewhere, she didn't attempt it. Which was why she was having such a difficult time even walking to the hedgerow.

On her first day, Cassie had told her that no one but those who lived at Dreagan were allowed past the hedges. But for her friends, for Kyle, she was going to break a rule.

Lily pushed away from the brick and squared her shoulders. She took two steps and stopped. It took another few minutes before she managed three steps. Each one brought her closer and closer to the hedgerow, but it was killing her spirit to do it.

With only ten more steps to go, Lily forced herself to take another three, and another three. She had to stop then, as her heart was pounding. At any moment she expected someone to grab her and tell her to get off Dreagan.

She took a deep breath, and walked the last four steps to the hedgerow. The leaves brushed her hands, the limbs interlocking so tightly she could barely see through them. Now she would have to find an entry point.

"Hey!"

Lily whirled around, falling into the hedgerow.

Denae rushed to her and helped her gain her balance. Denae was laughing as she said, "I didn't mean to scare you."

"It's all right," Lily said and shook out her skirt of imaginary debris. She felt more stupid than she had in a very long time.

"What were you looking at?" Denae asked.

Lily shrugged and glanced at the leaves. "Just looking at the shrub."

"You were quite absorbed. I've been calling your name. Oh, my God," she said with a gasp. "Lily, your face. What happened?"

"I fell," she said automatically. She repeated her story from earlier, happy that Denae, like Elena and Jane, believed her.

"Are you up for shopping?"

Lily wanted to be anywhere but Dreagan. "Yes, please."

"Good. I'm glad you're here early. Let's go," Denae said and started walking.

Lily kept up with her long strides. Right up until the moment she went toward the parking lot, and Denae went left.

"This way," Denae said with a smile.

Lily hurried after her, surprised when Denae disappeared around a hedgerow. Lily discovered that there were two hedgerows overlapping at that point so there was a path around them. It was designed so that only those who knew of the path would know how to get through the hedgerow.

As Lily emerged from the shrubbery, she gasped when she got her first full look at the manor. It was large, at least four stories, and spread wide with many windows, while the back portion of the manor disappeared into the mountain that rose up behind it. The dark gray stone didn't make the manor seem imposing at all, but rather ancient and important.

Then it occurred to her that she was seeing a part of Dreagan she shouldn't, a part that could help Dennis on his quest.

CHAPTER
TEN

Rhys halted when he caught a glimpse of black hair. He knew without having to see her face that it was Lily. It never occurred to him that Lily shouldn't be on the other side of the hedge. All that mattered was that he be near her.

Her head turned toward him, the wind pushing her hair out of her face. That's when he saw the bruise on her left cheek. When had that happened? There was nothing on her cheek when he left her last night. He took a step to go after her when he was hauled back.

Rhys jerked his head around and glared into Warrick's cobalt eyes "Let go," he demanded.

Warrick lifted a blond brow. "She's leaving with Denae, or did you forget that?"

"I didna." Actually, he'd forgotten everything, including the fact he couldn't shift again, once he saw Lily. "Did you see her face?"

Warrick sighed and dropped his hand. "Were you no' listening at all when Jane told us Lily's explanation just a few minutes ago?"

In truth, Rhys hadn't paid a bit of attention to anything anyone said. His thoughts alternated between wanting to find Ulrik and confront him or kill him—or both—and Lily.

The things he wanted to do to her body made him ache, made him burn with need. And that burn was quickly turning into a blaze. He craved her touch, pined for her smile.

Hungered for her kiss.

"That's a no then," Warrick said with a twist of his lips. "Why even bother coming to the meetings if you are no' going to pay attention?"

"Because Con drags me to them." Rhys turned his gaze back to Lily, watching her long skirt drag the ground as she follow Denae to the garage that held most of their cars. "How did she get the bruise?"

"She told them she tripped on her skirt and fell, hitting her face on the sidewalk outside her flat."

Rhys wasn't so sure he believed the explanation. He hadn't been staring at her cheek when he was with her last night, but he was sure he would've noticed if she were hurt. Besides, if what Cassie told him was true, then it was a man who had done that to her. Was it the same one Rhys saw leaving her flat? Was that what was wrong with her?

Anger ripped through Rhys. He'd been so intent on his desire he hadn't put two and two together. "That is a substantial bruise."

"Some humans bruise easily."

Rhys grunted as Denae drove off in the white Mercedes G-class SUV. "Surely those two are no' driving to Edinburgh." If so, he was going to follow.

Kellan walked up on Rhys's other side. "They're taking a helicopter I rented for my woman."

"Helicopter?" Warrick gave a long whistle. "I'm surprised you are no' trying to talk Con into buying one."

Kellan shrugged and crossed his arms over his chest. "No need. I bought one myself. It'll be here in a few weeks. Until then, I'd rather keep Denae off the roads if I can."

Rhys knew it was because Ulrik's men had sabotaged Iona's father's vehicle, killing him. "Our enemies could get to a chopper as well," Rhys pointed out.

"No' when they doona know which service she's taking," Kellan replied with a grin.

Warrick grunted. "You do know that since Denae is mated to you that she's immortal."

"That's no' the point," Kellan stated in a flat voice. "I doona like to even think of her being injured."

Rhys knew exactly how Kellan felt. But what nagged at him was the thought of not seeing Lily. "How long does Denae plan to be gone?"

Kellan dropped his arms and turned on his heel. "I've no idea."

Rhys watched him walk to the garage and get into a Range Rover before driving off. "He's following them."

"As would I if my mate left on such a trip after all that's been going on, immortal or not."

Rhys fisted his hands. At least Kellan could protect Denae properly. He was all but useless. Thanks to Ulrik.

Except for his magic. He still had his dragon magic, and that in itself was lethal.

He turned his head to Warrick. "Fancy a drive?"

"No' especially. You doona want to follow them as well, do you?" Warrick asked with a roll of his eyes.

"I'm headed to Perth."

Warrick's face compressed in concern. "Shite. Con will have your head."

"Let him take it," Rhys said as he started toward the garage. "I'd welcome it right now."

That wasn't completely true. He wasn't ready to let go of Lily. And that was the kicker. Rhys feared he would never be ready to let go.

"Is she your mate?" Warrick asked as they reached the garage.

Rhys was surprised Warrick followed. Warrick preferred to be on his own. Then again, each one of them wanted Ulrik to end his war. Rhys grabbed his keys off the hook. He didn't utter a word until he was behind the wheel of his red Jaguar F-type. He left the top up and started the engine.

"Maybe," he finally answered. Was being in love the same as knowing she was his mate? Rhys had a feeling it was.

Warrick got into the car and buckled his seat belt. He gave a shake of his head. "You're certainly acting like she is. Why no' just take her?"

Rhys jerked his head to Warrick. "You mean like I've done countless other women? Lily isna like them. She's a forever kind." He paused and took a deep breath, letting himself calm. "And I'm no' acting like she's my mate."

"Aye, my friend, you are. Make her yours."

"I'd disappoint her, and that would kill me more surely than what Ulrik has done to me."

Rhys put the car in reverse and backed out of the garage. Once cleared, he shifted into first and drove away from Dreagan.

"Several Kings have already been to see Ulrik," Warrick said after a long stretch of miles in silence.

Rhys gripped the wheel with both hands. "Perhaps. Then again, none of them had been hit with dragon and Dark Fae magic combined."

"He'll never admit to doing it."

"I think he will. I think he's waiting for me to confront him."

Warrick frowned. "Why do you say that?"

"Ulrik tried to recruit Tristan. It wasna long after that when I was struck with that evil mix of magic. The only one stupid enough to mix dragon magic with a Dark Fae is Ulrik. He targeted me for a purpose. He knows I'll go to him and demand to know his reasoning."

"I'm no' sure it's a good idea. I'm no' saying I wouldna be thinking the same, but why get that close to Ulrik? He's proven he can no' be trusted."

Rhys threw him a dark look. "Con can no' be trusted either, and yet we all put our faith in him." Rhys could feel Warrick's gaze on him, studying and watching. "Spit it out, Warrick."

"Are you going to side with Ulrik?"

Now that was a question that hadn't entered his mind until Warrick posed it. It would get Rhys inside Ulrik's group and could end up helping the Kings. Then again, Ulrik wasn't that stupid.

"Never."

Warrick rested his elbow on the door and rubbed his hand over the stubble on his chin. He opened his mouth to speak, but no words came out.

Rhys glanced at him the same instant Con's voice sounded in his head, a connection every Dragon King had.

"*Rhys?*"

Rhys ignored the King of Kings' call, realizing Warrick had heard him as well. Pressing his foot to the accelerator, Rhys drove faster toward Perth.

"You're no' going to answer Con?" Warrick asked.

Rhys shrugged. "Why? All he'll do is tell us to return."

"*Rhys!*" Con's voice reverberated in his head.

Blowing out a breath, Rhys opened the link and answered, "*You're no' going to get me to turn around. I have to see the bastard.*"

"*Fine.*"

Rhys blinked, unsure if he'd heard Con correctly. Since when did Con want them communicating with Ulrik? "*What's the trick?*"

"We think he knows where Henry is."

"That son of a bitch," Rhys said and swerved to pull the car off the road.

Warrick shifted in his seat. *"I was hoping we'd have heard from Henry by now."*

Con's sigh was audible. *"A human in the company of traitorous MI5 agents, Dark Fae, and Ulrik? How was he ever going to come out of it alive?"*

Warrick shook his head. *"He was trying to help."*

"He's a fucking human!" Rhys said. *"He should've stayed out of it!"*

Warrick's cobalt eyes grew icy with rage as he stared at Rhys. *"He's a friend to us. How many others are willing to help?"*

Rhys knew Warrick was right, but that didn't mean he had to like Henry putting his life on the line for them.

"It's because of Lily," Warrick said so the conversation was between the two of them.

Rhys looked out the windshield and felt the familiar pang in his chest whenever he thought of Lily. He'd never been more conscious of the fragility of a human's life than with Lily. It was no wonder the Kings who were mated wanted to have the ceremony done quickly.

Until the human was officially mated, she could die. Once she was bound to a King, she would never age, nor would she die unless her King was killed.

Con said, *"Go to Ulrik, Rhys. See what you can find out about Henry. Do whatever it takes to get the information out of him."*

"I doona plan to leave Perth until I have my answers."

"Good," Con said and disconnected their link.

Warrick chuckled as Rhys pulled back onto the road. "I guess we'll be staying in Perth for a while. You know as well as I that Ulrik isna going to give up that information easily."

"I hope he doesna," Rhys said coldly. He was itching for a fight, and who better to take his rage out on than the one responsible for his predicament?

"I'm looking forward to it."

Rhys shook his head. "I doona want Ulrik to know you're with me."

"Have you lost your mind?" Warrick asked angrily.

Rhys grinned. "Perhaps."

CHAPTER
ELEVEN

Henry wasn't sure if Rhi was a figment of his imagination or real. Since he was in Ulrik's home, he didn't trust anything he saw.

Rhi stopped next to the stuffed chair to his right and leaned an arm along the tall back. "Wow. And here I thought I'd get at least a smile from you, handsome."

"You aren't real."

She looked down at herself, then back up at him. "Pretty sure I am."

Henry lowered his gaze from her ethereal face to the white shirt that plunged low enough for him to see the swell of her breasts. He swallowed hard, his blood pounding. The shirt hugged her frame down to her small waist and the black jeans that fit her like a glove.

"If you're going to look me over, don't forget my new shoes," she said as she lifted her foot so he could see them.

He glanced at the tall heels with silver spikes. "Nice boots."

"Booties," she corrected. "They're Louboutins. The red sole is their trademark. Keep up, sexy."

Henry nodded in response. He couldn't care less about the damn shoes. "Why are you here? If it really is you."

"Trust me, stud. It's me," she said as she pushed away from the chair and gently sat beside him. Her face scrunched as she looked him over. "You look like hell. What did they do to you?"

"I don't recall much once the beating commenced."

"You're lucky to be alive," she said in a serious voice.

Henry shrugged then immediately regretted it. He gritted his teeth until the worst of the pain passed. "It was worth it if I can get the information I have to Banan."

Rhi set her hand atop his. Henry's skin warmed where their flesh met. In all his dreams, he would never have expected her to touch him. She was so far out of his league that he was content to just look at her. Oh, but to feel her. His pain was forgotten as desire flared thick and heavy.

"You're very brave," she said in a gentle voice.

Henry became lost in her silver eyes. He was floating, drifting. Soaring. "I did what I had to."

"No. You did what you could for your friends. You put your life in jeopardy for them."

"They deserve no less."

Rhi's smile held a hint of sadness. "You deserve life."

"I won't side with Ulrik," Henry said tightly. "It goes against everything I am."

"Of course you won't side with Ulrik."

Henry looked down at her hand atop his. "I'm prepared to die."

He wasn't just saying that because it was Rhi. Henry meant every word. Although having the Light Fae beside him bolstered his courage as nothing else could.

"I see that you are. A pity," she whispered and kissed his cheek.

Then she was gone, vanished as if she had never been. It happened so quickly Henry could only blink in response. Then the door opened and Ulrik entered. His gaze landed on Henry before he walked to the chair he had occupied earlier. "It's morning. Time for a decision."

Henry couldn't believe the time had already come. Not that it mattered. His decision was made the moment Ulrik gave him the ultimatum.

"That's good," Henry said. "I'm tired of being in this room."

"Want out, do you?" Ulrik said with a smirk.

"I sure do."

"The promise you give can be put into your own words. I'll use my magic to bind your promise."

Henry chuckled, amazed to find his ribs didn't hurt as much as they had a few minutes ago. "You're a piece of work."

Ulrik's smile vanished, his gold eyes narrowing on Henry. "Is that some kind of joke?"

"Joke? Not at all. I'll give you my promise. I vow that I'll never join you in any endeavor. I pledge that I'll fight against you from now until the end of my days."

"Which is imminent," Ulrik interrupted in a tight voice.

Undeterred, Henry continued. "I promise that I'll do whatever it takes to bring you down."

Ulrik stood so fast the chair toppled over. His arm reared back, his palm out. Henry watched it all in slow motion. He lifted his chin and prepared to die.

"Isn't this great?" Denae beamed from the passenger seat of the helicopter.

Lily nodded, though it wasn't her first time in a chopper. She'd always loved air travel of any kind, but the helicopter was her favorite. So much so, she had her pilot's license. How she missed flying.

She loved seeing the world from the vantage point of the clouds. There was something that altered a person when they looked down upon the ground from such a lofty height and realized how small things really were.

Lily basked in the pleasure as they soared. For a short time, she was able to forget about Dennis, forget about Kyle being threatened, and forget about betraying her friends. The one thing she couldn't forget was Rhys.

No matter where she was or what she was doing, he was a constant in her thoughts. His gentle but firm touch, his soft but insistent kisses. Her stomach fluttered remembering how tightly he held her as they kissed. She wondered if Rhys would enjoy flying, or was he afraid of it as so many were? Would he feel the freedom of it as she did? Would he love the exhilaration of going fast?

Time after time, she found herself wishing he were beside her so she could point out something below them, or laugh at how sedately they were flying. It was ridiculous really. She didn't even know Rhys, and yet, he was part of her world. A part of her.

How sad was she? Thank God no one else knew, lest they pity her. It was bad enough she ran from an abusive relationship, but to set her sights on someone that could never be hers? He made her want to find her lost courage, to break the invisible shackles that linked her to Dennis.

The chopper dipped, signaling that their ride was coming to an end. Lily looked down at her clothes. They weren't her. Just as her life with Dennis wasn't her. It was time to do more than just buy a few new items. It was time to erase Dennis from her life entirely. And she was starting today.

When the helicopter landed, Denae opened the door and stepped out. Lily followed, holding her hair in one hand so it didn't fly everywhere. Denae was all smiles as she waited for Lily. Together they walked to a black Mercedes where two men waited beside it for them.

"I hope all of this doesn't make you uncomfortable," Denae said after they were in the car.

Lily looked at her. "This?"

"The helicopter and the car waiting for us. I know I was unaccustomed to such wealth when Kellan and I got together. It's amazing how quickly I adapted," she said with a laugh.

For a second, Lily thought about telling Denae who she really was, but then she decided it didn't matter. "This doesn't bother me at all. It's nice that all of this is available to you."

"Kellan is a bit overprotective, not that I mind."

Lily looked away when she saw the love shining in Denae's whisky-colored eyes. "You're very lucky, you know."

"You'll find love yourself. I truly believe that."

"Of course." What else could she say?

When they arrived at the first store, Lily was anxious to shop. It felt like eons since she'd bought anything she liked. They walked through the doors of the store, and Lily paused and took a deep breath. She wanted to feel good in clothes again, wanted them to fit her, but more than that she wanted to stop Rhys in his tracks so he looked her up and down.

"I know that look," Denae said. "I've seen it on Shara's face often enough. That's a look of a woman who's ready to shop."

Lily returned her smile. "Oh, yes."

"Where shall we begin?"

Lily pointed to the shoes. "You wanted shoes."

Denae was shaking her head before she finished. "No way. Let's look at clothes. Shoes and jewelry are last."

Lily almost couldn't remember the last time she felt so carefree as she walked through rack after rack of clothes. Before she had time to find anything, a store employee was beside her. It took just a few items that Lily pointed out before the employee put her in a dressing room and began to bring outfit after outfit to her.

Lily shed the long skirt and shirt, wadding them into a ball. She stood in her bra and panties when the employee walked into the dressing room. Lily handed the hated clothes to the woman. "Burn those."

The young woman with a blond pixie cut eyed the clothes. "Are you sure?"

"I've never been more sure of anything." Just before the woman walked back through the curtain, Lily said, "I'm also going to need new bras and panties."

"I'll see to it," the woman replied with a bright smile.

Lily looked at herself in the mirror. Staring back at her was a hint of the girl she'd once been. She thought being on her own would give it to her, but she realized it was Rhys. He embodied the strength and fortitude she wished for herself. He gave her the courage to take a stand for herself.

It wasn't until she put on the first outfit of a pair of dark jeans and a red long-sleeved shirt that accentuated her breasts and her waist that she knew she would find the person she'd been before Dennis. The confident person who made her own decisions and didn't let anyone push her around—or hurt her.

Rhys hated waiting. For anything.

It didn't matter how long he lived, he hadn't mastered the art of patience. So the longer he had to wait for Ulrik to arrive at The Silver Dragon, the angrier he got.

He drummed his fingers on the hood of his Jaguar even as thunder rumbled in the distance. The first drops of rain were an annoyance, but he didn't budge even when the droplets became a steady downpour.

His thoughts turned to Lily. He wondered what she was doing and if she was having a good time. Her safety never factored in, because Rhys knew Kellan would move the heavens if he had to in order to protect Denae. Since Lily was with Denae, Kellan would protect her as well.

That's the only thing that kept Rhys from losing his mind with worry. He kept going over in his head the look on Lily's face when he reached her flat and when he took her home. Something was bothering her, and he wished she would tell him.

Not that he was one for sharing. He had yet to tell anyone about what was going on inside him with not being able to shift. It was tearing him in two as he sank further and further into a pit of despair. The only thing that kept the desolation from taking him was Lily. Her light, her smile . . . her kisses. She alone pulled him back from the edge simply by him thinking about her.

Rhys debated with himself whether to go after Lily as he wanted, or to be content to just look at her. Each time they kissed, it became more and more difficult for him to keep his distance. The fact he couldn't touch her without kissing her spoke volumes.

But he was no longer the Dragon King from before. He was . . . less. All because of Ulrik. Anger burned through Rhys. Ulrik had damaged him, ruined him. Never mind that Rhys still wouldn't think himself good enough for Lily even if he could shift again. Ulrik prevented him from protecting her as he should be able to.

Two hours later, Ulrik finally pulled up in his ice silver McLaren 12C Spider. The supercar rumbled to a stop on the opposite side of the street from Ulrik's antiques store. The door opened and Ulrik stepped out with his long black hair held in a queue, uncaring that rain soaked him and his expensive tailored suit instantly.

Ulrik shut the car door and walked away, locking the car with his key fob. He was halfway across the street when he suddenly halted. Then he slowly turned his head and looked at Rhys.

A distance of fifty feet separated them, but Rhys still saw the spark of anger in Ulrik's gold eyes. Rhys wasn't going to wait for an invitation. He pushed away from the Jaguar and strode toward his enemy.

Ulrik continued on to his shop and unlocked the door. It shut behind him, but Rhys didn't care if it was locked or not. He was going in.

Imagine his surprise when he tested the door and it opened. He walked inside to find only a few lights on.

"I doona suppose you'd leave if I told you to," Ulrik said as he walked from behind a wall to his desk at the front. He had removed his suit coat and released his hair, but remained in the wet shirt and slacks.

"Nay."

Ulrik gave a bored expression and pulled out his chair before he sat. "Then get on with it."

"With what?" Rhys asked skeptically.

"Whatever you came to say or accuse me of. The sooner you get it out, the sooner you can leave."

"As if you doona know why I'm here," Rhys stated.

"I doona."

The fact he said it so casually, as if it didn't matter that he had nearly killed Rhys. "Liar."

Ulrik shrugged. "As usual. After all the years you've been around you should've come up with something better."

"The word fits you. I almost think when it was created, the humans had you in mind." Rhys smiled when he saw Ulrik's nostrils flare, a sign that he was growing angry.

"I can always throw you out, you know."

CHAPTER
TWELVE

Rhys folded his arms over his chest, trying to determine what he wanted to ask Ulrik first. If the bastard was going to play stupid, then he'd let him. "Where is Henry?"

"Am I supposed to know the names of everyone that those at Dreagan know?"

"You know him. He was at your meeting with the Dark and MI5. He was spying on you, and somehow he was found out. Where is he?"

"I have no idea."

Rhys was undeterred. "Did the Dark take him?"

"Ask them," Ulrik said blithely.

"It was either the Dark or you. MI5 was too incompetent to even realize he was spying."

Ulrik raised a brow. "You seem to know quite a bit, though you're lacking relevant information."

"Henry is a good man."

"Who interfered in something he had no business with. As all humans do," Ulrik said with a sneer.

Rhys dropped his arms and walked to Ulrik's desk. He leaned his hands upon it and glared. "Then tell me why you felt the need to mix your dragon magic and Dark magic? Tell me why you wanted me to suffer! Tell me why you chose me to be stuck in a human form unable to shift!"

For long moments Ulrik simply stared at him. "Sounds like you got screwed. It sucks, does it no'? Tell me, Rhys, how does it feel to watch our brethren take to the skies now that you can no' join them?"

"It's hurts almost as bad as when we sent the dragons away." Rhys heard Ulrik's brogue slip back to his refined English accent, but he didn't mention it.

Ulrik pushed back his chair, the wheels rolling easily, and stood. "I want you to leave this store. Now."

"You did this to me for a reason. I want to know why."

"We all want something."

Rhys seriously contemplated killing Ulrik right then. He straightened, anger churning through him faster and faster. How dare Ulrik think he could do this to him and not answer for it?

"Your shadows doona scare me," Ulrik said with a hard look in his gold eyes.

Rhys hadn't even realized he'd called to his dragon power. All around him darkness billowed, shadows waiting to hide him—or devour an enemy.

"Did it ever occur to you that someone else could've done this to you?"

Rhys snorted loudly. He stopped his shadows from advancing, but he didn't pull them back. "All the Kings have been accounted for."

"Ah, but I'm no' supposed to have magic, remember."

"You do. We know it."

Ulrik simply smiled.

"Only you would be stupid enough to find an ally in the Dark to get back at Con."

"I want to kill Con, aye. But what makes you think I doona hold the rest of you accountable? You sided with him. You killed my woman together. All of you took my magic and stopped me from shifting. Each of you is responsible for what I am."

"So you turn the tables on me? Who's next? Is your plan to curse each one of us?"

Ulrik's smirk grew. "That is a nice idea. What would the mighty Dragon Kings do if none of you could shift?"

"You're one of us."

"No!" Ulrik exploded, his rage palpable. Gone was his mask of indifference. The fury clouded his face and darkened his eyes. "You made sure of that."

Rhys let his shadows grow closer to Ulrik. "What do you think happens to this realm if we are no' here to protect it?"

"I suppose we'll find out. Perhaps someone else will step in and take over."

"You?" Rhys asked skeptically. At Ulrik's shrug, he snorted. "Because if all of our magic is taken away, yours is restored. So you'll be the lone King who can shift. I'd like to see you battle the Dark alone."

"Who says I'd be alone or that I'll have to battle the Dark?" Ulrik's mask of coldness was back in place.

Now Rhys understood why Con wanted to kill Ulrik. Ulrik couldn't be reasoned with. He had a plan, and nothing was going to stop him from achieving it. "Why did you choose me?"

Ulrik remained silent, but squared his body, ready for an attack.

"Where is Henry?"

Ulrik's black hair fell over his shoulder as he bent his legs and leaned forward slightly.

"Why did you choose me?" Rhys asked again, this time sending his shadow to surround Ulrik. "Where is Henry?"

Again and again Rhys asked the question, but not once did Ulrik answer, mostly because he was battling the shadows. Rhys knew he couldn't kill Ulrik. He'd have to have his sword to do that, or shift into a dragon. But he could take some of his anger out on Ulrik.

One moment Henry was in the faintly lit prison, and the next he was standing in a large room with white marble floors and vases full of brightly colored flowers everywhere. He shielded his eyes from the light streaming in from the many windows.

He heard someone behind him, and tried to turn around and see who it was, but his eyes grew too heavy. Even as he fought to stay awake, he fell asleep.

The next time he woke, the light was even brighter. He turned his head and discovered the softest pillow in existence beneath his head. A part of his mind cautioned him to get up and discover where he was, and another urged him to sleep more. Henry found he couldn't fight the sleep. He gave in with a sigh and returned to his dreams.

Rhi stood in the doorway and watched Henry. He was a fighter. Maybe that's why she saved him. There was also a slim chance it was because he helped the Kings.

"It's a good thing you called me," Usaeil, Queen of the Light, said as she came to stand beside Rhi.

Rhi could've brought Henry to Usaeil's manor on the west coast of Ireland, but then it would reveal to one and all the power she'd managed to keep hidden from them. That was something she wanted to keep to herself.

So she got Henry out of the prison and to the outskirts of Dublin. From there, it was simply a matter of asking Usaeil for help. Now all Rhi had to worry about was finding out how much Henry remembered.

If he recalled seeing her teleport him out, then she would need to convince him to lie for her. Although Usaeil would want to know how Henry got out of his prison and how Rhi found him. Usaeil hadn't begun those questions yet. But they were coming.

"I'm glad you agreed to help," Rhi said.

Usaeil shoved her black hair over her shoulders and adjusted the coral sheath dress she wore. "He's aiding the Kings. Why wouldn't I help him?"

Rhi wanted to roll her eyes, but she didn't. "We might be Light, but we also use humans as the Dark do."

"We don't kill them."

"No, we sleep with them once and ruin them for any other mortal. We don't hurt them at all," she said sarcastically, giving Usaeil a cutting look.

Usaeil slid her silver eyes to Rhi. "I can easily toss Henry North out on his ass."

"Do it. What do I care?"

"I think you care more than you're ready to admit. Why else would you want to help him?" Usaeil sighed. "Rhi, we all know you went through hell at Balladyn's hands. We know it's going to take time for you to heal, but you *will* heal."

Rhi wasn't so sure. She could feel the darkness within her, coiling and shifting. She had to fight to remember what she should do, instead of what the darkness wanted her to do.

"Henry is healing nicely," Rhi said, changing the subject.

Usaeil nodded slowly. "His injuries were extensive. Had you not found him when you did, the internal bleeding would've killed him in a few hours. By the way, how did you find him again?"

This was what Rhi had been waiting for. Everyone knew she couldn't lie without feeling tremendous pain. She sank her nails into her palms, held Usaeil's gaze and lied. "I found him in Dublin. As I said, I don't know how he got there."

"So very odd."

The pain was gut wrenching. It twisted her insides and

squeezed her lungs so that she couldn't breathe. Pain exploded inside her head. She began to shake. It was time for Rhi to change the subject again. "You should tell Con we have him."

The queen twisted her lips. "If I do, Con will want to come here and finish healing Henry himself, or want us to bring Henry to him. I'm not in the mood for either."

"Henry will be finished healing soon. What then? You want him to remain? In a place full of Light Fae?" Thankfully, the pain began to dull enough that Rhi could breathe easier.

"No," Usaeil said with a frown. "Already his appearance has sparked interest. They're trying to get in to see him. He's a mortal, so he'll succumb to any Fae he encounters."

Rhi took exception to that. "He's stronger than that."

"He's human, Rhi. Not a single one can resist us. It's a fact. Henry is no different."

Rhi didn't argue, but she knew she was right. Henry was different. She'd seen it the first time she met him in Con's office months ago. He took in the fact his friends at Dreagan were actually dragon shifters with a nod, his solemn hazel eyes seeing things anew.

She bit back a grin as she recalled how he'd become a little flustered when he saw her and learned who she was. Henry's smile was charming, sweet . . . honest. He looked at her as if she were the only woman in the realm.

Even though Rhi understood that it was the fact she was Fae that intrigued him, enthralled him, she took an instant liking to the human who never backed down.

He might be mortal, but he was a skilled adversary, a dangerous foe with espionage skills that far surpassed even Denae's.

As an ally, Henry was clever, shrewd, cunning, and brilliant. A perfect partner for the Kings.

"I'll take him to safety if he's such a danger here," Rhi told Usaeil.

The queen lifted a black brow. "You surprise me again."

"It's my new thing." Rhi looked down at her black nails with two small hearts painted in red—Big Apple Red— on each ring finger.

"I don't want him waking up here. It's bad enough the mortal knows as much as he does. He doesn't need to see this place. Or me."

Rhi rolled her eyes. "You're the one who wanted to become a famous movie star."

"I like movies," Usaeil said defensively.

"Yep. And it's *suuuch* a good idea for the Queen of the Light to be so recognizable," she said.

Usaeil's silver eyes glared for a heartbeat before she sighed. "I think I like you sullen and silent better than the smartass you've become."

"I've always been a smartass. I just hid it."

"Not nearly as much as you think. I'll have a group of Light bring Henry back to Dublin."

Rhi straightened from the doorway. "No." She cringed when she heard the harshness in her voice. Licking her lips, she tried again. "You said yourself that others were taking an interest in him. We don't need a Light going to find Henry once he's been healed and having sex with him."

A pained expression came over Usaeil's face. "Point taken. I'll bring Henry myself. Where do you want to go?"

"The Caledonian Hotel in Edinburgh."

Usaeil walked to the bed where Henry lay sleeping.

Rhi met her queen's gaze. "I'll be waiting."

She teleported to The Caledonian and the luxury suite on the top floor. A moment later, Usaeil arrived with Henry. Rhi hurried to her queen's side and helped get a naked Henry in the bed.

Usaeil dusted off her hands as Rhi covered Henry. "Now he can wake and call the Kings."

"I'm going to remain."

"I don't think that's a good idea."

Rhi sat in the chair close to the bed and looked at Usaeil. "I'm sure it's not, but it's what I'm going to do."

"Will you then travel to Dreagan?"

Rhi cocked her head to the side. "Why do you always ask that in the same condescending tone? What is it about the Kings that you want to keep from me?"

"Nothing," Usaeil said quickly.

A little too quickly by Rhi's thinking. There was nothing for Usaeil to hide. She was queen. The only thing someone in Usaeil's position would hide would be an ally or . . . a lover.

It was like a kick in her stomach. Twice.

Rhi stared at Usaeil and tried to keep her face devoid of any expression. Before she confronted her queen, she would need to dig more. She wanted proof, to see Usaeil and her lover with her own eyes.

Usaeil walked to the mirror and checked her appearance. "I've got an interview I need to get to," she said and looked at Rhi through the mirror. "Just promise me you won't spend too much time at Dreagan. It always depresses you."

"You think I'm there for *him,* don't you?"

Usaeil blew out a breath and turned to face Rhi. "You still hold love in your heart. No matter what you tell yourself, every time you go to Dreagan, you go for him."

"He doesn't want me."

"No. He doesn't."

"I don't want him either." It about killed Rhi to say the words, but they were needed. She had to know if Usaeil was sleeping with a Dragon King—and which one it was.

Usaeil looked out the windows of the expansive room. "Do me the courtesy of not lying."

"I'm not."

That got the queen's attention. "You're really over him?"

"Yes."

"Maybe some good came from Balladyn taking you after all. It's never a good idea for a Light to mix with the Dragon Kings. Return to Ireland soon, Rhi."

Rhi waited several minutes after Usaeil vanished to make sure the queen hadn't veiled herself. Then Rhi let her fury show. There were only a handful of Kings who would sleep with a Light, much less contemplate taking on the Queen of the Light.

Kellan was at the top of her list, but since he was mated to Denae, she mentally scratched off his name.

Next up . . . Con.

The King of Kings would take Usaeil as a lover. The bastard.

"Rhi?"

She was jerked out of her thoughts by the croak from the bed. Rhi jumped up and leaned over Henry who was looking at her through eyelids opened into slits. "How are you feeling?"

That made him frown. "I don't hurt anymore, but I'm so bloody sleepy."

"I know. I'm sorry. We had to."

"We?" he asked as he tried to sit up.

Rhi helped him up. "Yeah, stud. You were surround by Light Fae who healed you."

"And I slept through the whole damn thing? Just my luck," he mumbled grumpily.

She sat on the edge of the bed and smiled. "Well, on the plus side, you're no longer in that prison."

His hazel eyes went wide as his memories returned. "I need to get to Dreagan. Now."

CHAPTER
THIRTEEN

Lily was idly scrolling through quotes on her phone while Denae was trying on another pair of shoes. She came across one that struck her soul so profoundly that she never wanted to forget it.

Where there is no struggle, there is no strength.

"There's one more stop I want to make when we're done here, if you don't mind," she said.

"Not at all. Is it wrong that I want all of these shoes?" Denae asked with a grin.

Lily laughed as she shook her head. "Are you really asking me that? Look around me," she said, indicating the obscene number of bags with all her purchases—clothes, underwear, shoes, and makeup.

"I was hoping you'd buy something, but damn," Denae said, her Texas accent thickening on the last word. "You really surprised me."

Lily had surprised herself. "I needed to do it. It's been a long time coming."

"Because of your past?" Denae asked as she stood and looked in the full-length mirror to test the Jimmy Choo shoes.

Lily didn't respond. She simply looked at Denae.

Denae's face crumpled as she threw up her hands. "I'm sorry. It's a habit from my days at . . . from a past job. I don't know anything, I swear. It's just things I've picked up from your words and actions."

"No, I'm the one who should be sorry. I'm too defensive about something I want desperately to forget." Lily squeezed her eyes shut and wished she could make Dennis disappear so easily. When she opened her eyes, Denae's gaze was locked on her.

Denae walked to Lily and sat in a chair beside her. "We're your friends, Lily. You can talk to us."

"Like you feel comfortable telling me about what you did before?" Lily asked with a small smile. "You kept that from me for a reason, just as I'm keeping my past from everyone."

Denae sighed and glanced away. "I keep it from you not because I want to, but because it protects Dreagan."

"And I'm protecting myself and my family."

"Fair enough, but if there ever comes a time you want to talk, please know you can come to me. I won't let you down."

Staring into Denae's eyes, Lily knew she wouldn't. Though she didn't know Denae well, there was an honesty about her, a toughness that Lily wished she had. "You don't happen to know any karate or anything, do you?" Lily asked, thinking how she'd love to be able to defend herself against Dennis.

Denae's gaze intensified, watching Lily as if she were sizing her up. "I know several forms of martial arts. What do you want to know how to do?"

"Anything. Everything. I've always wanted to learn." It wasn't a lie. Lily had always wanted to be one of those independent women who could seriously kick some ass when needed. "I'm a woman living alone. I'd feel better if I could defend myself."

Now that was a partial lie. Today was the first step in preparing for the time when she would kill Dennis. She needed to find the old Lily, and then she needed to learn enough moves to surprise him.

Dennis would never see it coming. He thought of her as helpless, weak. Vulnerable.

Those were three traits she had allowed to manifest within herself, and she was cutting them out—painfully, completely.

"I'd be happy to teach you," Denae said as she stood and walked back to the mirror to look at the shoes on her feet again. "How about after dinner tonight?"

Lily looked at her watch and cringed. Dennis would be waiting for her at her flat.

"Do you need to return home?" Denae asked.

Lily shook her head. She had to remember she wasn't going to be scared of Dennis anymore. He wanted something from her. She knew him well enough to know he wouldn't harm her family—yet. This was her one chance to find a way to get them free. She had to use it wisely. Because once she returned to her flat, she would have no choice but to help him. "I'm free as a bird."

"Good, because I've got a surprise for you."

They shared a smile. Lily did feel free, and it was exhilarating. Why hadn't she done this sooner? Why had she held onto the person Dennis turned her into?

Because I was fearful.

The truth slammed into her. She was scared, but Dennis had control over her only as long as she allowed him to. And she had accepted and tolerated all manner of things from him, even after she left.

Lily was so deep in her thoughts that when she looked

around again, Denae was at the counter purchasing three pairs of shoes. Lily rose, adjusted her purse on her shoulder, and gathered all her bags in both hands. She was walking toward Denae when the two men in black suits stopped beside Denae. One of the men gathered Denae's purchases while the second approached Lily.

Lily handed her bags to the man. His blond hair was trimmed close to his head along the sides, and the top of his hair wasn't much longer. His blue eyes looked at everyone with suspicion. He gave Lily a small smile as he greeted her with a "ma'am" and took the bags.

Denae walked to her, laughing. "I called our driver as I was paying."

"Those men aren't just drivers."

Denae turned and began to walk out of the store. "Nope. They sure aren't. Dreagan has enemies, Lily, and Kellan wanted to make sure we were safe."

"I'm surprised he let you come without him."

"Oh, he didn't," Denae said with a chuckle. "He's near."

Lily wasn't surprised by her admission. Kellan was the protective sort. Despite the fact Denae said she could defend herself. To have that kind of relationship. Rhys's face flashed in Lily's mind, her soul aching to kiss him again, to touch him and hold him.

"Lady Lily?" said a high-pitched female voice behind them.

Lily froze, her heart thumping wildly in her chest. Her breath came faster, the world spinning. It had been so terribly long since anyone had called her that.

"Oh, my God. It *is* you," the woman said as she walked around Lily and stood in front of her. "It's me, Elizabeth Dabney, though I'm Attwater now."

That meant she had married James Attwater, Earl Attington, one of the men who once courted Lily. It seemed like a lifetime ago.

Lily plastered a smile on her face. "Hello, Elizabeth. I always knew you would make a lovely countess."

"He was supposed to have been yours," Elizabeth said, though there was no heat in her words. "Where have you been, Lily? We've not seen you in years."

Lily's throat closed up as images of her time with Dennis ran through her mind. Something bumped into her from the side, and she saw Denae out of the corner of her eye. Lily grasped at the opportunity. "Elizabeth, let me introduce you to my friend, Denae."

"Hi," Denae said and stuck out her hand. "It's nice to meet you."

"An American," Elizabeth said with a brow raised.

Denae glanced at Lily. "I'm from Texas, yes."

"Are you visiting?"

"I live here. Have for some time actually."

Elizabeth was intrigued now. "Really? What do you do?"

Denae's smile was slow. "I'm married to one of the owners of Dreagan Industries."

"Oh," Elizabeth exclaimed, her eyes looking at Denae with new interest. "How exciting. My husband loves Dreagan whisky. We must have you and your husband to dinner if you're ever in London."

"Of course."

Lily watched the exchange with curiosity. Denae could handle herself with the peerage, especially someone like Elizabeth who liked to flaunt the fact she was a countess. Then again, Denae seemed comfortable in any scenario.

"Please forgive us," Denae said. "Lily and I really must go. We have another appointment."

Elizabeth stepped aside. "It was good to see you, Lily."

Lily waved, throwing a good-bye over her shoulder as she followed Denae out the door and to the car awaiting them. Once they were inside, Lily drew in a deep breath and said, "I can explain."

"No need," Denae interrupted her. "Your past is your past. You'll share when you want to."

Lily looked away, tears gathering in her eyes. She had fully expected Denae to grill her on Elizabeth calling her Lady Lily, and yet Denae didn't say a word. "I didn't run away from my family," she suddenly said, needing to fill the silence.

"When is the last time you saw them?"

Lily looked straight ahead. "Four years ago."

There was a stretch of silence before Denae said, "I know there's somewhere else you want to go. Before that, I wanted to tell you my surprise."

"Which is?" Lily asked as she looked at her.

"We have rooms at Radisson Blu Hotel. We've had a long day, and I'm exhausted. That is, if you want to stay. If not, we can return to Dreagan right now."

Lily shook her head, grinning again. "I think it's a fabulous idea."

They talked of nothing and everything during the ride to the hotel. It wasn't until Denae was out and all the bags had been unloaded that Lily remained standing in the open door of the car.

"Is everything all right?" Denae asked.

"That one other place I wanted to go? Do you mind if I do it alone?"

Denae gave her a comforting smile. "Tell the driver where you want to go. He'll take you anywhere and bring you back."

Lily waited until Denae was inside the hotel before she got back in the car. She pulled out her phone and touched the screen so the quote was visible. "Take me to the best tattoo place you know, please."

CHAPTER
FOURTEEN

Rhys pushed his shadows again and again at Ulrik, but no matter how much Ulrik was injured, he didn't answer a single question Rhys threw at him.

Rhys stood amid the shadows watching them tear at Ulrik. The King of Silvers fought them, and if Ulrik had all his magic, he could easily best them. What Rhys was learning was that Ulrik somehow was able to have a portion of his magic, but not nearly as much as Rhys originally feared.

Suddenly, Ulrik shot Rhys a cold smile. "Did you really think you could have Warrick sneak in without me knowing?"

There was no way Ulrik should've known Warrick was there. Rhys had kept Ulrik detained, and yet Ulrik knew not just that there was someone else there, but who it was. "How do you know it's Warrick?"

Ulrik threw out his hands, and Rhys's shadows were shoved away. Rhys pulled them back, waiting to see what Ulrik would do next.

Ulrik ran his hand through his hair, smoothing it down as he glared at Rhys. "Warrick, why don't you come join us?"

A moment later Warrick came around the front to stand near Rhys. "Ulrik. It's been a long time."

Ulrik looked at him as if he was absurd. Then he looked back at Rhys, and dropped all pretense of his British accent. "You'd think Con would learn that he willna see inside this store. No' through cameras he put in himself, or through any Kings he sends."

"How did you know it was Con who installed the cameras?" Warrick asked.

Ulrik cut his eyes to Warrick. "I'm smart like that."

"You're going to tell me why you took my ability to shift," Rhys stated.

Ulrik straightened his shirt. "And I need to know why the Kings feel the need to continue coming to my store."

"We come because you've aligned with the Dark," Warrick said.

Rhys glanced at Warrick and nodded. "We come because you want to expose us. You want us to stop paying you these visits? Then quit what you're doing."

"Doing?" Ulrik said with a laugh. "I warned Con that judgment day was coming. He must pay for what he did."

Warrick snorted in derision. "We all did it, Ulrik. You should be coming for all of us."

"Oh, all of you will pay for taking my magic, but I'm going after Con for something else."

Rhys felt as if the ground had been yanked from beneath him. "What are you talking about?"

"Con knows. Ask him."

"You know he willna tell us," Warrick said.

Ulrik turned and walked around his desk. "That's my problem how? You're the ones who allow him to keep such secrets. Perhaps you should think about who is ruling the Kings."

"We rule ourselves," Rhys said.

Ulrik looked up, a smirk pulling at his lips. "I remember the moment Constantine decided he wanted to be King of Kings. He was ruthless in his endeavor to get that position. Would he no' be just as ruthless in keeping it?"

Every ounce of anger left Rhys. He was frustrated, exhausted, and weary. He wanted to see Lily, to have her near and soothe his anger. The idea of remaining in human form for eternity was appalling. "What do I need to do for you to reverse the curse on me?"

Ulrik looked him up and down. "Get out."

Rhys briefly thought of remaining and calling to his shadows again, but all it would do was bring their battle to the attention of the humans. This fight needed to remain private. As much as Rhys wanted to know why Ulrik had targeted him, it wouldn't change his circumstances.

He glared at Ulrik. "This isna over."

Henry sat on the edge of the bed still a little amazed he wasn't in any more pain. He blinked at Rhi. "Did you hear me? I have to get to Dreagan. I need to talk to Banan."

"First, I need to know what you remember about your capture and imprisonment."

Henry's lips turned up. "You mean Ulrik? He gave me a choice to join him or die."

"You chose death."

"Of course," he said with a frown. "I'd never sell my soul to someone like him."

Rhi's wealth of black hair moved as she nodded. "No, you wouldn't. Why not? Most humans would do anything to remain living."

Henry paused as he considered her words. "Do you have such a bad view of us mortals?"

She shrugged one delicate shoulder. "I've been around a long time and seen many things. You're different than other humans."

"In my line of work, every day could be my last. I

stopped worrying about dying and concentrated on helping my country. That's the only way I could be a spy. I'm now focusing my energy on helping Earth, not just my country."

"So you expect to die?"

Henry chuckled and glanced down at himself to see he was naked, with only the edge of the sheets covering him. "Yes, and I suspect it'll be violent and painful. Now, where are my clothes?"

Rhi snapped her fingers and a pair of dark jeans and a black sweater appeared on the bed, along with socks and a pair of black boots.

Henry raised his brows as he looked at her. "Really? With just a snap of your fingers?"

"Yes," she replied with a vibrant smile that made his breath hitch. "Oh, one more thing," she said with another snap of her fingers.

A pair of black boxers with a silver skull and crossbones across the front appeared.

He looked at the clothes. "This is what you see me wearing?"

"Would you rather another gray suit?"

Actually, he wouldn't. "Thanks, Rhi."

"My pleasure," she said and turned her back to him as she walked to the windows and looked out over Edinburgh.

She was waiting for him to continue with his answer. Henry dressed, shaking his head at how well everything fit, and then sat to put on the socks and boots. "I was in a lot of pain at Ulrik's. I tried to find a way out, but there were no windows, just that one door."

"You remember me coming to you?"

"Yes." Henry stood and then pulled on the sweater. He ran his hands through his hair. "I thought I was dreaming you. What were you doing there?"

"I . . . don't know."

"Did you go to visit Ulrik? Is that why you knew where I was?"

Her shoulders sagged. "No, I wasn't visiting Ulrik. If you must know, I check in on you from time to time. When I couldn't find you, I called in a favor from a friend."

"A friend? Who the hell would know where I was? If Banan couldn't find me, how did you?"

Rhi turned and leaned back against the window. "His name is Broc. He's a Warrior and able to locate anyone, anywhere."

Henry nodded, remembering how Banan had explained about the immortal Highlanders who had primeval gods inside them and their Druid wives. "Ah. How did you get me out?"

"You don't remember?"

"No," he said and frowned. "One minute I was there, and the next I was . . . I don't know where. The place was bright. It hurt my eyes."

Rhi didn't hide her relief quickly enough from Henry. She had something to do with his escape, but whatever it was, she didn't want him to know the particulars.

"Are my answers satisfactory? Can we get to Dreagan now?"

Rhi pushed away from the window. She seemed to consider something for several minutes. "Can I trust you, Henry?"

He crossed his arms over his chest. "I'm a spy, Rhi. You either trust us, or you don't. There isn't any middle ground." When she didn't immediately reply, he dropped his arms to his side. "You saved my life. I know it was you who got me out of Ulrik's hold. I don't know how, and it doesn't matter. I owe you. If you need a favor or for me to keep a secret, it's the least I can do. And I'm very good at keeping secrets."

"That you are," she said with a sly grin.

"Then trust me," he beseeched. "Let me begin to try and repay you for saving my life."

Rhi walked to him, her long legs encased in black and the five-inch heels of her black boots only making her legs look longer. "I've never trusted a human before."

"I won't let you down."

Her silver gaze held his. "No, I don't think you will. Have you ever teleported, stud?"

"No."

She smiled, her voice going husky. "Feel free to hold on tight then."

"Wait," he said as he took a half-step back. "What do you mean, teleport?"

"One moment we'll be here, and the next, wherever I take us."

Henry squeezed the bridge of his nose with his thumb and forefinger. "Just how many other kinds of magic are out there?"

"This is a kind of . . . power . . . that only a select few Fae have. Oh, and Fallon MacLeod has it because of the god inside him."

Henry was going to have to keep a ledger of all the Warriors and their powers. He couldn't keep up with it all when the Druids, Dragon Kings, and the Light and Dark Fae were added in. He tried to pretend that knowing there was a world of magic and immortals within his own was just another day at the office, but the truth was that it scared the hell out of him.

But he knew Banan, trusted Banan as he trusted few people. He knew the Dragon Kings were good, decent men, and it was easy to detect the villains—Ulrik, the traitors within MI5, and the Dark Fae.

Rhi, well Rhi he yearned for as he'd never wanted another thing in his life. She was a walking sex goddess. With a smile or a single look, she had him hard as granite. He didn't know if she was using him or not, but as long as he got to Dreagan, that's all that mattered.

As for the Warriors and Druids from MacLeod Castle, he knew of them, and it was only a matter of time before their paths crossed.

"The Warriors are good people," Rhi said. "If you can't get to Dreagan, find MacLeod Castle. They'll help you."

Henry dropped his hand and looked at her. "Those at MacLeod Castle trust you?"

"Definitely," she said with a knowing grin. "Now, are you ready?"

"No," he said, but Henry closed the distance between them. He tried not to look at the swell of her breasts. Then he gave up and let his gaze feast on her beauty, causing his balls to tighten and his blood to heat.

Rhi wrapped his arm around her and looked up into his face. "I warned you to hold on, handsome."

He stared into her beautiful, unusual, silver eyes. Henry vaguely realized the hotel faded away. When he blinked, he was standing outside Dreagan Manor.

"That wasn't so bad, was it?" Rhi asked.

Before Henry could answer, the front door was yanked open as thunder rumbled around them. He glanced from the faces at the door and back to Rhi. "It certainly wasn't. Too bad I can't do that trick."

"Too bad I can't teach you," she whispered.

Henry's arm tightened around her. Only in his dreams did he get to hold her, but now she was in his arms. He wasn't sure he could let her go.

"Remember, stud, you must keep my secret."

"The Kings don't know?"

She shrugged. "They do, but I don't want it spoken about. It's just better if you don't mention it," she whispered.

Then she leaned up and placed her lips on his. The kiss was simple, light, and quick, but it seared Henry to his very bones. He was dazed as he opened his eyes while she stepped out of his arms.

Rhi then turned to the group who had come outside. She nodded to Banan. "No more need to search. Henry is safe."

"How did he get here?" Con asked as he came to stand beside Banan.

Henry cleared his throat. "I don't really know."

Banan's forehead was furrowed as he looked from Henry to Rhi and back to Henry. "Are you all right?"

"I am now," Henry said. "Ulrik had me after I was beaten by the Dark. I passed out, and then I woke up, healed, not far from here."

"We're glad you're here," Con said.

Henry found it odd the King of Kings didn't so much as look at Rhi. Though Banan, Tristan, Ryder, and Guy certainly did, each with confusion and worry.

"Rhi," Banan said. "Can you fill in the blanks?"

CHAPTER
FIFTEEN

Lily looked down at her right inner forearm and smiled. Never again would she forget the quote. She would see it every day.

Where there is no struggle, there is no strength.

It was her new motto. She'd made it her own, made it part of her. It was just another step in the remaking of her life. Lily's arm throbbed from the tattoo, but she felt amazing.

It must have shown, because when she emerged from the tattoo parlor onto the sidewalk, three men were walking down the street and smiled, each eyeing her with interest. Lily returned their smiles and walked to the car where the driver awaited her.

He opened the door and nodded in greeting. "Is it your first tat?"

"Yes," Lily answered and held out her hand. She kept her long-sleeved shirt pushed up so it wouldn't touch the irritated skin.

He read the words. "Verra nice."

She paused before getting into the car. Lily glanced at the sky. It was late, and she didn't want to keep Denae waiting any longer. She briefly thought about buying a gun, but she didn't want anyone to witness her purchase. "Let's get back to the hotel so you can get some dinner."

He closed the door after she got inside. It was a short drive to the hotel, and with every minute that passed, Lily felt more confident than ever. It was almost as if those years with Dennis never happened.

Although, if that were the case, she wouldn't have need of her new tat.

Lily said good night to the driver and walked up the steps to the hotel. She entered the lobby and approached the desk. As soon as she told them her name, they handed her a room key as well as a note from Denae.

She waited until she was in the lift to open the note. Lily glanced at her watch to realize she had less than twenty minutes to get dressed for dinner and meet Denae down at the restaurant.

Lily used the key to get into her room and stopped when she saw all the bags from her purchases set neatly in the living room of the suite. She dumped her purse and key on a small table and hurried to the bags, sifting through them, looking for the red dress and matching shoes.

After a quick shower to wash off the day, Lily put on some makeup, careful to cover the bruise on her cheek. She pulled out her new makeup. It had been awhile since she'd used more than eyeliner and mascara. She had fun using the eye shadow to give herself a sultry look.

With her new red bra and matching panties on, Lily then slipped into the dress. She kept her hair down, pulling it over her left shoulder. Next, she dug in her purse, finding the secret compartment she had made and withdrew the diamond stud earrings she'd received from her parents on her twenty-first birthday. They were the only pieces of jewelry she wore.

Lily put on her shoes and a dab of lip gloss before she

looked in the mirror. The reflection staring back at her no longer had trepidation and fear in her eyes. She was in charge of her life.

She almost left the room without the black clutch. Lily tossed the lip gloss, room key, and her phone into the clutch before she walked out of the room.

On the ride down to the lobby, Lily decided to tell Denae who she was. Elizabeth had, after all, already spilled some of it. The doors to the lift opened and Lily walked out. She smiled when a man holding the door for her looked her over with an appreciative eye. It felt amazing to be noticed.

But not nearly as good as it would be if it were Rhys who gave her such a look.

Lily was almost to the restaurant when a hotel employee stopped her. "A phone call?" she repeated in surprise.

"Yes, ma'am," the older man said, nodding his gray head. "If you'll follow me."

There was no one that knew where she was, and no one that wouldn't try her mobile first before calling the hotel. Curious, she followed the man to the first desk where she was handed a phone.

"Hello?"

"I really hate to be left waiting," Dennis said.

Rhys was driving out of Perth when someone nearly ran into him. He looked over, ready to tell the wanker off when he saw it was Kellan.

"Better see what he wants," Warrick said.

Rhys followed Kellan as they pulled over and turned off their vehicles. Both Rhys and Warrick got out and met Kellan outside.

"Sorry," Kellan said before Rhys could talk. "I kept trying to get your attention, but you were rather focused."

Warrick glanced at Rhys. "I doona blame him. I was the same."

Kellan's gaze narrowed as he looked between the two of them. "I had a feeling the two of you would be here. Did you get your answers from Ulrik, Rhys?"

"No' even close. Is that why you almost hit me? To rub it in?" Rhys asked, his anger spiking again.

Kellan's lips flattened before he said, "First, I've heard from Banan. Henry is at Dreagan."

"That's a relief," Warrick said.

Kellan nodded to Warrick before he looked back at Rhys. "I was going to ask you to join me for dinner, but now that I've seen you, I doona want you around Denae. And I doona think Lily would want it either."

As soon as he said Lily's name, Rhys's entire body went taut. Lily. The one person in all the realms who made him catch his breath with desire and yearning. "You're having dinner with Lily? She's no' back at Dreagan already?"

"The girls had a long day. Denae wanted to stay the night, and Lily agreed. I'm supposed to meet them in thirty minutes. I'd have been there sooner if I hadna been looking for you."

Rhys ran a hand down his face. Then he looked at himself. He was in jeans and a shirt. Not the attire he wanted when meeting Lily. "I'm no' dressed for dinner."

"That can be remedied," Warrick said.

Kellan regarded Rhys with an intense look. "If you want it to be."

He did. Rhys knew he shouldn't, but there was no way he was going to pass up a chance to have dinner with Lily and get to know her better. If he got to touch her again, even better. It was too great of a temptation to pass up. They wouldn't be completely alone, but it was better than every other King watching them.

"It's obvious you want to, so do it," Warrick urged. "It might be good for you."

His unspoken words of "especially after today" hung

in the air. Rhys licked his lips and thought of the bruise he had seen on Lily's cheek that morning. "Aye."

Warrick slapped him on the back. "Looks like I'm flying home. See you lads later," he said before he walked into the night.

Kellan looked at his watch. "Warrick is happier alone anyway. Follow me, Rhys. We'll have to hurry. I doona like to keep my woman waiting."

Rhys strode back to the Jaguar and pulled in behind Kellan onto the pavement. They drove like the roads were their own personal racetrack, making it into Edinburgh in record time. Ten minutes later, Rhys walked out of the store in his newly bought clothes and jogged to the car. Kellan was already on his way to the hotel, two blocks away.

Rhys sped down the street and pulled up behind Kellan in front of the hotel. Rhys exited the car and tossed the keys to the valet as he buttoned the top of his jacket and fell into step with Kellan.

Rhys's gaze scanned the lobby looking for any sign of Lily. Then he realized she was most likely in the restaurant with Denae. When he and Kellan reached the restaurant and were then led to the table, the disappointment that flared at not seeing Lily was tremendous.

He needed her as desperately as he needed to shift. Rhys fisted one hand as anguish filled him. If this was how he felt waiting on Lily, how would he ever cope if she was killed? The room spun, causing him to grab hold of the back of a chair to keep himself standing. He managed to stay on his feet and keep following Kellan. Lily couldn't die. If she did, he would cease to exist.

Rhys knew it with the same certainty that he knew he loved her.

Denae smiled and stood when they walked up. She kissed Kellan and then greeted Rhys. "Lily is here, though she got in just a little while ago."

"You were no' with her?" Kellan asked when they were all seated.

Denae sat and took a sip of her wine. "There was somewhere she wanted to go herself."

"So she might no' come down," Rhys said, worry causing his voice to deepen. "Is that what you're trying to say?"

Denae adjusted the napkin in her lap. "Yesterday I'd have said that, but after today, I think she'll be here."

"What happened?" Rhys needed to know every detail. If Lily was in danger or hurt, he would kill the person responsible. If something else had changed . . . well, he wanted to know that as well.

"A lot actually. She's . . . different."

Kellan motioned to a waiter and ordered a drink for himself and Rhys. "Different how?" he asked Denae.

Denae shrugged helplessly. "You'll see when she comes down. While we were shopping, an old friend of Lily's stopped her."

"Did they upset her?" Rhys asked.

"In a way, though it was more like she was embarrassed the woman recognized her."

Kellan touched his cheek as he said, "Because of her bruise?"

"I might be speaking out of turn, but I think it's because the woman knew Lily as well as her family. Lily admitted to me that it has been four years since she spoke to her family."

Kellan let out a whistle.

Rhys reached for the whisky as it was set in front of him and brought it to his lips. That was an interesting bit of news he hadn't known. The glass was at his mouth when his gaze was snagged at the door by a flash of red.

He shifted and then froze as his eyes feasted on Lily. Every ounce of blood went straight to his cock when he saw the way the red dress hugged her incredible curves.

The dress stopped above her knees, and the sleeves hit just beneath her elbows.

Her long, lustrous black tresses hung over her left shoulder. She held her head high, the high heels bringing notice to her gorgeous legs. As she approached, he caught a flash of a diamond at each earlobe.

Rhys set aside his drink and got to his feet, only vaguely aware that Kellan was speaking. The closer Lily got, the more he saw the frown of worry, the same hint of fear as the night before. Then her gaze slid to him.

The anxiety on her face was replaced with a slow, dazzling smile that made something shift unexpectedly in his chest. "Rhys," she said, the voice throaty, utterly sexy.

"I was in the city. I hope you doona mind," he said as held out her chair.

"Not at all."

Their hands touched, sending a current of electricity through him. They were close enough for him to bend and place his lips on hers. There was nothing that he wanted to do more, but he recalled they were in public. It took every ounce of his control, but he remained where he was.

She sat and reached for her napkin. That's when Rhys saw what was obviously a new tattoo by the redness around the words. He waited until Lily finished greeting Denae and Kellan before he held out his hand and nodded to her arm as he asked, "May I?"

Lily hesitated, but after a moment she turned her arm to him. "Of course."

Rhys sat and gently wrapped his fingers around her wrist. Blood pounded through him in a storm of need when he heard her quick inhale when their skin touched.

By the stars, what this woman did to him. His blood pounded through him, her nearness making everyone else fade away.

He had to read the tattoo twice before his desire-filled

brain could comprehend the meaning. "Where there is no struggle, there is no strength," he said aloud.

Rhys didn't need to ask to know there was meaning behind it. He looked into her dark eyes, drowning in the possibility of what could be.

"You look very handsome," she said, her words soft, encouraging. "I've never seen you in a suit."

"I doona often wear one." He abhorred them. Usually. Then again, he wanted to impress Lily, to show her he was more than a man who had a different woman on his arm every night.

She looked down, her smile growing. "I love when a man is as comfortable in jeans and a tee as he is in a suit." Her gaze returned to his. "Especially when a man can wear a suit as well as you."

If Rhys weren't already hard, he would be now. He rubbed his thumb along the skin at her wrist. "Red looks fetching on you. The frock does as well."

Her eyes twinkled at the compliment. "Thank you."

"Rhys?" Kellan interjected. "Are you going to let Lily order a drink or hold her arm all night?"

"Why can I no' do both?" Rhys asked with a wink to Lily. It was the first time in weeks that he felt almost himself. That's what Lily did to him. She healed the scars left from Ulrik's magic.

Lily's bright smile was a salve on his battered soul. She had no idea how her mere presence could soothe and calm him as nothing else could.

And that alone scared him much more than the thought of never shifting again.

CHAPTER
SIXTEEN

Lily couldn't remember ever being so nervous—or so excited.

She pulled her arm out of Rhys's grip, his fingers trailing seductively along her skin. As if she needed reminding of how he made her body respond to him. He commanded her as easily and surely as the moon ruled the tides.

His close proximity made her heart thump. His heat made her body crave his touch. His aqua ringed dark blue eyes seared her skin with his intense gaze, causing her to be conscious of how her dress molded to her body.

He was virile, persuasive, and masculine. His rugged good looks turned heads, but in a suit, he looked dashing and powerful. A combination no woman could ignore. And he was sitting next to her. Lily wanted to run her fingers through his long dark brown waves and pull his head down for a kiss.

And if he didn't quit looking at her as if he wanted to take her right there, she just might.

By the time she had her hand back in her lap, her lips were parted and her chest rose and fell rapidly.

Rhys could do that to her with a simple touch. An innocent, modest touch.

Lily took a deep breath and lifted her eyes only to clash with Denae's gaze from across the round table. Denae directed a small, knowing grin at her.

It took Lily a second to realize the waiter was standing beside her, waiting on her drink order. She had been quite shaken up by Dennis's call, and then she saw Rhys. With Rhys filling her mind, she didn't have the wherewithal to think about Dennis or his demands.

Lily desperately wanted some alcohol. She was searching her mind for what to order when her gaze snagged on a woman across the way drinking champagne. "I'll have a glass of champagne, please."

"That sounds decadent," Denae said. "I'd like one as well."

Rhys lifted a finger to get the waiter's attention. "Bring us a bottle of Dom Perignon."

When the waiter walked away, Denae leaned forward and nodded to Lily's new tat. "So that's what took you away."

"Yes," Lily said and carefully moved the hem of her sleeve away from the sensitive skin.

"It must be important," Kellan said, his celadon eyes watching her.

Lily shifted slightly in her chair. "Don't we all have things we need to conquer?"

Kellan bowed his head slightly, a small grin playing at his lips. "That we do, Lily."

She was saved from further questions when the waiter returned with the champagne and flutes. Denae talked about all the stores they had visited while their drinks were being poured. Lily discovered that her hand shook when she went to grab her glass. She fisted her hand to try to get control of herself, but she couldn't stop the shaking.

Rhys leaned over and whispered, "No one can see your hand."

"I don't know why they're shaking."

"Do I make you nervous?"

She looked into his dark blue eyes. "Yes."

Disappointment flashed in his eyes for the briefest of seconds. "Would you like me to leave?"

"No."

He stared at her for a heartbeat, then two, before one side of his mouth kicked up in a smile. "Good."

Lily really needed a drink then. She brought the champagne flute to her lips and took a sip of the golden liquor. The bubbles danced on her tongue before she swallowed. "It's been a long time since I've drank champagne."

"Today has been quite full then."

She knew he was fishing for information, but she didn't care. Lily took another drink, feeling herself relax, her muscles loosen with each swallow. "I've needed today for a long time. I just didn't realize it."

Her body warmed with Rhys's gaze on her. She was sitting between two incredibly gorgeous men, but she only had eyes for Rhys—as it had been since she first arrived at Dreagan. He dominated a room full of people, her attention gravitating to him no matter who was with her or where they were.

Their conversation was halted once more to place their food order. Lily handed the menu to the waiter and sipped her champagne as Rhys and Kellan ordered. After the waiter left, Rhys and Kellan exchanged a quick look that left Lily wondering what was going on.

"Did you get all that you needed?" Kellan asked Denae.

Denae shot him an apologetic look. "Yes, and a bit more."

"Good," Kellan said.

Lily laughed and shook her head as all eyes turned to her. "Denae, you've got a keeper there for sure. Usually men cringe when women talk about shopping."

Kellan reached over and took Denae's hand. "She changed me. In more ways than one."

"I'll say," Denae said with a bright smile. She turned her attention to Lily. "It wasn't that long ago that he was quite set in his ways, refusing to even consider another option."

Lily watched the love brimming between them. "Is what Denae said true?" she asked Rhys.

Rhys sat back in his chair as if he were in his own home. "Oh, aye. We didna think anyone would ever be able to tame Kellan. Then Denae came along."

"He resisted me," Denae said with a hurt look that was ruined when she laughed as Kellan pulled her to the side so he could kiss her.

Kellan was smiling as he turned to Lily. "I tried to resist her, but she had no idea I was falling for her from the verra beginning. She had me wrapped around her little finger."

"You're so lying," Denae said, laughing.

"No' at all, my love. If you'd known, you could've destroyed me."

All the smiles were gone as Denae cupped Kellan's cheek. "Without you, I would've died."

"I wouldna have let you."

Lily knew there was a deeper meaning to their words, and by the look on Kellan's face, Denae's mention of death wasn't metaphorical. She wished she knew their story, but it was private. Would she ever have such a story? She glanced at Rhys, wishing with all of her might that her story involve Rhys.

"They always tend to forget other people are around," Rhys said as their food arrived.

With smiles back in place, Denae and Kellan rejoined the conversation. The four talked of everyday things. Laughter was never far, and the smiles were frequent.

Lily drank two glasses of champagne while she ate. The atmosphere made it easy to forget why she'd gotten the tattoo, why she wore the dress, and why she was determined to find the person she once was.

All too soon the meal was finished. Lily feared that would end the night, but she was pleasantly surprised when they remained at the table, ordering a second bottle of champagne.

"This has been a truly fabulous day," Denae said as she lifted her glass to Lily.

Lily responded in kind. "It was. Thank you for inviting me."

Denae winked at her, even as Kellan pulled her chair closer to his so he could drape his arm on the back of it and gaze adoringly at her.

"You watch them as if you've never seen such affection," Rhys said in a low tone.

Lily turned her head to him, wondering how his chair had gotten so close to hers. Which she was quite pleased with. "Actually, I was thinking how much those two remind me of my parents."

"In what way?"

"In all of it." She turned her gaze back to the couple. "The way Kellan has to touch her, even if it's just their fingers. He needs to have her near, but Denae also desires to be near him. She gravitates toward him. Then there's the way they share those smiles, as if they know exactly what the other is thinking."

"He's thinking he wants to take her to their room," Rhys said, a grin in his voice.

Lily glanced at him and chuckled. "No doubt, but there's deeper meaning in those looks and smiles as well. It's a connection between two people who truly love each other. It's amazing to watch."

"Have you ever been in love?"

His question threw her. The smile died on Lily's lips as she hastily took a drink.

"Doona answer that," Rhys said a second later. "I had no right to ask."

Lily shifted in her chair so that she was turned toward him. "I'll answer it if you will."

Rhys slowly nodded his head.

Lily licked her lips. "There was a short period of time when I thought I was in love. I was vastly mistaken."

"I've never been in love," Rhys said. His fingers touched the ends of her hair before his hand dropped back to his lap.

"I find that hard to believe."

Rhys lifted one dark brow. "Because of the women you see me with?"

"Because women flock to you. You're a beacon, a magnet for women. It's your good looks, yes, but you're charming and kind and . . . gentle. Women sense that."

There was a beat of silence as his eyes dropped to her mouth. "Is that how you see me?"

"Yes."

He cleared his throat and looked up before chuckling. "Looks like we've been ditched."

Lily followed his gaze to see Denae and Kellan walking arm in arm from the restaurant toward the elevators. "Good for them." She turned back to Rhys. "If you need to go—"

"I doona," he interrupted before she could finish.

Warmth infused Lily. She couldn't hold back her smile. While Rhys poured the last of the champagne into their glasses, Lily glanced around and saw women of all ages throughout the restaurant gazing at Rhys with longing.

Rhys handed her the glass, their fingers touching. Lily's stomach clenched in excitement.

His head cocked to the side, a question on his face. "What?"

"Look around," she dared him. "There isn't a woman here who wouldn't gladly leave with you." She waited for him to notice, but his gaze was locked with hers.

"I'm no' interested in any of them."

He stood and held out his hand to her. "Walk with me."

As if she could say no. Lily put her hand in his and got to her feet. He looped her left arm through his while she held her glass in her right. She didn't know where they were going, and she didn't care. It was the best day of her life, and she never wanted it to end.

They walked to one set of large double glass doors that were opened, allowing the cool night air to fill the area. Rhys guided her out the doors to the balcony that over-looked the city.

"You wear those clothes like a woman born to them."

Lily jerked her gaze to him, startled. "Why do you say that?"

"You're comfortable in that designer dress. I may no' know brands, but I know couture." He motioned inside the restaurant with his chin. "See the blonde in the black dress? She keeps rubbing the dress as if she can no' believe it's real."

Lily nodded as she caught sight of the woman. "She's doing the same thing to the huge engagement ring. Her fiancé must come from money."

"And she doesna. I'm no' trying to be crude, just honest. There is a difference between someone like her and someone like you."

"Did Denae tell you about what happened today?"

"She said you ran into an old friend, but that's all."

Lily turned and leaned back against the stone railing

of the balcony. "My family does have money. As I told her, I didn't run away. I've just been on my own."

He closed the distance between them and smoothed down a lock of hair that got caught in the wind. "If you doona wish to tell me, then doona, but I ask that you doona lie."

"I didn't exactly lie." She blew out a breath and looked away. "I didn't run away from them, nor am I hiding from them. I've also been on my own for a bit."

Her heart missed a beat when Rhys placed a finger on her chin and gently turned her face back to him. "You owe me no explanations. You doona owe anyone anything."

Their faces were so close that she thought he might kiss her again, but then he took a half step back. It was enough to end her hope of a kiss.

"Are you happy?"

She considered his question. That day was the happiest in a very long time, and she was content in her job. But was she happy? No. She still had so much to cut out of her life for good. She couldn't be truly happy until Dennis was dead.

Lily thought about Rhys. Was he happy? He seemed more relaxed that night than he had in a long time. There was so much she didn't know about him, but that always took a backseat to the passion that blazed each time he was near.

"I'll answer if you will," she countered.

Rhys gave her another crooked smile that made her melt. "Agreed."

"I'm getting to a place where I can be happy with every aspect of my life."

His grin was full of sadness as he said, "I used to be, but I fear I'll never be again."

The honesty of his words left her reeling. She suspected something had happened to him. Now she knew for certain. Her heart hurt for the brief glint of misery she saw. It was gone quickly, as if it never was.

Lily was about to ask another question when two couples joined them on the balcony. Rhys's face darkened with annoyance. She grabbed his hand and pulled him back into the restaurant. He quickly took her arm and led her past their table and out of the restaurant.

Only then did he stop and face her. There was hopefulness in his eyes when he asked, "Shall I leave you for the night? Or shall we continue our conversation?"

As if she needed to think. She took out her room key from her clutch and held it up. "Let's continue."

CHAPTER
SEVENTEEN

Henry was still reeling from Rhi's kiss, so he was taken aback when she disappeared. He stared at the place she had been and sighed.

"What the hell happened?" Banan asked as he walked up.

Henry was soon surrounded by Dragon Kings. He looked up at Banan and shrugged. "I fucked up."

"Let's get inside and discuss this," Con stated and strode back into the manor.

Henry licked his lips, remembering the softness of Rhi's mouth. She had helped him, showed him her secret, and kissed him. Why him? Why was someone like her even paying attention to him?

"Doona get attached to her," Banan warned in a low voice beside him.

Henry frowned. "Why not?"

"No' only is it no' a good idea for any human to have sex with a Fae, but Rhi was once involved with a King."

"Is she still involved with him?"

Banan's forehead furrowed. "Well . . . no, no' exactly."

"Then it isn't a problem."

"Rhi is a friend, Henry, just as you are. There are things

you doona know about the Fae. They're beautiful and sexual. They lure humans."

"No one lured me," he pointed out.

They reached the library on the first floor. The door was shut as the last of them filed in. Con motioned for Henry to sit, and since his strength was still returning, he accepted the offer. Banan handed Henry a glass of whisky. Con sat on the other side of the sofa with Henry while the chairs were taken by the remaining Kings.

Con let out a breath slowly. "Henry, you've been a friend to us that we never expected. You've aided us in multiple ways. All of it you did at the peril of your own life."

"It's what I do," Henry said, watching Con.

Tristan spoke up then. "Which is why we're grateful."

"You should've told me you were going to infiltrate the traitor group in MI5," Banan told Henry, his voice laced with irritation.

Henry had known this was coming. "Why? Because I'm human? Because I can die? I've always known that. We needed to know what was going on in that meeting."

"Who is we?" Con asked.

Guy leaned forward, his face dark with anger. "Con."

Henry held up his hand. "It's a valid question, and Con is doing what any leader would. The 'we' I'm referring to is us," he said circling his finger to mean him and everyone at Dreagan.

"You still should've told me," Banan stated.

Henry ran a hand down his face. "Probably. Look, mate, it's already done."

"Can you tell us what happened?" Ryder asked.

Henry tossed back the contents of his glass and let the whisky work its way down his throat to settle in his stomach and spread warmly. "My cover was solid. No one knew I was spying, no one. We arrived at the meeting place first. Daniel Petrie, the leader of the MI5 team was nervous. It wasn't long after that the Dark showed up. We stared at each other for what seemed like eons before a lone figure appeared."

"Who was it?" Guy asked, scooting to the edge of his seat.

Henry rubbed his chin. "He never said his name. No one did, but he was obviously in charge. It was Ulrik. He calmed the Dark and MI5 with just a few words. And then he told them I was a spy."

"Shite!" Banan exploded and got to his feet to pace the library. "It's a damn miracle you're alive."

Tristan leaned forward in his chair. "Were you able to talk your way out of it?"

"I wish," Henry said with a snort. "No, I was attacked first by my fellow agents, and then the Dark took over. The Dark wanted to take me prisoner. I soon passed out. When I woke, I was in a room much like this one."

"Obviously you were no' with the Dark," Con said as he placed an arm on the back of the couch.

Henry shook his head. "No, I was with Ulrik. He put me in a plush room with some water, but that was all. He offered to let me live if I agreed to work with him."

Guy dropped his head into his hands while Tristan's lips thinned.

"When I called him by his name, he grew furious and told me never to say it again," Henry said.

Ryder slapped his hand angrily on his leg. "You were right, Con. It is Ulrik."

"I know Ulrik," Con said to Henry. "He wouldna have just let you go."

Henry touched his ribs. "My injuries were worse than I knew. I had several broken bones, including ribs. I couldn't fight my way out. Hell, I could barely stand. When Ulrik came for my decision, I told him in no uncertain terms to kiss my ass. He started to throw magic at me, and the next thing I knew, I was in a place full of so much light I couldn't open my eyes."

"I'll be damned," Banan murmured.

Tristan shook his head in amazement. "The Light Fae healed you."

Ryder said, "Now we know how he got here and why Rhi was with him."

"Hmm," Con said.

Banan rested his hands on the back of the chair he'd vacated. "Is there anything else you can tell us?"

"Yes," Henry said. It was the most vital piece of information and he'd nearly forgotten. "Ulrik has a man who is forcing a woman to get him onto Dreagan to look for some weapon."

Con's face, usually devoid of emotion, grew thunderous. "Did he say that exact word? Weapon?"

"He did." Henry swallowed hard at the fury suddenly filling the library. "He didn't mention what the weapon was, who the man was, or the woman for that matter."

"We doona have that many women working for us who are no' a mate," Guy pointed out.

Con stood. "Then it should be easy to determine who it is. I want them discovered immediately and watched."

"What?" Henry asked. "Wouldn't it be better to fire them?"

"And let Ulrik know that we've discovered his plan?" Con asked with a cold smile. "Nay. We'll play his game."

Henry watched Con stalk from the room.

"Well. This has gone four ways to hell," Ryder said and got to his feet. "Glad you made it out all right, Henry."

Tristan was the next to stand as he nodded at Henry. "This information is verra important. Great work."

Ryder and Tristan walked from the library together, leaving Henry with Guy and Banan. He looked between the two Kings to see that neither appeared happy.

"We know the bad guy is Ulrik. Shouldn't you be happy?" he asked.

Guy turned his face to the fire in the hearth. "You doona know what Ulrik looks like. How can you be sure?"

"I called him by the name. It was only the second time I said it that he got so irate."

Banan's head hung, his chin against his chest. "What color hair did he have?"

"Black as pitch," Henry answered.

Guy's shoulders slumped. "His eyes?"

"Gold."

Banan cursed beneath his breath and spun around to pace the library once more. "We have no choice but to kill him now. Dammit, Ulrik!"

That's when it dawned on Henry that not all of the Kings hated Ulrik. Ulrik had been one of them, and now he was the enemy.

"I'm sorry," Henry said. "I didn't realize Ulrik was a friend."

Guy scrubbed a hand down his face. "He was a friend to all of us. Some have forgotten that."

"And Con?" Henry asked.

Banan stopped before the fire. "They were the best of friends, closer than brothers. Ulrik wants to kill Con, and Con wants to kill Ulrik. Whoever wins, it'll tear the Kings apart."

Ulrik sat for a long time after Rhys and Warrick left. He didn't think he would see another King after his last encounter with them, but he should've been better prepared.

The day had gone to shit with nothing turning out as he wanted it. It was rare when his plans didn't fall into line, and when it happened, it put him in a foul mood.

He set straight a painting of some chap from the sixteenth century and growled when he saw the frame cracked in the corner from his encounter with Rhys and his shadows. The fact Kings continued to come to his store was not a good sign.

The more they meddled, the longer it was going to take for his schemes to happen. Yet he couldn't leave. The moment he didn't appear to be at The Silver Dragon, Con would search for him. That time would come, but it wasn't now. Soon, so very soon Constantine would get what was coming to him.

Ulrik was finishing straightening the store when the bell chimed above the door at the same instant as an image of an attractive woman with blue eyes and light brown hair cut to her jawline filled his head.

"Abby," Ulrik said as he faced her.

She smiled and closed the umbrella, adjusting the strap on her shoulder holding the briefcase. "Hello, sir," she replied in the perfected British accent he required she use. She looked around the shop, standing straight in her black pencil skirt and soft pink sweater. "Is now a bad time?"

"No' at all. Come to the back, and we'll go over everything."

He waited until she walked around to the back, and then he locked the door and followed. Abby was never late. She arrived precisely on time, every time. Ulrik found her punctuality refreshing. She didn't ask any more of him than he offered, though she let it be known she was interested in taking him to her bed.

For the last ten years, Ulrik had kept from giving in to that particular desire, but Abby was a very desirable woman. And he had needs.

She lifted her blue eyes to him after she sat. "As usual, everything is playing out just as you said it would."

Ulrik nodded in response. For all of Abby's attributes, she knew only a quarter of his plans. Trust wasn't something he gave. Ever. It had been a hard lesson, but Constantine taught it well.

"Good. And the shipment from Russia?"

Abby flipped open the briefcase and pulled out a manila folder. She scanned the pages. "The Astron has put into port in Norway right on schedule. They'll take on your additional cargo there before heading to London."

"That's good news. Go ahead with your other reports now."

Abby went through them one at a time, naming who was showing leadership and who was weakening. Ulrik could have no weak links in his plan.

It was an hour later before Abby finished. She finished putting away the folders in the briefcase. "Do you have any orders for me?"

"No' today. I'll be taking care of a few issues over the next day or so. I expect you back two days from now."

"Yes, sir," she said with a nod and stood.

Ulrik rose with her. When she started to grab her things, he put a hand on her arm to stop her. Their gazes met. He weighed her interest, glancing down to her cleavage visible in the curved neck of the sweater.

Her eyes widened a fraction, her breath hitching. It was all the indication he needed. After the day of disappointments, he needed to ease his body. Ulrik turned and shoved her against the wall, roughly taking her lips as she clawed at his clothes to remove them. He had no such desires.

He yanked up her skirt, shoving aside her panties to feel her wetness. In no time at all he had his pants undone and his cock free. Holding one of her legs up, he plunged inside her. She screamed, her nails digging into his back as she kissed him like there was no tomorrow.

CHAPTER
EIGHTEEN

On the lift up to Lily's room, she and Rhys stood in the back while a group piled on with them. Rhys looked down at her while she watched everyone else.

Lily's eyes were so full of . . . eagerness that Rhys found himself watching her to see the play of emotions on her face. There were times she hid her feelings well, but others when she wore them on her sleeve for the world to see.

Tonight, they were visible, and he was glad. One by one the other occupants reached their floors. When the lift arrived at her floor, Lily glanced at him and walked out when the doors opened. Rhys followed, appreciating the sway of her hips—and thankful for the dress that no longer hid all of her beautiful curves.

It wasn't until the door shut behind him in her suite that she laughed. "Shall we resume our conversation now?"

Rhys wanted to continue his perusal of her—with her clothes off. Desire ran thick and hot in his veins. It was a mistake to think he could be alone with her in her room. He'd nearly taken her last night on the trail. There was no one to interrupt them in her suite, no one to stop him from marking her as his.

"Rhys?" she called his name, a small frown marring her face.

He looked beyond her to the living room and the numerous bags that filled the space. She followed his gaze and groaned aloud.

"I can't imagine what this looks like. I haven't done anything like this in years," she said while shoving aside bags so they could sit on the sofa.

Rhys stopped her and gave her a little push so she sat. He walked to the bar area and claimed a stool. The broader the distance the better if he was going to have to think and carry a conversation. "Forget the clothes. Let's continue where we were below."

"All right." She sat back on the sofa and crossed one leg over the other after she kicked off her heels. "Tell me something about yourself."

"I have enemies."

Her gaze lowered to the half-empty glass of champagne in her hand. "So do I."

Now that wasn't something he had expected her to say. "What do you fear?"

"Not finding my courage when I need it."

Once more he was taken aback by her words. "Why would you need courage?"

"My enemy, remember," she said with a wink. But the truth was there in her words. "Your turn."

Rhys wanted to ask her so many more questions, but he'd begun this game. "I fear that I willna gain back part of myself that I've lost."

"Hmm," she said with a nod as she drank. "I can relate. What do you hope for?"

"To vanquish my enemies."

"I want to be free." Her voice was full of wistfulness.

He thought over his next question for a moment, then asked, "If you could be anywhere, where would you be?"

"Here. With you. You?"

He stared into her eyes, his balls tightening with need. "Right here."

"Tell me something you've never told anyone else, a secret we would share between us."

Rhys set aside his warm champagne. He couldn't tell her his biggest secret—that he was really a dragon. But he wished he could. "That I'll fail those who need me most."

"My given name is Lilliana Eleanor Ross, the Earl and Countess of Carlisle's third daughter."

"You're nobility?" he asked in shock. That certainly wasn't something he saw coming. It explained why she wore the clothes as she did, as well as her elegance.

Lily bowed her head of black hair and pushed the length off her shoulder. "I am. The friend I saw today called me Lady Lily. I just knew Denae was going to ask about it, but she didn't."

"That's no' her style."

"No, it's not."

"That is some secret," Rhys said. "I feel my response was quite inadequate."

Lily laughed and finished off her champagne before she set it on the coffee table. "You could tell me more."

"My friends count on me. I . . . I'm no' as I once was. I'm more focused on vengeance."

"You're still there for your friends. That's what matters."

Rhys glanced away, because he knew that unless he could shift, he was useless in the coming battle. But he shoved those thoughts aside as he remembered who he was with. He thought of her new tattoo and the scar Cassie mentioned seeing. Suddenly, he wanted to see the scar himself. "Show me something no one else has seen."

Lily held his gaze for several seconds as she swallowed nervously. Then she rose gracefully and walked to him. She turned her back to him and moved her hair. "Unzip me, please."

Rhys hesitated, his hands shaking at the thought of touching her bare skin. He revisited their kisses every night in his dreams. He couldn't have her this close and not take her, but if Cassie was right and Lily was once abused, he had to let her make the first move.

He grasped the zipper and slowly pulled it down. The neck of her dress gapped and creamy bare skin became visible. Then he saw her red bra. He swallowed, desire riding him hard.

Lily shifted so that the dress fell from her left shoulder. Rhys saw the vertical mark that ran over four inches from her shoulder down her back, spanning about an inch wide. The scar was leathery, indicating it was a burn.

Fury, deep and dark, surged. The longer Rhys stared at the wound, the more he wanted to find the bastard and envelop him in dragon fire. Nothing burned as hot as a dragon's fire.

Rhys ran his hand along the scar. He knew the answer, but he asked, "Who did this to you?"

"Someone I trusted. Someone I gave my love to. A boyfriend I lived with."

Rhys was about to zip up her dress when he spotted something else on her back. He gently moved aside the dress from her right shoulder and saw more scars. They were thin, white, indicating they were older.

His hands shook from the ferocity of his wrath. "He did all of this?"

"Yes."

"With what?"

Lily took a deep breath. "The largest scar was from a fire poker. The others were from whatever was in reach. Sometimes his pocket knife, sometimes his cigarettes."

Rhys finished unzipping her dress and got the full view

of her back. It was riddled with scars. Some burns, as she said from the ends of a cigarette, and others cuts.

"Only your back?" he asked around the emotion thickening his throat. He couldn't understand why someone would want to hurt a person as sweet and beautiful as Lily.

Lily stepped away before she faced him. She let the dress drop. "He made sure never to hurt me where others could see."

In all his eons of years, the only time Rhys had ever felt such outrage was when he had sent his dragons away. Now, as he looked at Lily's stomach, as scarred as her back, he couldn't comprehend anyone doing something so heinous.

The amount of courage it took her to show him was staggering. When Rhys asked his question, he wasn't sure what he would show her. Now he knew. Now there was no doubt what he would let her see.

Rhys took off his jacket and carefully folded it to lay it across the stool next to him. Then he unbuttoned his shirt and removed it. He didn't take his eyes from Lily's face, so he was able to see her lips part and a look of awe fall over her face.

Lily couldn't stop herself from closing the distance and putting her hands on such an amazing piece of artwork. The dragon, a curious mix of black and red ink, was intricate, the shading masterful.

She was mesmerized by the tattoo, running the pads of her fingers along it. The head of the dragon was on Rhys's right pec. The body of the dragon stretched across Rhys's impressive chest almost as if it were lying down with its wings tucked. The tail however, went over Rhys's left shoulder and then wrapped around his left arm, stopping at his elbow. The planning and drawing of such art must have taken months, not to mention the time it took to get the tattoo.

Lily lifted her gaze to Rhys's blue eyes. "This is . . . I

don't have adequate words. I've never seen such beautifully elegant, and yet fiercely intense work. Still, I can't be the only one to see this."

Though she hated to admit it, Lily knew Rhys had bedded other women. They had to have seen the tattoo.

"I doona willingly show this."

"Why?" she asked in disbelief. "It's gorgeous."

Rhys shrugged. "I have my reasons. When I take a woman to my bed, it's either too dark for her to see, or I take her from behind."

Lily returned her gaze to the dragon, but that's not what she saw. She indulged herself in the perfection that was Rhys. Hard sinew, flawless and impeccably shaped, warmed beneath her palms from his thick shoulders to the washboard stomach to his narrow waist.

She slid her hand along the bulging muscles of his arm where the dragon tail was and imagined those arms around her, holding her close. Not so long ago that dream had been reality. It was a fleeting moment in time, but it was branded upon her mind for all eternity.

"If others have seen this, it wasna because I wanted to show it," Rhys said in a low voice.

"This art was meant to be seen. Why would you get this and then hide it?" she asked and tilted her head back to look at him.

Rhys's chest expanded as he drew in a breath. "It's . . . complicated."

"I show you scars. You show me beauty."

"Those scars are part of you. They tell a story of your courage and strength."

Lily felt her eyes sting with unshed tears. "It took me years to get up the nerve to leave him."

"But leave him you did."

"Yes." If only she'd found someone like Rhys—no, if

only she'd found Rhys—instead of Dennis, how different her life would be. "I walked away from my family for him."

"Focus on the part where you left him."

It was good advice, because the last person Lily wanted to think about being so close to Rhys was Dennis. The bastard had no place in her life in any way, shape, or form.

Rhys's gaze intensified as he stared down at her. "It takes a special kind of bravery to do what you've done."

"If I was as strong as you think, I'd take what I really want."

"Which is?"

As soon as the words left his mouth, she rose up and placed her lips on his. Lily wasn't sure where such daring came from. Perhaps it was standing in her bra and panties after allowing him to see the ugliness of her body. Perhaps it was how gently he ran his fingers over her scars, causing her eyes to fill with tears. Because how could anyone look at or touch her and feel passion?

Perhaps it was because he showed her his tat.

Regardless, she wanted another kiss, and she wasn't going to let the night end without it.

Lily began to pull away when Rhys wrapped an arm around her, bringing her close. He rested his forehead against hers while he let his fingers trail lightly down her arm.

"I've been craving that all night," he whispered.

Chills raced over Lily's skin. She slid her arms around his neck, shivering when his caress traced down her side to her hip and around to her buttocks. Her breath was coming rapidly, her body heating from the need coiling within her. She sucked in a breath when he cupped her ass and pulled her against the hardness of his arousal.

Rhys's other hand shifted upward, delving into her hair. "Doona tease, sweet Lily."

Lily realized then that he was letting her take the lead. A man who was always in charge was giving her the reins. She knew it was because of her past, but that didn't matter. The simple fact that he was thinking of her when no one else had made her breath catch.

Rhys was able to reach into her very soul in one instant and repair the years of damage Dennis had wrought. If there was any doubt in her mind that Rhys was unique and exceptional, it was gone now.

She looked into his eyes. Her heart thumped, her blood hammered in her ears. The desire was no longer hidden in his gaze. It shone bright for all to see. This was her moment, her shining instant when her wish to have Rhys was granted.

Lily lifted her mouth to his, but it wasn't for the chaste kiss from a moment ago. All of her desire, all of her longing . . . all of her yearning was poured into the kiss.

And Rhys's answering moan was all it took to spur her onward.

CHAPTER NINETEEN

Rhys knew it was a mistake kissing Lily again, but it didn't matter how many times he told himself that, he still couldn't leave. She was in his blood, in his psyche. She roamed through his dreams, teasing and tantalizing him with her seductive black eyes and hair.

Her first kiss had been a meeting of lips. The second time had been full of longing and passion. The third time she kissed him, he was unprepared for the force of it. The kiss was fiery, fierce, sensual, and altogether carnal.

His cock ached to be inside her, to fill her again and again until she was limp from the pleasure. He wanted the world to know she was his. The very fact that someone like Lily was with him made his throat tighten with emotion. She knew what kind of man he was, and she still opened herself to him.

Rhys rocked her against his arousal once more and heard her throaty moan. It made his rod jump in anticipation. He pulled her tighter, loving the feel of her warm skin against his. Her hands roamed over his shoulders and back the more their kiss sizzled and burned.

With a small movement, Rhys undid her bra, the straps

loosening on her shoulders. She ended the kiss, a grin upon her lips as she leaned back to remove the garment. Rhys's mouth went dry as he stared at her breasts. They were full and round, her dusky pink nipples already hard.

Rhys cupped both breasts and watched as Lily's eyes slid closed on a soft sigh. That sigh turned into a moan when he ran his thumbs over her nipples. Her nails dug into his arms and her head dropped back, exposing the long curve of her neck.

Unable to resist, he leaned forward and kissed along her neck as he massaged her lovely breasts. But it wasn't enough. He wanted all of her bared so he could put every inch of her to memory.

It was Lily who stepped out of his arms. Her lids opened to show her dark eyes were dilated, her breathing heavy. The curve of her lip was seductive, alluring as she turned and walked to the door of the bedroom. There she paused and shimmied her panties over her hips and down her legs. She stepped out of the red satin and disappeared into the bedroom.

Rhys removed his shoes and socks before he stood. As he followed her, he unbuttoned his pants. At the doorway, he stopped and looked inside to see her standing at the floor-to-ceiling window with her back to him.

"You've no idea how beautiful you are," he said as he removed his pants and came up behind her.

She leaned back against him, her palms on the window. "My body is on fire, and yet the glass is cool."

Rhys reached around and set his hand atop her breast and slowly ran his hand down her stomach to the black curls nestled between her legs. He held her up with his other hand wrapped around her waist while he spread her curls. A satisfied smile formed when he found her wet to the touch.

To his surprise, she reached behind her and wrapped

her hand around his cock. Rhys hissed in a breath as she ran her hand up and down his length.

Rhys wouldn't be able to hold onto his control if she continued, and he wanted the night to be about her. He wanted to show her that he was different, that she mattered. He spun her around, pushing her back against the window. Her breath came out in a huff, but her eyes were alight with excitement.

Bending his head, he fastened his lips around a nipple and sucked. Her arms came around him, his name falling from her lips in a strangled whisper.

Rhys suckled, teased, aroused first one breast, and then the other until he had to hold Lily up. Her eyes were closed, her lips parted as moan after moan fell from her full lips. Only then did Rhys drop to his knees. He moved one of her legs until her thigh rested on his shoulder. At the first touch of his tongue against her sex, she jerked and then sighed.

Her hips began to move as he found her clit with his tongue and swirled around it. He licked, he laved mercilessly, bringing her to a fever pitch only to back away at the last second before she could peak.

"Breathe," he told her. "Close your eyes and concentrate on how my tongue feels against you."

She complied instantly. Rhys paused for a moment, and then he licked her slowly. Lily shivered, gasping and clinging to the window even as she begged for more.

"Please," Lily pleaded.

Rhys slid a finger inside her as he continued his assault. The moment her body began to tighten around him, he stopped once more. He looked up at her and used his tongue to swirl around her clit faster and faster, matching the rhythm of his fingers pumping inside her.

Almost instantly her body tightened, getting ready to

climax. Rhys added a second finger to stretch her. She moaned loudly, her palms on the window. When Rhys pulled away once more, Lily groaned, her hips rocking from the need to fulfill the pleasure. He stood and waited for her to open her eyes to look at him.

He lifted her up so she could wrap her legs around his waist. Rhys kept her raised above his cock, her back against the window. Then, slowly, gradually, he let her slide down his arousal.

When she was fully seated, he held still, gazing into her dark eyes. "How do you feel knowing that anyone who looks can see us?"

"I feel sexy, carnal. Free," she whispered in a throaty voice.

He pulled out of her and then thrust deep. She clung to him, their eyes locked as their bodies moved against the other. He progressively increased the rhythm, plunging deeper, harder each time. Soon sweat glistened over their bodies.

Suddenly her body went taut as the orgasm took her. Her mouth opened on a silent scream, her body convulsing from the strength of it. Rhys carried her to the bed and gently laid her down. He smoothed back her hair and grinned as she gazed up at him in contentment.

Her legs tightened around him, drawing him deeper inside her. Rhys rose up on his hands and rotated his hips before he began to move again. She met him thrust for thrust, pushing him higher, urging deeper.

His climax hit him unexpectedly. He plunged deep and shouted her name as the tidal wave of pleasure overtook him, sending him into a sea of ecstasy he'd never experienced before.

Her arms wrapped around him, brought him down to her. She held him as they were wrapped in a bubble of bliss that no one could fracture.

* * *

Ulrik stood on the roof of his building staring off toward Edinburgh. His sources told him Rhys went there with Kellan while Warrick flew back to Dreagan under the cover of clouds. Rhys and Kellan weren't alone, however. Denae, Kellan's mate was there, as was a mortal named Lily.

"Lady Lily Ross. Nobility mixing with the Kings." Ulrik grinned. He could imagine Con would have a field day with the news.

Constantine, the one who refused to let go of tradition, the one who clung to an old way of life that no longer served the Dragon Kings. Then again, Con was as outdated as his beliefs.

It was time for the Kings to have a new leader.

It was time for a great many new things.

Ulrik looked to the sky. He might have some of his magic back, but he still couldn't shift. Every minute of every hour of every day that passed and he couldn't take to the skies made him hate Con even more.

He was so close to getting his revenge that he could taste it. Many humans would die. Many Kings would die. But he would finally have all of his magic returned. He would finally take to the skies and soar among the clouds as he once had.

More importantly, his Silvers would at last be free from their perpetual sleep. It didn't matter what he had to do, or who he had to hurt to get back what was taken from him.

Rhys only had a taste of what he himself had endured through the millennia. If Rhys was this crazed after only a few weeks, what would he do years or decades from now? Ulrik was *almost* tempted to wait and find out. Con would get to see firsthand how a King could lose his sanity by being forced to remain in human form.

It was an ugly, violent, and dangerous spiral that took everyone and everything near.

That was one way to take down Con, and there was a very real chance Rhys could do it. However, Ulrik suspected that Con would lock Rhys away before anything like that could ever happen.

By doing that, Con would alienate many of the Kings, because though Rhys was a hothead, he was loyal to a fault and he had many friends. It was no secret that Rhys and Con butted heads often. So it would work in Ulrik's favor that some would see Con's actions as retaliation against Rhys.

But that was a chance Ulrik didn't want to take. No, he had planned out his vengeance to the last detail. Now that everything was coming together was not the time to change anything.

How many years did he lose in his insanity? How many did he squander, scraping among the humans' filth trying to ignore the dragon within him begging to take to the skies?

How many years did he exhaust until he learned to take whatever he wanted?

Only then was he able to start planning this moment. Thousands upon thousands of years of networking and laying the foundation of Con's ruin. Just a little more time and all would be set right once again.

Ulrik turned away and walked barefoot to the door that led back inside the building. He walked down the ladder and then to the doorway of one of the spare bedrooms. Abby still slept, not that he expected her to be awake. He'd used her until she was limp and unable to move, much less utter a sound.

He closed her door and stood in the hallway. Abby, like most people, would assume that the room was his. In fact, Ulrik's bedroom was hidden. No one but he had ever seen it.

Or ever would.

He was tempted to go there and rest, but there could be no rest for him. Instead, he decided to go downstairs and get some work done. Ulrik was halfway down the spiral staircase when he was alerted that someone was inside the store. It left him uneasy that there was no face to go with the alert.

On silent feet, he made his way down the rest of the stairs and out the hidden door. As he stepped into the back of the store, he paused. All the lights were still off with just a few on dim to cast away most of the shadows.

Ulrik came around the corner to see a man sitting in one of the overstuffed chairs. His back was to Ulrik, so he couldn't see the man's face.

For a second, Ulrik thought it might be Con finally come to try and kill him. Then Ulrik realized that Con wouldn't come alone. He would want others watching.

"Looked your fill yet?" the man asked.

Ulrik frowned. There was something about the voice he recognized, a vague memory of something long buried that he should know. He didn't have any friends. Which meant whoever this man was, he was an enemy. Ulrik prepared to kill him as he gave the chair a wide berth and walked around it until he stood diagonal to the man.

The light on the table beside the chair clicked on. "Hello, Ulrik."

Ulrik stared in shock at his uncle.

CHAPTER TWENTY

Lily had her eyes closed, but sleep was the furthest thing from her mind. She was nestled in the comfort—and security—of Rhys's arms.

It was surreal. Amazing.

Incredible.

The night before she thought was the end of everything, and twenty-four hours later, it was the best day of her life. How could two such varying incidents occur so close together?

With that thought, her mind drifted to Dennis and what he was forcing her to do. But it wasn't just her. It was those at Dreagan—Denae, Cassie, Jane . . . Rhys.

Then there was Kyle.

If she helped Dennis onto Dreagan, she would never be able to look at Rhys again. How could she after making love to him, and then betraying him?

Yet, how could she ever look into the eyes of her parents if she didn't save Kyle? She would be responsible for him turning into Dennis.

It was a no-win situation. She had to choose between family and Rhys.

The decision was even more difficult now that she knew what she would be missing. Rhys was everything she wanted and needed. He was strong, gentle, encouraging, and loving. He was a man who would support her in whatever she did.

He reminded her so much of her father, which only made her want to cry. She knew her father would like Rhys. All of her family would like Rhys. How unfair fate was to give her a man who could heal her wounded soul only to force her to decide between Rhys, who could be the love of her life, and her family.

An image of her family flashed in her mind. It was four years since she last saw them. Was her father still watching his food for his high-cholesterol? Which diet was her mother on now? Did her eldest sister at long last have the baby she'd been dreaming of? Were her other sisters married?

Lily's heart hurt with the unanswered questions. She wanted to think that Dennis wouldn't have gotten to her this time if she had only returned to her family when she left him, but she knew it was a lie. Dennis would've found some way to get what he wanted. He always did.

If she chose Rhys, then her family would suffer unimaginably. Not to mention what sweet, funny Kyle would endure.

If she chose to save Kyle, Dreagan would miss some piece of artwork or something that could quickly be claimed by insurance and replaced. No one would die, and no one would be turned into an assassin.

Only she would be the one to lose either way.

The fact she knew she would have to leave Rhys, Dreagan, her friends, and her new life behind only pushed her to want to see Dennis dead sooner. If only she'd listened to her mother about Dennis. If only she hadn't let him rule her life. If only she hadn't been so weak to remain with him.

If only . . .

There was no amount of looking back that would change her past. It was done, decisions already made. The only thing she could do was ensure her present and her future.

And after what she was about to do to Rhys, she didn't deserve him.

She wanted to tell him what was coming, but what would that accomplish? He would try to stop Dennis, which would only end up getting someone at Dreagan killed and her brother lost to her forever.

No, it was better not to tell Rhys anything. He would know her involvement when she didn't return to work. Lily knew Dreagan might seek her out for damages, and she was prepared to face whatever legal action they would take.

"That sigh didna sound good," Rhys said into the silence of the room.

Lily hadn't even realized she had sighed. She listened to the beat of his heart beneath her ear. "Just thinking."

"Anything I can help with?"

How she wished he could. Lily opened her eyes to look at his handsome face, a shadow of a beard darkening his jaw. "Unfortunately, no."

"You're no' thinking of that wanker of an ex while in bed with me, are you?" he asked as he cracked open an eye and smiled at her.

She chuckled. "I would never."

"Good, because that could severely damage my confidence."

"Nothing could damage your confidence."

He looked at the ceiling and put his other arm behind his head, his smile gone. "I'm a good listener. If you need to talk."

"You've heard the worst of it."

"Have I?" he asked softly and looked at her before lightly

touching her bruised cheek. "How did you really come by this?"

Lily couldn't answer. She didn't want to lie again, especially not to Rhys. And yet the words stuck in her throat.

"The bastard found you." Rhys turned so that they faced each other. "Why did you no' tell someone? I'd gladly have taken care of him. Hell, anyone on Dreagan would."

If only his "take care of" meant kill, but Lily would never ask that of anyone. It was her soul that would be stained with Dennis's death and no one else's.

"It's been a year since I left him. I thought I was free of that part of my life, but I was wrong." When Rhys entwined his fingers with hers, she gained courage to continue. "He's only hit me in the face a few times."

"There's a special place in Hell for men like him," Rhys said angrily. "I'd love to get my hands on him. Is he still around?"

Now Lily had no choice but to lie. How she hated it. Just another reason to want to cut Dennis out of her life for good. "I hope he got the hint after I refused to take him back."

"Next time, call me. I'll make sure that son of a bitch never bothers you again."

She looked into his blue eyes, unable to hold back the wash of tears. Even though Rhys couldn't help her, the fact he was willing to try was enough. The tears were forgotten as Rhys pulled her against him and kissed her. The last time she was in control. This time, it was all him.

He seized her lips, captured her breath. He conquered and dominated her with just his kisses. Lily submitted, wanting him and eager to see where he would take her. His hands were everywhere, caressing, stroking. Seducing. From her face to her feet, every inch of skin felt his touch. He was demanding and yet gentle, commanding yet tender.

His rule in the bed was absolute, unequivocal. And Lily found she was more than willing to acquiesce to his experienced hands and skilled lips.

The world fell away, forgotten as if it was but a dream. Rhys claimed not just her body and mind, but her soul. He challenged her without words to give herself up to him with no questions asked. Lily hesitated for only a heartbeat. Then she freely and unconditionally gave herself to him.

If she thought his kisses before were heavenly, then the scorching kiss now was as sinful as it was pure. The hunger inside her grew, expanded until it consumed her.

She tried to delve her hands into the silkiness of his dark brown locks, but he took her hands and held them above her head. Then he ran his free hand over her breasts, stopping to roll a nipple between his fingers.

Her back arched, desire curling through her, heating her blood. Pleasure spread each time he pinched her aching nipples. Her breasts swelled, throbbing for more of his touch, to feel his big hands cup them, his long fingers massage them.

She moaned when he pushed open her legs. Her body quivered, waiting for his touch to soothe the fire within her. There was no stopping the blaze, no controlling the inferno Rhys had begun.

This fervor was something new, some energy that hadn't been there until the amazing man beside her brought it to life. He knew how to coax her, entice her . . . tempt her.

She was frightened of this new force. But she also found herself growing stronger, more self-assured.

His fingers lightly grazed her dark curls, just skimming her swollen sex. Lily moaned and lifted her hips seeking him, but he was gone.

"Close your eyes," he demanded when she lifted her head to see where his hand was.

Lily complied and dropped her head back on the mattress. Her other senses came alive then—smell, hearing, and feeling.

She knew the second before his hand rested on her inner thigh, the warmth of his skin penetrating hers. By degrees he moved his hand closer and closer to the juncture of her thighs until his fingers sunk into her wetness.

A sigh left her, but whatever relief she got quickly evaporated as a new need replaced it. Lily tried to shift so that his fingers went deeper. He held her still with a firm grip on her hands.

Lily cried out from the pleasure when his fingers swirled around her clit. She was panting, her body covered in sweat and shaking from the desire.

"You're mine," Rhys whispered in her ear. "Your body is mine to tease and seduce. Tonight, you're all mine."

Excitement grew, expanded. It was his deep voice filled with control and hunger. It was his words, those profound, mysterious words that dared her to imagine more than just a night belonging to such an enigmatic man.

"Say it, Lily. Say you're mine."

She was breathing heavily, her sex aching for relief. His slow circling of her clit was robbing her of thought. "I'm yours. All yours."

He continued his unhurried stimulation of her aching clit while she shivered and whimpered from the pleasure. With his light, steady touch, Lily found herself hurtling toward a climax.

A moment later, he released her hands and lifted her up and over him as he fell on his back, the blunt head of his arousal sliding inside her. Lily braced her now free hands on his chest and stared down at Rhys. His face was hard, controlled, his need clearly visible.

She rocked her hips, hissing at the exquisite feel of him deep inside her, stretching her, filling her. Wanting more, she repeated the movement again and again, moving faster, more sensually each time.

His large hands reached up and grasped her breasts. As he tweaked her nipples, spurring her desires, his eyes glowed with longing.

Lily looked down, momentarily stilled when she saw the dragon tat move. Rhys sat up, taking her mouth in another intense kiss that made her forget what she'd seen. His hands gripped her hips as he moved her hips faster. Lily sank her hands into his long hair and returned his kiss, their tongues moving in time with their bodies.

She tore her mouth from his and screamed as the climax ripped through her. Lily was unprepared for the force of it, the sheer intensity of it.

Her body was limp, jerking with the effects of such a powerful orgasm while Rhys prolonged it by continuing to thrust into her. Just as the orgasm began to end, another rolled through her. She clung to Rhys as the bliss consumed her, the passion and pleasure making her feel as if she were floating, flying.

"Lily!" Rhys bellowed as he gave a final thrust and buried himself deep within her as he climaxed.

The happiness she found in Rhys's arms was dimmed by the fact that she was going to lose him.

He shattered the walls caging her in, giving her a glimpse of what her life could have been.

And she was going to destroy it all.

CHAPTER TWENTY-ONE

Rhi was veiled as she stood on the balcony of the hotel and looked through the window at Rhys and Lily cuddled once more on the bed. Of all the Kings, Rhys was one of her favorites.

He was one of the first to welcome an ally with the Light Fae, and then when she fell in love with her Dragon King, Rhys supported her. Rhys was cocky, impulsive, reckless, and wild. But he was brave, valiant, bold, and daring.

It was going to take a certain kind of woman to tame him, and she suspected that the woman now lay in Rhys's arms. But did Rhys realize that?

If Rhys hadn't had his ability to shift taken from him, Rhi imagined that he would've gone after Lily and made her his own in quick order. The fact he had spent weeks away from Dreagan so as not to see her didn't bode well. However, seeing them in bed naked was definitely a step in the right direction.

The question now was would Rhys take what was meant to be his? Or would he run?

The Dragon Kings were frustratingly idiotic at times. They were fearful of trusting humans, and rightly so after what had happened to Ulrik. Despite that, they found love among the mortals.

Well, some did. Kiril was the odd one who'd found love with a Fae.

A stab of pain lanced through Rhi's chest every time she thought of Kiril and Shara. It wasn't that she didn't like Shara. She was the first Dark Fae to turn Light, and she made Kiril happy.

No, Rhi was hurt because they had what she was told could never be—a union of the Kings and Fae.

The overwhelming tide of heartbreak still had the ability to take her breath away. For thousands of years she'd lived with the pain of her one-sided love. There was a way to turn it off. It was there, inside her, waiting. All she had to do was search out the darkness within her and she could shake free of the hold her lover had on her.

She could move on with her life, forget the love they shared and the happiness that had been hers for a short time. She could wipe away the promises he'd made her—and broken. She could ignore the pull Dreagan had on her.

Usaeil and the Dragon Kings all thought she was her old self. They assumed because she broke the Chains of Mordare that had held her and escaped Balladyn that the dark couldn't penetrate the light inside her.

They were wrong.

At all times she knew were Balladyn was. The darkness inside her sought him out, searched for him. She almost went to him once while in Rome.

Even with Balladyn becoming a Dark Fae, he was the only family she had left. He hated her though. He blamed her for his becoming Dark. It was her fault. She shouldn't have left him. He wouldn't have left her, even in the middle of battle.

Rhi was tired of the weight of her unreturned love. She

was tired of pretending the darkness wasn't part of her. She was tired of fighting the inevitable.

The Dragon Kings had a good chance to win the war, but that chance was growing slimmer by the day. The writing was on the wall. Ulrik would win. The Kings would be defeated, and the Silvers woken.

As soon as the Silvers woke and took to the skies, the humans would die. The Dark Fae believed they would still have mortals to feed off of, but Rhi recognized the truth.

Ulrik wanted to rule this realm as it once was—with dragons. He would kill any King who didn't side with him, and he would find a way to return the dragons to this realm to eradicate mortals once and for all. Earth would no longer be inhabited by humans, and the Fae—Light and Dark—would have no reason to remain.

Rhi jerked as she felt the darkness pulse inside her. Balladyn was in the city. She located him and teleported nearby, remaining veiled.

It was lucky that she could keep the veil up for long periods, unlike most Fae. She peered around the corner of the building and spotted Balladyn talking to another Dark who wore glamour to appear human, hiding his red eyes and black and silver hair.

Balladyn finished the conversation and turned on his heel to walk away. He took ten steps before he halted and turned his face in her direction. He was only twenty feet from her. She could see his red eyes in the light of the streetlamp. His long black and silver hair was pulled back in a series of small braids that formed one thick plait down his back.

His customary black leather pants were sculpted to his muscular legs, and the deep red V-neck tee showed off the thick sinew of his chest and arms.

"Rhi?" he called softly in his Irish accent. "I can feel you. Talk to me."

She remained veiled, barely breathing.

"You've sought me out for a reason," he continued. "I've been searching for you. Let me see you."

Rhi teleported away before she gave in.

Rhys woke suddenly, immediately reaching for Lily as the morning sun filled the room. His hands met cool sheets. He lay there on his elbow looking at the empty bed, his heart thumping in his chest.

Not once had he remained all night with one woman, and he certainly had never woken to find himself alone. He didn't like the desolation, the void that filled his chest.

He jumped from the bed and walked naked to the doorway. His steps slowed when he saw the light on in the bathroom. Rhys looked inside to find Lily with the white hotel robe on, standing at the sink looking at the tattoo on her forearm.

Whatever had tightened around Rhys's chest released so that he could breathe easier, the relief palpable. He leaned a shoulder against the doorway and watched the subtle play of emotions crossing Lily's face. There was despair, misery, sadness, and finally anger.

She inhaled deeply and slowly released it as she looked up in the mirror. Their eyes clashed, held, and a slow smile pulled at her lips.

Rhys's gaze raked over her disheveled hair and her swollen lips. He'd never seen a more beautiful sight. "I'm pretty sure you should still be in bed," he said with a grin.

She turned to face him and shrugged, the movement causing her robe to gape and expose a tantalizing side of her breast. "I'm an early riser."

"I'm going to have to change that."

Her laughter filled the bathroom when he closed the distance and pulled her against him. "I didn't wake you, did I?"

"Nay," he replied, not wanting her to know it was her absence that pulled him from sleep. "Are you hungry?"

"Starved."

Rhys reluctantly released her and went to order breakfast as she grabbed a brush and began to run it through her long tresses.

"I don't even know what time I need to meet Denae to go home."

Rhys glanced at his suit jacket where his mobile was. He was sure if he checked there would be a message from Kellan asking him to take Lily back to Dreagan. It was a task Rhys relished. "We'll find out," he called.

He ordered room service and replaced the receiver. He was on his way to his suit when a robe hit him in the chest. Rhys instinctively caught it and looked up at a grinning Lily.

"You can't be walking around naked," she said. "What will the hotel staff think?"

He winked at her. "They'll think you're a verra lucky lass."

"They wouldn't be wrong."

Rhys put on the robe and loosely belted it at his hips before he checked his mobile. Sure enough there was a message. Denae and Kellan indeed wished for him to drive Lily back to Dreagan.

He heard the shower turn on and caught a glimpse of Lily as she let the robe fall. She looked over her shoulder through the door and smiled before she stepped into the shower and shut the glass door.

Since he hadn't heard any more about Henry, Rhys called the one person who would know. Banan. It took four rings before Banan answered.

"I gather you're having a good time," Banan said testily.

Rhys frowned and walked out onto the large balcony.

"Aye. Tell me about Henry. All Con told me last night was that he was at Dreagan."

"First, it is Ulrik doing all of it."

"Tell me something I doona know."

Banan sighed. "Ulrik told the group of Dark and MI5 that Henry was a spy. The Dark attacked him, but somehow Henry ended up with Ulrik, who wanted Henry to join forces with him."

"What?" Rhys stated with a snort. "Ulrik has no love of mortals, Banan. You know that."

"I do. I also thought it sounded a bit . . . strange."

Rhys leaned on the balcony railing. "But you believe Henry?"

"He wasna lying. For whatever reason, Ulrik offered Henry that deal."

"Are you sure Henry didna take it?"

There was a slight pause and then a sigh from Banan. "I doona think he did. He was injured badly, Rhys. Several broken bones and at least two broken ribs, not to mention I suspect there was internal bleeding the Light healed."

"Light? What?"

"Somehow the Light got Henry away from Ulrik and healed him."

Rhys knew it was Rhi who had saved Henry. What was she doing with Ulrik? "How did Henry get away?"

"He says he doesna know, but he's keeping something from us."

Rhys immediately thought of Rhi and her ability to teleport with a passenger. "Rhi got him to Dreagan."

"Obviously."

Rhys dropped his forehead into his hand and closed his eyes. Rhi was like a sister to him. She drove him nuts at times, but she was loyal, a skilled warrior, and had a quick wit that always made him smile.

If he hadn't been so consumed with his own misery, he

would have been there to help her through whatever was going on. Not only had Ulrik carried her out of Balladyn's fortress, but Rhi was visiting him. Her constant wearing of black nail polish said more than her words ever could.

She was being torn in two.

There was a time, not so long ago, that he had been in a similar position with the wound Ulrik had inflicted upon him. It was Rhi who had eased the pain and given him the ability to shift one more time if he so chose. It was a miracle that she had, otherwise he would not have had the pleasure of Lily's body.

"You know something." Banan let out a string of curses. "It has to do with Rhi."

Rhys opened his eyes and straightened. "Trust me when I say that Rhi is on our side." He hoped.

"Con isna going to like this."

"Con doesna have to know a damn thing," Rhys bit out.

Banan gave a bark of laughter. "That's true, but I have to say I doona like being kept in the dark."

"Rhi has always helped us. She's no' going to turn her back on us now."

"Why no'?" Banan asked. "In her shoes, I certainly would have. Long, long ago. After what he did to her . . ."

"I know," Rhys said into the silence.

Banan cleared his throat. "There's more."

"More?" This didn't sound good in the least.

"It involves one of Ulrik's men. The mortal is using a woman who works here to gain entrance onto Dreagan and search for the weapon."

Rhys's ears began to ring as he thought of the bruise on Lily's cheek. She'd told him her ex-lover had returned after a year, but she'd never said why he came back.

"Rhys? Did you hear me?" Banan asked.

Rhys ignored him and asked instead, "Who is it? Who is the woman?"

"We doona have many working for us," Banan began slowly.

"Who?" Rhys demanded harshly.

The silence grew as Banan hesitated.

"Just spit it out." Rhys knew in that instant, knew with a certainty that rocked him, that it was Lily.

"We've narrowed down the names to two," Banan finally said. "Lily's is one of them."

CHAPTER
TWENTY-TWO

Lily bathed, hating to wash off Rhys's scent. She was deliciously sore from their repeated lovemaking. If only they could remain in the hotel and halt time. If only she had some kind of superpower to stop Dennis so she could have her family *and* Rhys. But she wasn't a superhero, and no one was going to save the day for her.

Lily finished rinsing her hair and turned off the water. She grabbed a towel and opened the shower door to find Rhys. A small shriek sounded from her as she put her hand to her throat. "You scared me."

Rhys's lips lifted in a lopsided smile. "I was just about to join you."

That's all it took. A few words from his sexy voice, and her body began to throb.

"Then our breakfast arrived."

Lily was more than a little disappointed. Her stomach growled as she dried off. "Right on time."

He walked out of the room, and Lily put the robe back on and ran her fingers through her hair before she joined him at the table that was loaded with food.

"I didna know what you liked," Rhys said with a shrug.

There was a little of everything. Lily laughed and eyed the Belgian waffles and bacon. She chose her dishes and tucked a foot beneath her on the chair as she poured both of them coffee. Rhys took the seat opposite her and picked the omelet and a piece of toast. They ate silently for a few minutes as she studied him.

"I need a shave," he said when he caught her staring.

She lifted a shoulder in a shrug. "It's not bad."

"I'd scrape your delicate skin if I tried to kiss you."

"Want to find out?" she asked with a mischievous smile.

His gaze darkened. "Doona tempt me."

"I'd do anything to remain right here forever."

"Would you?"

Was it her imagination, or had there been a hint of something in his voice? As if he knew about Dennis. But that was silly. There was no way he could know. Rhys was intelligent, but Dennis was careful and she hadn't told Rhys anything. No, it was just her imagination at work. "I would."

"What about your job?"

Lily swallowed her bite of food. "I don't have to work. I do it because I enjoy it. Many of my jobs were about having the satisfaction of supporting myself without having to fall back on my family's money. But Dreagan . . ." She paused and glanced at her plate. "This may sound silly since I've not been there long, but Dreagan has become a home for me. I found true happiness there. And friendships. That doesn't happen often."

"Interesting."

She winced as she caught sight of the bags of clothes from the day before. "I was only going to spend my money yesterday, but then I wanted to erase all parts of the last four years."

"It's understandable."

"I know how all of this makes me look. I needed to make a clean cut, to eradicate the past."

"You can no' erase it. It's part of you. It made you who you are today," he said as he leaned back in his chair and pushed his empty plate aside.

Lily rubbed her left wrist that was beginning to ache. A reminder of one of the first instances of abuse from Dennis. "My scars will be a constant reminder, yes, but I have to remove the parts that keep me from being who I really am. The clothes, the attitude. The fear."

"He chose your clothes?"

It took her two tries to answer. "Yes. He didn't like anyone looking at me, so he had me wear loose, baggy clothes. I forgot what it was like to feel good in something until yesterday."

"Did he break your wrist?"

Lily stopped rubbing it and stared at him.

Rhys's gaze dropped to her left wrist for a moment. "You've no' stopped rubbing it for some time. Does it hurt?"

"Only when it's about to rain, and yes. He broke it a month after I chose him over my family."

"Why did you no' go back to them then?"

Lily wrapped her now cool fingers around the cup of coffee to warm them. "My mother was a commoner. She had no connections to the upper class, and yet my father fell head over heels for her. My grandfather wasn't pleased at all. He wanted his children to marry in the upper class, but especially his heir. My parents snuck off and married, much to the dismay and anger of my grandfather. It wasn't until my eldest sister was born three years later that my grandfather would even speak to my parents."

"All because your father chose your mother?"

Lily nodded and scrunched up her face. "Sad, isn't it? My parents told all five of their children that it didn't matter who we fell in love with, be it prince or pauper, if we loved them, then they would be welcomed into the family."

"Then what went wrong with your lover?"

"Dennis won my parents and brother over initially. He could be very pleasant when he wanted. One weekend my father and brother went hunting and invited Dennis. When they returned, my father was agitated. He told me I was still young and that I shouldn't be ready to settle down so soon."

A frown furrowed Rhys's brow. "No explanation?"

"None. My sisters never liked Dennis. They were always rude to him, and yet he was so congenial. But they saw the evil inside him that I never did. Until it was too late. After the harsh words to my family when I left, I was too proud to go back to them then. I only wish I had."

Rhys's aqua ringed dark blue eyes held a hint of anger when he said, "The bastard will get his day."

"Yes. He will."

Rhys tossed his napkin on the table. "What do you want to do today?"

Lily glanced at the clock and cringed. "I was supposed to be at work fifteen minutes ago."

"Everyone knew Denae brought you to Edinburgh. Your job isna in jeopardy."

"Are you sure?" she asked as she rose and searched for her clutch that had her mobile phone in it. "Perhaps I should call."

"Denae already has. They left a few hours ago."

Lily slowly straightened from picking up her clutch. "Oh." Was Rhys taking her back? She prayed for it even as she hoped that he had another engagement. Being so close to him was a harsh reminder of what she had to do.

"I'm to drive you back to Dreagan."

She swallowed, her mouth suddenly dry. "You don't mind?"

"Only if you do."

Lily lowered her gaze to his chest, visible in the gaping

robe. She frowned when she saw the dragon move again. That couldn't be right. Tattoos didn't move.

"Lily?"

She jerked her gaze to him. "Yes, that's fine. When did you want to leave?"

"We doona have to. Would you like to remain another night?"

More than anything. It was on the tip of her tongue to say yes. Then she thought of Dennis's phone call the night before and his threat to Kyle if she didn't get him the information. "They might excuse me today, but I doubt I'd have a job tomorrow if I didn't come in."

"As you wish."

With their conversation now strained, Lily stared at her plate. A magical night was now spoiled by Dennis. Could her hate grow any more? Apparently it could.

Lily rose and nervously looked around. "I guess I better get ready."

She walked to the bedroom with a heavy heart. Without even trying Dennis had shattered her dream, destroyed the one day that would get her through the rest of her life. Loathing grew and spread through her. She could feel it seeping into every nook and crevice of her mind, smothering anything good. But she didn't care. In order to kill Dennis, she was going to have to be methodical, meticulous. And cold.

Lily removed her robe and put on another new set of bra and panties, a pretty nude lace confection. She decided on a pair of jeans and a blue and white striped nautical long-sleeved fitted shirt and a navy sateen jacket with gold accents. A pair of black boots with four-inch heels completed the outfit.

She looked at herself in the mirror and ran her fingers through her still damp hair. The clothes were her armor, a reminder that she made her own decisions and chose what was best for her. Every time she dressed now she would be severing another tie to her past. And it felt wonderful.

Lily walked out of the bedroom and found Rhys still sitting at the table. His smile of appreciation set butterflies off in her stomach.

"I feel like I should take you sailing."

She laughed and glanced down at herself. "So that's what I inspire, huh?"

"Nay." Rhys stood and walked to her. He stopped in front of her and set his hand on her hip, their bodies brushing. "I was thinking how much I'd love to strip those clothes from you and keep you in the bed for the rest of the day."

Lily forgot to breathe as a mental image flashed in her mind of their bodies entwined. She reacted instantly, desire tightening, coiling within her until her chest heaved. Rhys wasn't just sexy. Every movement, every smile, every look of his beautiful eyes was erotic, stimulating. Suggestive.

He was the god of sex, skilled and proficient in the many ways to bring a woman to her knees with a seductive smile.

"If I got back in that bed, I wouldn't ever want to get out."

Rhys's grip tightened on her waist. "Is there anything wrong with that?"

"No, but it wouldn't be long before those at Dreagan came looking for you."

"And you."

No, it wouldn't be anyone from Dreagan looking for her. It would be Dennis. "You're the one important to Dreagan."

"You doona think you're important?" he asked with a slight frown.

Lily rested her hand atop his arm holding her. "I meant at Dreagan."

"You're important to us. We doona hire anyone that doesna fit."

"I'm just an employee."

Rhys raised one dark brow. "If you think that, then why did Denae ask you to accompany her yesterday?"

Lily didn't have an answer.

"You're part of the Dreagan family. And we doona let just anyone in."

A sharp pang of guilt and regret pierced her. She couldn't believe she was going to betray people who considered her a part of their family. But she had to remember her true family, she had to remember that it was Kyle's life that was on the line. As much as she loved working at Dreagan, her brother was more important.

"I love it at Dreagan. I don't ever want anything to change that."

"Then doona let it," Rhys whispered.

That was the second time Lily got the feeling Rhys knew what she was about. She shifted her feet nervously, but didn't look away from his gaze. "I never willingly would."

Rhys's mobile rang, splintering the silence. He sighed and dropped his hand from her waist. "There are really times I hate those damn things."

She smiled as he walked to the bar and answered the phone before taking it into the bathroom with him. He closed the door, and a moment later the sound of the shower reached her.

Lily sank down on the couch and put her head in her hands. That's when she began to plan how she would ensure Dennis never bothered her again.

CHAPTER
TWENTY-THREE

Ulrik wasn't just shaken at seeing his uncle, he was alarmed. All the dragons were supposed to be gone. All except the Dragon Kings, and his uncle was never a King.

"Sit, Ulrik," his uncle said in a smooth voice. "Let's talk."

Ulrik was tempted to remove Mikkel from the store, but he was intrigued. Not to mention there were questions he wanted answers to. So Ulrik took the chair opposite him. He looked Mikkel over in his tailored black suit and white shirt opened at the neck. His uncle's hair wasn't quite as long as his, but it was the same inky shade of black, just as his eyes were the same golden color as Ulrik's.

Whatever happened to Mikkel, he had stopped aging as well. He looked only a handful of years older than Ulrik. There was only one thing that would stop him from aging.

"Mikkel, what are you doing here?"

"I never left," he said with a smile that held a healthy dose of smugness. "Oh, Con tried to send us all away. I fought it, because I knew if the dragons ever left, we'd never return. This realm is ours."

He said the last part in a hard tone. Ulrik didn't disagree with him, mostly because he felt the same. Earth was the dragons' home eons before humans ever arrived. "It doesna explain how you're here. Or why you're in human form."

"Ah. That," Mikkel said in distaste. "The Dragon Kings were so obsessed with taking your magic they didn't know what I was about. When your magic was suppressed, the Silvers needed a King."

Anger crackled through Ulrik, but he kept a tight rein on it. There was only one King of the Silvers, and he was it. Until he knew what his uncle was about, he wasn't giving anything away. But how it burned to know Mikkel was a Dragon King.

Though that wouldn't be for long. As soon as Ulrik had all of his magic back, he would take the title once more. Mikkel hungered to be a Dragon King, but his magic and power didn't come close to comparing to Ulrik's.

"No outrage?" Mikkel asked with a small smile. "You really have become soft after all these millennia of being in human form."

Ulrik simply stared at Mikkel. "You've been here all this time as a Dragon King. Why no' challenge Con? Why no' go to Dreagan?" He purposefully left out the Silvers caged in the mountain at Dreagan, because he wanted to see how much his uncle knew.

Mikkel's laugh was that of an adult humoring a child. "All in good time. I intend to take over Dreagan and remove Con from existence."

"Con is mine," Ulrik said in a low tone, the silent warning dripping from his voice.

Mikkel's gold eyes expressed his doubt. "You don't have any magic. You can't go against a Dragon King without your magic."

"But you can?"

Mikkel gave a halfhearted shrug. "I've got my ways."

"So you can shift?"

"Let's focus on you right now."

Ulrik began to laugh, the sound empty. "You can no'."

Mikkel's pleasant expression faded to one of fury. "Nay, I can no'!"

Ulrik didn't think his uncle realized he'd slipped and used the brogue. Mikkel had been so careful to speak in his British accent, and Ulrik knew it was by no accident.

"Does that please you?" Mikkel asked, once more in control.

"Immensely. However, I'm curious. If you're a Dragon King, why are you unable to shift?"

Mikkel crossed one leg over the other. "When your magic was locked and I became the King of the Silvers, I immediately shifted into human form."

Ulrik watched the aversion on Mikkel's face, and almost laughed. "Aye. That's what happens to all Kings. That's how one becomes a King."

"Exactly. I knew something must've happened to you, so I remained in this form and went to find you. I saw Con in dragon form standing over you, and then I saw him fly away with the others following."

"So you watched me walk away?" Ulrik said, a new bout of anger emerging.

Mikkel gave a shrug of indifference. "You were no longer King."

"I was alone," he said tightly.

"You survived."

It took everything Ulrik had to keep his fingers relaxed and not rip the arms off the chair. "Then what happened?"

"I tried to shift." Mikkel stood and began to walk around the area while he spoke. "No matter how many times I tried, I couldn't get away from this human form. The magic I had wasn't as strong either. It was like something dampened it."

Ulrik knew it was the spell Con and the others used on him that somehow affected his uncle as well. "All these thousands of years you've been right here. Why show yourself to me now?"

Mikkel stopped behind the chair he had vacated and smiled. "Because I want you to join me. You've no idea how long I've been planning this, or how much I've already done."

"Tell me."

"I've come to an understanding with a group of mortals. They like to think they're in control of things, and I allow them to believe that. You might know them as MI5."

Ulrik recalled the visits from the Dragon Kings as things began to make sense now.

"There is also another alliance I'm particularly proud of," Mikkel said. "The Dark Ones."

"I might no' have been a King during the Fae Wars, but even you know what occurred during those years. You can no' trust a Dark."

Mikkel's lips twisted as he considered Ulrik's words. "I have an understanding with Taraeth."

The king of the Dark. Mikkel really was playing with fire. Ulrik himself had made friends in the Dark Fae world, so he knew all the participants.

"With the Dark and MI5 on my side, I've been able to do a great many things."

Ulrik rubbed his hand over his chin, feeling a day's growth of stubble beneath his palm. "Like what?"

"My people have infiltrated Dreagan multiple times."

"To what end?"

"I've convinced MI5 that those at Dreagan need to be exposed for the dragons that they are." Mikkel chuckled. "You should've seen their outrage and fear to know they aren't the only beings on this realm."

"They know of the Dark now."

Mikkel's eyes narrowed as his smile faded. "Of course. They must work together."

"How did the mortals take the Dark?"

"Not well, actually. Neither do the Dark like being so near humans and not able to take them as they normally do."

Ulrik knew there was more, and he wanted to know all that his uncle had been doing. "What else?"

"There is a weapon on Dreagan that can kill a Dragon King."

Of all the things he thought Mikkel might say, this one took him aback. "What?"

"A weapon that Con has kept hidden from all."

Not all. Kellan would know as Keeper of the History, but Ulrik didn't bother to tell Mikkel that. "What kind of weapon?"

"That I don't know. Yet. I've a man who will get on Dreagan any day now and find it."

"Why no' have MI5 or the Dark get it?"

Mikkel made a sound at the back of his throat as he waved his hand. "Damn mortals screw it up every time. The Kings know as soon as someone crosses their boundary. Same with the Dark. The patrols the Kings set up night and day prevent the Dark from getting onto Dreagan unnoticed. We did find a way, a secret doorway. You might know where that doorway is located since it's the spot the Kings killed your woman."

A slow blaze of rage enveloped him. No one spoke of her. No one.

Mikkel put his hands in the pockets of his pants. "That doorway is the only place someone can get onto Dreagan without the Kings knowing it. Can you believe the Kings made a pact with the Campbells years ago to guard the piece of land that borders Dreagan?"

Ulrik glared at his uncle.

"Apparently one of the Campbells is a Warrior. I know you must have run across those bastards over the last few hundred years. Mortals who allowed a primeval god inside them to give them power and immortality. Then there are the Druids the Warriors are married to." Mikkel grunted. "The Druids use their magic to alert whatever Campbell lives on the land that someone is there."

"So you can no' get on Dreagan."

Mikkel grinned then. "The Kings are used to people coming to take a tour of the distillery. My man is going to get on Dreagan that way."

"The plan will fail. Those who work for Dreagan are loyal."

"Not if you use the right motivation," Mikkel said softly.

Ulrik blew out a long breath. Mikkel had always had a way of getting what he wanted. The only thing that slipped through his fingers was becoming a King. "I guess you have been busy."

"That's not all I've done. My most impressive feat yet is the beginning of the end of the Kings."

Ulrik feared he already knew what it was. "Care to explain?"

"I mixed Dark Fae magic with my own during a battle between the Kings and the Dark. Rhys never knew what hit him. Not until it was too late. I never did like that reckless idiot."

"You made it so he can no' shift."

Mikkel rubbed his hands together, his gold eyes alight with merriment. "Oh, yes, I did. It was fabulous. I don't imagine Rhys was without pain. He learned soon enough that he could either stay a dragon forever, or remain human to the end of his days. Odd how he chose the human form."

"You condemned him to what we've suffered."

"Rightly so," Mikkel said in anger. "One by one, I'll

ensure the Kings know what it means to suffer. Con will be the last."

"And the mates of the Kings?"

Mikkel's disdain was evident as he scrunched up his face. "The women will die with their mates. That's how it works. They'll remain immortal until their Dragon King is killed."

"True."

"Besides, they're humans. The mortals only want our power and immortality."

"No' all of them."

Mikkel laughed and stepped aside. Ulrik's gaze landed on Abby who came to stand beside his uncle. She looked adoringly up at Mikkel as if he were her savoir.

"Yes, all," Mikkel said.

Ulrik was rarely outplayed. It happened so seldom that he at first didn't recognize the jolt of outrage. His gaze skated away from Abby to look back at his uncle. "Abby has been working for you this entire time."

"One of my many brilliant plans," Mikkel said and kissed the top of Abby's head before giving her a little shove away. "She kept an eye on all you had going on. All the while, I was setting my own plans in motion."

"Why no' just come to me yourself?"

Mikkel cocked his head to the side. "I had to know whose side you were really on. You considered Con a brother once."

"Until he killed my woman and banished me from Dreagan."

"Your woman needed to be killed! She was betraying you."

Ulrik lifted one shoulder in a shrug. "So she did. Whatever I felt for Con and the other Kings died the day I was banished and my magic taken."

"I know." Mikkel's smile was wide, triumphant. "I've

watched you carefully, Ulrik. Which is why I think it's time for you to join with me. Just think. Constantine will never know what hit him. Already he believes all that's been happening is your doing."

"Con will come soon and try to kill me."

"That won't happen," Mikkel stated. "I won't let it. The days of Constantine being King of Kings is numbered. I'm going to take his place. I just need you beside me. You deserve your own retribution."

Ulrik stood and looked at his uncle's outstretched hand. The minutes stretched as he stared at the hand. With a deep breath, he clasped it, sealing his promise.

CHAPTER
TWENTY-FOUR

Lily stood on the balcony of her suite and looked out over Edinburgh. The streets teemed with people even as the sky refused to chase away the clouds gathering. All of her bags had been collected by a bellman and were on their way to her flat since they wouldn't fit in Rhys's car. Lily shivered in the cool breeze. Rain was coming, and soon, if the increasing ache in her wrist was any indication.

She began to turn to go back inside when her vision caught sight of something across the block. Her heart plummeted to her feet when she saw Dennis standing on a balcony smiling at her.

"No," she whispered.

She didn't want Dennis to know who she was with. There was no telling what he would do. It was the worst possible scenario. Dennis put his mobile next to his ear, and a moment later hers rang. Lily's hands shook, and it took her two tries just to answer it.

"What do you want?" she asked.

"You know what I want."

"I'm returning today."

"Hmm. I see you've moved on. Who's the bloke?"

Lily glowered at him from across the expanse. "I'll get you what you want."

"I've no doubt."

"Then leave me alone."

"I think you need proper motivation," Dennis said, a smile in his voice. "Here I thought threatening one of those pretty women was the key. Looks like I should've been threatening to kill your new lover. Does he know how to make you scream, Lily?"

She was still shaking, but it now was from anger, not fear. She glanced down at her arm and read the tattoo. It reminded her of the courage she possessed. "I'll do what you want."

Dennis laughed, the sound grating on her nerves. "They'll know it's you when this is all over. Surely you're not stupid enough to know you can't stay there."

Lily disconnected the call and spun around to hurry inside. She closed the door and jerked the curtains closed so Dennis could no longer see in. Her hands hung on the curtains as she felt tears beginning to fall. If she gave in now, the dam would break and she would cry a river.

Rhys stood in the doorway of the bathroom and watched Lily. Her distress was evident by the way her shoulders shook. He heard her sniff, and knew she was crying. It was the silence of her tears that cut through him as nothing else could.

She was in trouble, and she was desperately attempting to handle it on her own. The fact was, she was failing. He could help if she but let him. It wasn't just that he could aid her, he wanted to help. The night they'd had was . . . spectacular, mind-blowing. Utterly incredible.

After little hints he dropped throughout the morning, it was obvious Lily was the one who was going to get Dennis onto Dreagan. But she wasn't happy about it. Their solitude and happiness had been shattered as completely as if Dennis was standing in the room with them. Rhys was in turns furious and distressed by what Lily was being put through. He never thought to find a woman like her, and yet here she was. There was nothing he wouldn't do for her. It was too soon to let her know of his love. He would show her in other ways though.

She thought she hid her emotions well, and for the most part she did. However he was looking for the slightest chink, and he had found it.

Lily was being forced. It was the same thing Rhys told Con on his mobile when he'd walked into the bathroom earlier and turned on the shower. Rhys was willing to stake his life on it. Constantine wasn't so sure, but he was willing to allow Rhys's plan to play out after much convincing by Rhys.

He wanted to peel the skin from Dennis's body over what he put Lily through—and for what was being done to her now. It wasn't fair that Lily had to suffer so much. Rhys hated that she was going to endure it alone for a little longer, but there was no other way. What Lily didn't know was that she would never be by herself. There would always be a King watching over her. Most times it was going to be Rhys.

The question was whether he could refrain from killing Dennis when he saw the asshole. It was Con's concern as well.

Frankly, it was a valid one.

"Lily."

She jerked upright and released the curtains, though she kept her back to him. "I didn't hear you. Are you ready to leave?"

If he had his way, Rhys would never let her out of the room. "Almost."

"I've got something in my eye," she lied. "The wind is

beginning to pick up. I'm afraid it'll be raining on the drive back."

"I'll get you to Dreagan safely."

She finally faced him. The only evidence of her tears were her spikey lashes and watery eyes. "I've no doubt."

Rhys finished buttoning his dress shirt from the night before and tucked it in. Then he grabbed his jacket and slipped it on. "What?" he asked when he caught her staring at him with an odd expression on her face.

She smiled shyly. "I'm putting you to memory in that suit."

"You keep talking like that and I may begin to mimic Con and wear the things every day."

"A well-fitted suit is to a woman what lingerie is to men."

Rhys walked to her and gave her a soft kiss. "Looks like I need to go shopping then."

"Just because I think you look good in a suit?" she asked with an astonished expression on her face.

"Is that so implausible?"

"Yes."

He was really going to have to work on convincing her that her opinion mattered, just as she did. After their night together, he knew there was no turning back for him. Of course he'd learned that in the middle of the night when he didn't want to get up and leave as he had all the other women. With Lily he only wanted to pull her against him and make sure that he could feel her at all times.

The thought of leaving her—or her leaving him—made him go a little crazy. Whether he wished it or not, Rhys had found his mate.

His mate.

It boggled his mind. Of all the Kings, he'd never expected to find anyone who would fill his heart the way Lily did. He enjoyed women. Or he used to. Now he only had eyes for his Lily.

As he gazed into her black eyes, he wanted to beg her to trust him and tell him everything. Which wasn't right when he couldn't tell her everything about himself. Even if he could, she wouldn't believe him since he couldn't prove he was a Dragon King.

Con had asked if Lily was his mate, and Rhys had lied and said he wasn't sure. If Con had a hint that Lily was his mate Con would tell her everything, and Rhys knew that might be all it took to frighten her away. If anyone was going to tell her, it was going to be Rhys.

"I like the way you look at me," Rhys told her.

She glanced down, but the tears were fading. "I'm surprised you ever noticed me. I'm nothing like the women you usually take out."

Rhys inwardly grimaced, because he'd known his past would get brought up. "I noticed you, Lily. I noticed you from the first moment you came to Dreagan, but I stayed away because you were a different kind of woman. The kind that changes a man. The forever kind."

"Oh."

He smiled at her surprised expression. "I've never stayed an entire night with a woman."

"Never?"

"Never. And trust me when I say that's a verra long time."

"Why?"

Rhys gave a shake of his head. "It's the lifestyle I chose."

The sound of rain hitting the window drew her attention. "Here comes the storm."

"We can outrun it." He held out his hand, waiting for her to take it.

When she did, they walked hand in hand from the room. There was a smile on her face until they got into the lift. By the time they reached the lobby, her grip on his hand had tightened and the worry in her furtive glances told him that Dennis was there.

Rhys hurriedly put her in his Jaguar and drove away from the hotel before he went to search for the bastard. When they reached the edge of the city, she released a sigh and seemed to relax.

Whenever Rhys got his hands on Dennis, there was not going to be anything to save him. Human or not, Rhys was going to kill the wanker.

Con sat at his desk, staring at it, though his mind was going over his conversation with Rhys. Ever since the dragon and Dark magic was used on Rhys, he'd been different.

Reserved. Withdrawn.

Cautious.

As much as he hated to admit it, they needed the old Rhys back. The reckless, outrageous Dragon King who questioned Con at every turn.

For many weeks, even before the magic was used on Rhys, Con observed the lovely Lily watching Rhys. And Rhys watching her. Con knew Rhys well enough to know he would keep himself removed from the mortal. Which is why it was such a surprise that Rhys joined Denae and Kellan with Lily in Edinburgh.

Rhys had a keen mind, and he was rarely wrong. Yet Con was worried that he wasn't seeing things clearly when it came to Lily's involvement with Ulrik.

Forced or not, Lily had a choice to go to someone at Dreagan and tell them what was being asked of her. She hadn't. That in itself worried Con. Dreagan was a job to her and many others on the land. To those who lived there— the Kings and their mates—it was home.

People willingly died defending their homes.

Very few were willing to put themselves in danger for a job.

"Got a minute?" Warrick said as he entered Con's office.

Con motioned to the chair. It was always a surprise when Warrick came to him. The King of the Jades preferred to keep to himself. It was a rare thing to find him with any of the other Kings, and even rarer when he sought Con out. "What is it?"

"I wanted to tell you about our visit with Ulrik."

He ran a hand through his hair. "I wondered if you were going to get around to it or make me wait for Rhys to return."

Warrick's cobalt gaze narrowed. "It's no' that I didna want to talk to you about it. I wanted to mull it over in my mind."

"I was a wee bit surprised you went with Rhys."

Warrick paused for a moment and ran a hand over his chin. "The Rhys walking around now isna the same one I've always known. I wasna certain what he would do to Ulrik. I went to make sure Rhys returned to Dreagan."

"And? What happened with Ulrik?" Con urged.

"I've got a bad feeling."

That made him sit up straight. "How so?"

"Ulrik didna act surprised when we asked about Henry or what was done to Rhys. Neither did he gloat over it."

That was interesting news. "It could be that Ulrik was doing it on purpose, to keep us guessing."

"Why? You know he wants to kill you. You want to kill him. Both of you have made those statements many times. Why would he no' rejoice in our suffering?"

"That's a good point, and one I can no' answer." Con wasn't at all pleased at this new development.

Warrick shook his head. "I watched him while Rhys was interrogating him and using the shadows. Ulrik never backed down. All the while, I expected some kind of come-back from him about how we deserved it."

"There's no one else on this realm who has dragon magic, Warrick. I know for some of you it would be easier to know there was another adversary out there instead of Ulrik, but we need to face the facts. Ulrik will see us exposed and back in another war with the Fae. We can no' battle the humans and the Fae."

"Hate Ulrik all you want. Hell, I blame him for our having to send the dragons away, but doona be so hasty to put all our resources to taking down Ulrik."

"If he's dead, then all of this goes away. Those with mates can rest easier, and we can stop worrying about the humans discovering who we are."

Warrick got to his feet. "When are you going after Ulrik?"

"Right after we catch the bastard who thinks he can come onto our land and take something from us."

CHAPTER
TWENTY-FIVE

Rhys was an hour from Dreagan when he heard Kiril's voice in his head. Since he'd been ignoring his mobile that dinged with texts and calls repeatedly, he knew he couldn't disregard Kiril now.

A glance over at Lily showed that she was sleeping. There hadn't been much talk between them since they left Edinburgh. With the city behind them, she hadn't been able to keep her eyes open.

"Aye?" Rhys said as he opened the link between him and Kiril.

There was a frustrated sigh from Kiril. *"About damn time, dick. If you didna answer I was going to come looking for you."*

"I didna want to wake Lily, jerk."

"More likely you didna want to chance her hearing anything." Kiril grunted. *"I remember doing the same with Shara."*

Rhys didn't respond. If he tried to claim Lily wasn't his mate, Kiril would see through him. But he wasn't ready to tell anyone else she was his, either.

"I can no' imagine how you're feeling with Lily's name on the list of suspects," Kiril said.

"It's her, Kiril. Lily is the one Ulrik spoke about."

"Aw, fuck. Con's going to want to talk to her."

"No' happening," Rhys said, giving enough heat to his words so that Kiril would know it wasn't just Rhys wanting to give Con a hard time.

There was a beat of silence. *"I see."*

"Nay, you doona. She's being forced. Lily told me her history with the guy, and I believe he was in Edinburgh watching her."

"Have you considered the possibility that she's . . . acting?"

"If you'd seen the scars all over her back and stomach, you wouldna be asking me that."

"What?"

The shock in Kiril's voice only mimicked what went through Rhys when he had seen the scars himself. *"She's no' faking. Lily left him a year ago. I believe he returned recently. He's also the reason she has the bruise on her cheek. She didna say as much, but it wasna difficult to piece together."*

"Shite. This just keeps getting crazier and crazier. Have you told her you know?"

"Nay."

"I've some experience in this since I went through something similar with Shara in Ireland. Tell her, Rhys. Tell her everything."

Now it was Rhys's turn to be shocked. *"Have you lost your damn mind? She's mortal. I can no' tell her* everything."

"You can. Banan told Henry."

"That's different. Henry is helping us."

Kiril's sigh was long and loud. *"So could Lily. I thought you would want her to know since she's your mate."*

Rhys was so unprepared for that statement that he nearly missed his turn. He and Kiril had always known what the other was thinking, but Rhys had made sure to be so careful and not mention anything about Lily around him—or anyone for that matter.

"Doona even try to tell me I'm lying," Kiril said. *"I know you. I've seen you looking at her with the same hunger that I look at Shara."*

"Lily is mine. I didna try to fight the inevitable. It's no' that I doona think she's strong enough to handle the truth or willna accept it. I think . . . she's been through too much already."

"You're making a grave mistake. Trust me. If Lily is being coerced, then she'll know she can trust you. If she isna, then you'll know that as well. Besides, if she's your mate, you'll have to tell her sometime what you are."

"And what is that?" Rhys asked angrily. *"What am I but an immortal who can no longer shift? She'll really believe I'm a dragon when I can no' prove it to her."*

"Tell her, Rhys. You know it's the right thing to do. For everyone."

Kiril closed the link, leaving Rhys with his words reverberating in his head. Was it the right thing to do? Probably.

The fact of the matter was that he was afraid to tell Lily. Not just fearful of how she might react, but terrified of her turning away from him. It was a proven fact that some humans couldn't handle that there were other beings on the earth with them. Rhys wouldn't be able to handle it if Lily turned away from him.

He had already lost his ability to shift. If he lost her . . .

But he wanted her to trust him. If she knew that he could protect her, then she might very well tell him everything. As much as he wanted to think this was all about him, it wasn't. What was happening involved not just the Dragon

Kings, but the mates there, as well as everyone who worked for Dreagan.

As hard as it was to think about, Rhys was going to have to take the chance and tell Lily while hoping that she trusted him enough to respond in kind.

Instead of turning off the main road and driving to Dreagan where Con, Kiril, and the others would be waiting, Rhys decided to go somewhere else to talk to her. He briefly considered her flat, but no doubt Dennis would be there.

Thinking about the bastard had Rhys sending a mental shout to Ryder.

Thankfully, Ryder answered immediately. "*I hope you get here soon. Con is chomping at the bit to talk to Lily.*"

"*I'm sure he is.*" And it was the main reason Rhys decided against Dreagan. "*I need you to look into Lily's past and see if anyone with the name Dennis shows up. Look in the last four years.*"

"*Give me a sec.*"

Rhys slowed the Jaguar and took a left turn down a narrow road. He stopped the car to allow another vehicle coming from the opposite direction over the one-lane bridge before he drove across and then continued along the curving road.

"*I found something,*" Ryder finally said. "*A Dennis Adams.*"

"*Do you have a picture of him?*"

"*Aye. I'll send it to your mobile now. What's going on, Rhys? Why are you looking for this guy?*"

"*Because I believe he's the asshole who's going to try and come onto Dreagan. Send that picture to every King and mate.*"

"*Consider it done. How did you know about him? Did Lily admit to conspiring? I was hoping she wasna guilty.*"

Rhys clenched his jaw tightly. "*Dennis is her ex-lover,*"

*and he physically abused her. I'm sure if you look, you'll
find the first incident on record with a broken wrist."*

"Aye, I see it, but there's nothing after that."

Of course there wasn't. Dennis had made sure to hurt
her only enough to keep her frightened. There was no trail
of injuries for anyone to follow.

"You doona think she's part of it, do you?" Ryder asked.

Rhys found the stream he was looking for and pulled
slowly off the road to the clump of trees that hid his car.
"I know she's no' willingly participating."

"Is there anything else I can look for to prove that?"

Rhys dropped his head back against the headrest. *"Look
into her family. Dennis is likely to use them somehow."*

"I'll find out what I can."

"Thanks."

"As if I'd let a fellow King lose his mate."

Rhys frowned. *"How did you know?"*

*"I didna until you just admitted it. Anything else you
need?"*

*"Aye. Have someone go to the village. I want Lily
watched after I drop her off, and I can no' stay."*

"On it now. Talk to you soon."

Rhys severed the link and shut off the car. He sat
staring out the windshield to the wide stream that flowed
before him. There were two trees on opposite sides of
the water that bent toward each other, as if seeking to
touch.

"We stopped," Lily said as she opened her eyes. She covered her mouth as she yawned and looked around. "Where
are we?"

"We're about thirty minutes from the distillery. The rain
will be here soon. Come see this." Rhys got out of the car
and walked to the water. For long moments, he waited to
hear the sound of the door opening. When it finally did,
he was able to release the breath he had been holding.

Lily came to stand beside him at the shoreline. "It's beautiful. Another place I had no idea was here."

"The glen hides it." He didn't bother to tell her they were on Dreagan land.

A flash of lightning lit up the sky, foretelling the approaching storm. Lily turned to look at him, her gaze direct and candid. "You have something on your mind."

"Am I that easy to read?" he asked with a small grin.

She crossed her arms and shivered as a gust of wind blew around them. "I can see the line of worry around your eyes. I find it's just better to come out and say whatever it is you need to."

Rhys didn't bother to hide his scowl. "Just what do you think I have to say?"

"That you don't want to see me again. I assumed as much would happen after we left Edinburgh."

"You must have a verra low of opinion of me."

Her smile was sad, the dejection visible. "I'd like to think I'm a realist. Last night was . . . it was everything I ever dreamed of, a fantasy come to life."

"So you doona want any more of me, aye?" Rhys tried to keep his tone light, but he was hurting too much to succeed.

Lily's black eyes stared at him a moment, as if she were trying to decipher his words. "What?"

"Did it never occur to you, Lily Ross, that I'm no' nearly finished with you? That you might be my fantasy come to life?"

"I . . ." She swallowed and shook her head. "No, that never occurred to me." Her gaze dropped to the ground for a moment. When her eyes lifted back to him, there was a glimmer of exhilaration that she appeared frightened to show. "Is that what you want? To see more of me, that is?"

Rhys pulled her into his arms and gazed into her dark eyes. The feel of her against him had desire clawing at him, urging him to take her right there against the tree. "I most certainly want to see more of you. I'm no' sure I'll ever be ready to have you out of my life."

Her lips parted and a glow of delight infused her. Rhys bit back a moan when she rested her hands on his chest. There was still a smile upon her lips, but it was sensual and full of promise.

"Why me?" she whispered.

"There are too many reasons to list."

She tilted her head back and laughed, the long strands of her inky hair lifting in the breeze. Rhys was mesmerized. Lily had no idea of her appeal, of the tantalizing way she seduced him every second of every day. Of how she made him eager to face each day as long as she was with him.

Suddenly her smile dropped as she tried to pull out of his arms. Rhys held her, refusing to release his hold on her.

"This can't work," Lily said, looking at his chest.

Rhys inhaled deeply. He'd known this was coming, but it didn't make it ache any less. "Why?"

"Too many reasons to list." She threw his words back at him.

"Try me."

"I can't," she whispered, her anguish visible.

Rhys tilted her face up to his. "Is it because of Dennis?" When her face went blank, he continued. "I know, Lily."

"Of course you know. I told you about him."

"Nay, lass. I *know*."

She shook her head, her chest rapidly rising and falling as she began to grow agitated. "So this was all a ruse? You were trying to get me to fall for you so I would tell you everything?" she demanded angrily.

Rhys easily held her and wished there was a simpler way to handle such a situation. "Lily, listen to me," he said and gave her a little shake. "This wasna a ruse. I spent the time with you in Edinburgh because I could no longer deny the fact that I craved you as I do the air in my lungs."

She stared at him in disbelief.

"The enemies I spoke of in the city happen to be a mutual one—Dennis's boss. He wants to bring Dreagan down, to expose us."

"Expose you how?" she asked skeptically.

Rhys's heart knocked against his ribs. For the first time in his very long life, he feared, truly feared. "We're no' human. We're Dragon Kings, rulers of the dragons that used to inhabit this realm. We're immortal, shifting between human and dragon form."

He waited with bated breath for her to speak, to show some kind of emotion that she'd heard him. Minutes ticked by as she simply looked at him.

Then she said, "Oh."

CHAPTER
TWENTY-SIX

It was a dream. A very bad dream. Lily wanted desperately to wake up. There was no way that Rhys would've made love to her so sweetly, showed her his tattoo, and then declared that he wanted to date her. There was no way fate would hand her a man like Rhys—handsome, intelligent, gentle, and strong.

The only explanation for his announcement that he was a dragon was that he was either daft as a loon, or it was a dream. She knew Rhys wasn't a nutter, so it had to be a dream.

"Oh?" he repeated, with a deeply furrowed brow. "That's all you have to say?"

Lily shrugged, pinching herself, but still she didn't wake. "What else am I to say?"

"You doona believe me."

It wasn't a question, but a statement. The hurt in his blue eyes was like a knife sinking into her heart. "What you're saying isn't possible."

"Expand your mind, Lily. Quit thinking that in this vast universe humans are the only beings around."

"I have no doubt there are other things out there. In space. Not here."

Rhys closed his eyes and heaved a sigh. "This willna work if you doona believe."

"Then prove it. Show me what you look like as a dragon."

His eyes snapped open, their intensity making her want to cower. "I can no'," he said tightly and dropped his hands from her.

Lily missed his touch instantly. It was like she went through withdrawal after being so near to him. His pain, however, was visible. Whether she believed him or not, he believed it. "Why? Why can't you show me?"

Rhys paced away from her. He was silent for several moments until he stopped before her, his face set in hard lines. "Listen verra carefully. What I'm about to tell you isna told to humans unless they're a mate."

"A mate?"

He waved away her words. "Aye. The females who marry one of us. I'll get to that in a moment. Whatever I tell you here can *never* be spoken to others."

"All right." Lily was intrigued, curious.

"The dragons were the first to rule this realm. We've been here since the beginning of time." He glanced at the sky, a serene smile on his face as he delved into his memories. "Imagine looking up and seeing dozens of dragons in the sky." He looked back at her, sadness filling his aqua ringed dark blue eyes. "We dragons were numerous with the smallest the size of an eagle and the largest bigger than you can fathom. Each species of dragon was designated a color, and within each color was a king. The strongest dragons, the ones with the most magic of that color were chosen as kings."

Lily was enraptured by his tale and the way the emotions

drifted across his face as he spoke. There was joy and delight, but it was tinged with sorrow and gloom.

"I was King of the Yellows," Rhys continued. "The Yellows were daredevils, willing to fly higher than others, and laugh in danger's face. The dragon world was structured so that no one dragon faction could rule the others. Which is why there is a King of Kings."

In her mind, Rhys's words were coming to life, creating a place that seemed fantastical and beautiful, vivid and magnificent.

"Out of all the Kings, only the most powerful could be King of Kings. Most times there's a fight to the death to rule. Other times, the only one who could challenge decides not to."

"Doesn't everyone want to be King of Kings?" she asked.

Rhys shook his head. "I considered it for a time, but I doona have the patience to keep everyone else in line."

"So the King of Kings rules the Kings?"

"He likes to think so," Rhys said with a flattening of lips. "But, aye, in a way, he does. His decisions are for the dragons as a whole instead of mine which are thinking of only the Yellows."

"What happened to change everything?" she asked.

Rhys looked away to the water. "Humans. No longer were we the only beings on this realm. Suddenly we had to share this planet. In response, every King was given the ability to shift to human form so we could communicate with the mortals. We were given the duty to protect no' just this realm, but the dragons and humans living here."

Lily had a feeling the tale was about to take a bad turn.

"For a time"—he turned back to her—"everything was fine. Some Kings took mortal females as their lovers, and some even as their mates. Things couldn't have been better. Until a female decided to betray a King."

Lily licked her lips and ignored the raindrops she felt. "Were you the King?"

"Nay. His name is Ulrik. He was the only one who could've challenged Con to be King of Kings, but he chose no' to. He was happy with his duties and about to ask his female to become his mate."

"Why would she betray Ulrik? Did he mistreat her?"

Rhys shook his head of dark brown hair, a lock falling into his eyes. He shoved it back by running his hand through his hair. "Ulrik never mistreated anyone."

"Then she had no reason to betray him." Lily couldn't believe that she was talking as if she now accepted Rhys's tale, but in fact, it was hard not to.

Rhys looked at his hands. "None of us know why she betrayed him, even all these millennia later."

"You didn't ask? I'd have wanted to know."

"The female was going to start a war between us and the humans, and Con wanted to stop it. As soon as we discovered what the female was about, Con sent Ulrik on a mission, and every Dragon King descended upon her, sinking our swords into her."

Lily was astounded at such an action. "You killed her?"

"In the hopes that whatever war she wanted to start would never come to fruition."

"And?"

"And it all went to hell." Rhys kicked at a river rock. "Ulrik returned and discovered what we'd done. He was . . . irate. His anger was ferocious, his rage vicious. He was enraged that he didna have a chance to talk to his woman, and that we'd killed her. That savageness found an outlet with the humans. Ulrik felt so betrayed by both his lover and the other Dragon Kings that he sought revenge on the very species who wanted the war—the humans."

"How could humans even think to fight against dragons?"

Rhys grunted. "Better than you think. They found the small dragons and slaughtered them. Hundreds upon hundreds of dragons were butchered. And with every dragon that was killed, Ulrik and his Silvers decimated human villages."

"My God." Lily might never have been in a war, but she saw enough news to be able to comprehend the sheer destruction that could be wrought by humans, and it wasn't that far-fetched to think about what a dragon could do.

"No matter how many times Con pleaded with Ulrik to stop, Ulrik refused to listen. The humans then began attacking larger dragons. Kellan is King of the Bronzes who were the Bringers of Justice. Kellan stationed them around a large village to protect the humans in case Ulrik attacked. Those same humans the Bronzes were there to guard killed them."

Lily clutched her stomach and squeezed her eyes closed. This story was too gruesome not to be real. The more she listened to Rhys, the more she began to believe him. How could she not when she looked into his eyes and saw not an ounce of deceit or falsehood?

"The Bronzes were some of the largest dragons, and yet they didna fight the humans. All because Kellan asked his dragons to protect them."

"Stop," Lily said feeling her eyes fill with tears.

Rhys wrapped an arm around her and brought her against him. "At that point we knew if something wasna done to put a halt to the war that the peace and happiness that coexisted would be gone. The humans refused to talk of ending the war. They wanted every dragon killed because they feared us and our magic, as well as our power. It was Con who came to the decision that we had to send our dragons away."

Lily buried her head in Rhys's chest. She didn't need to look at him to know how difficult that statement was for him. She heard it in the catch in his voice, the way his words stumbled over themselves.

"We opened a dragon bridge, which is a portal to another realm and watched our beloved dragons leave. The Dragon Kings remained behind, because we were the only ones who could stop Ulrik. Despite our sending the dragons away, four of the largest Silvers remained with Ulrik. And they were wreaking havoc."

Lily turned her head so that she could see the stream and hear the trickle of water. "What did you do?"

"We combined our magic to bind Ulrik's. We banished him from Dreagan, forced him to wander the realm for eternity in human form, never able to shift into a dragon or fly again. We trapped his four Silvers and spelled them to sleep. The humans still were no' satisfied. We had no choice but to put a magical border up around Dreagan and hide there for centuries until the Dragon Kings were forgotten, a tale told to frighten children. We stay in human form, blending in with you now, and only taking to the skies at night over Dreagan."

Lily stepped out of Rhys's arms. "Say I believe your tale, because it's hard not to. I want to see you in dragon form."

"I wish I could show you. Through the millennia, we kept watch over Ulrik. He was harmless, just living life as a human. It seems that somehow his magic returned, or at least some of it."

"And?" she urged when he paused.

"Ulrik wants revenge on us. He wants to make every Dragon King pay for what we did to him, and part of that is exposing us to humans. He's allied with MI5, who fear us. He's also joined forces with the Dark Fae."

Lily drew in a shaky breath. "When you say Dark, does that also mean there's Light Fae?"

"Aye. We are amiable with the Light Fae, especially one named Rhi. I trust her completely. The Dark Fae, however, are as evil as they come. You can recognize them by their red eyes and black and silver hair."

"And all this time I thought the only thing I needed to worry about was being invaded by aliens who wanted to drain our planet of water." Lily put a hand to her forehead and filled her lungs with air before slowly releasing it. "Light equals good, Dark is bad. Got it."

"It's too much for you."

"Yes," she admitted and dropped her arm to her side. "But I want to hear all of it. Please. So Ulrik joined with the Dark Fae."

Rhys rubbed a hand along his jaw and regarded her silently for a few seconds. "Aye. I was in Ireland, which the Fae have claimed as theirs, with Con and Kiril. Kiril had been captured by the Dark, and Con and I went to free him."

"Wait," Lily interrupted him. "Shara is Irish, and she has a large silver streak in her hair."

"Shara comes from a powerful Dark Fae family, but just as a Light can turn to the Dark, she became Light."

Lily digested that information, and then asked, "So is Shara Kiril's mate?"

"She is. All the women married to someone from Dreagan are mates."

No wonder all the women seemed to have a secret among them. Now Lily understood why the bond between the group of women was so strong.

Rhys continued, saying, "We were in a battle with the Dark when I sustained an injury. You must understand, Lily, that the only way a Dragon King can be killed is by another Dragon King. There is no other way for us to die."

"That's . . ." She couldn't even finish the sentence. It was all so preposterous, and yet, she couldn't deny she was accepting Rhys's tale. "You said you were injured. How?"

"With magic. I expected it to heal quickly as all wounds

do, but it didna, and the pain was excruciating. I lost consciousness while returning to Dreagan. When I woke, my wound was healed, but the pain remained, reminding me that something wasna right. I was able to shift back to this form, but when I next changed into a dragon, I almost couldn't. The agony was insufferable, but the worst was when I tried to shift again."

Lily could have hit him when he paused. "What? What happened?"

"It was killing me."

The breath left Lily as if sucked out. She stared in complete devastation. Even before she was told Rhys was immortal, she'd expected him to be invincible, indomitable.

Unconquerable.

CHAPTER
TWENTY-SEVEN

The distress on Lily's face was a balm to Rhys. He wanted to wrap his arms around her and simply hold her. That's all it would take to wipe away the torment of the past few weeks.

"You said you couldn't die."

He smiled at her. "The injury I sustained was from a mix of Dark Fae magic and dragon magic. I told you the only way a Dragon King could be killed was—"

"By a Dragon King," she said over him. "So a Dragon King gave you the wound."

Rhys nodded. "Rhi used her Light magic to halt the cycle I was in and give me a choice. I could remain in dragon form for all eternity, or I could shift one more time."

"You shifted one more time," she said, her brow furrowed. "Why? If you're a dragon, this must be a version of hell for you."

"You've no idea. I watch every night as the others take to the skies while I am stuck down here."

"Then why did you shift again?"

If he told her the truth, she would know just how deeply he cared for her. But if he didn't, she would never realize how much she meant to him, or how much he was willing to do for her.

"For you. It was the night your flat was broken into."

Her eyes went large as she covered her mouth with her hand. She gawked at him a minute, then dropped her hand. "I don't understand."

"Yes, you do," he said softly.

"We rarely spoke. You barely even looked at me. You were gone to Ireland and wounded, and I didn't even know about it."

Rhys fisted his hands so he wouldn't reach for her. "I looked, Lily. Every damn day. I sought you out while you were working. I hid in the shadows and looked my fill, because I knew if I ever got too near, I would never want to leave."

He waited for her to respond, but she simply gazed at him. Rhys cleared his throat. "Say something. Anything."

"I'm afraid to."

"After all I just told you, you're afraid to speak?" he asked, a rueful smile pulling at his lips.

She licked her lips. "I don't want to hope too much."

"Hope, Lily. I willna let you down. I'm telling you all of this because I have feelings for you." He wanted to tell her she was his mate, that he loved her more than life itself, but he was afraid of scaring her off.

She blinked, her black eyes gazing at him with wonder. "You've always made me hope."

He touched her face, in awe of the woman before him. "Ulrik is the one who hurt you?"

"He is."

"He's the one Dennis works for?"

Rhys nodded again. "We know Dennis is using you to get onto Dreagan. Tell me what's going on, and I can help."

She turned her back to him and put her hands on her hips. It was everything Rhys could do to remain in his spot and not go to her, beg her to believe him and return his feelings. There wasn't a doubt in his mind that she wasn't willingly helping Dennis, but he wasn't so sure of her feelings. She'd enjoyed their night together. However, so did plenty of other women.

How ironic that the one woman he wanted above all others might not want him.

It was an eternity later when Lily faced him once more. "Dennis was the one who broke into my flat."

"I guessed as much."

"He was in my flat the day before yesterday when I arrived home. That's when he told me I was going to help him get onto Dreagan. When I refused, he threatened to kill someone from Dreagan."

Rhys twisted his lips. "The women. As mates to a Dragon King, they're immortal as well, only dying if their King is killed. So you doona need to worry about that. That means you doona have to help Dennis."

"I told him I would tell one of you what he was doing, and I knew that there was no way those at Dreagan would allow anything to happen to any of the women. Dennis apparently knew what I would say, because he had another threat."

"Your family," Rhys deduced.

Lily dashed a hand at her eye. "My little brother, Kyle. Dennis has befriended him."

"So he threatened to kill him?"

"Worse. He said he would bring Kyle into what he was doing and turn him into an assassin. I was afraid then, but not knowing who Dennis is involved with, it's much worse than I ever imagined. I can't let Kyle become mixed up in that world."

Rhys shook his head in frustration. "Damn."

"I have no choice. Dennis knows where I am at all times. He knew I was in Edinburgh and followed me there."

"I assumed as much when I caught you crying this morning. I wish you would've told me."

Lily threw up her hands. "I figured Dreagan had enough money to cover whatever it was Dennis wanted to steal. It never entered my mind that you all were dragons!"

"So you believe me?" he asked, trying his best to hide the hope welling inside him.

She sighed with a smile. "I can't believe I'm saying it, but yes."

"Will you let me help you with your Dennis problem?"

"Didn't you hear me? He's probably watching right now. He follows me."

Rhys smiled, anticipation of spilling blood thrumming through him. "That's exactly what I'm hoping for."

That brought Lily up short. "What?"

"I needed to tell you all of this and gain your trust. I suspect Dennis will show up any moment. And I have a plan."

She blinked. "A plan."

"Whatever happens, know that you're no' alone." Now that things were swinging back in his favor, Rhys closed the distance between them, sliding his hand behind her neck, and claiming her lips.

Rhys could feel eyes on them. It was the only thing stopping him from making love to Lily. He ended the kiss and looked down at her as the drizzle turned into droplets and quickly whispered his plan into her ear.

"Ready?" he asked and looked down at her.

She squared her shoulders. "No. Something is going to go wrong, but I want this over with."

"It'll be over. Verra soon. That I promise."

"Dennis is—" she began to argue.

Rhys raised a brow. "I'm a Dragon King, Lily. It's asking a lot for you to trust me, but I promise I willna let him hurt you or your family."

"I'll never forgive myself if something happens to Kyle. Dennis told me that if he dies, there are men who will take Kyle."

"I willna allow that to happen."

She gazed up at him and nodded. "I believe you."

It was obvious she wanted to trust him, but she was worried and scared. Dennis had done that to her. It infuriated Rhys that he couldn't kill the bastard. At least not until the Kings had Kyle—and all of Lily's family—to safety.

Then Rhys was going to enjoy putting Dennis through every bit of pain he'd ever inflicted on Lily. Except Dennis would suffer it all in one night. If that didn't kill him, Rhys would ensure Dennis didn't breathe a moment longer.

With the rain coming harder, Rhys took Lily's hand and they ran to the car. He put her inside, then walked around the car to the driver's side. Rhys didn't look behind him where he knew Dennis was watching, nor did he mention it to Lily. She had enough to worry about.

He got behind the wheel and started the car, then pulled back onto the road and drove to Lily's flat. Rhys glanced over to see her hands clasped tightly in her lap and her gaze straight ahead. He laid his hand atop hers. She turned her head to him and smiled slightly. That's all he needed to warm his heart. She wouldn't smile if she didn't trust him.

"Thank you," she whispered.

"Thank me when this is over. I'm picturing us on Australia's Gold Coast soaking up the sun for at least a week."

She shifted her hands so that both of them now held his. "That sounds heavenly."

"Consider it a date," he said and threw her a smile.

All too soon, they reached the village. The rain was coming down steadily when Rhys pulled up against the curb outside of Lily's flat. He put the car in park and turned his head to her.

"I doona want to leave you."

She brought his hand to her lips and kissed his knuckles. "But you have to."

"I can stay."

"I can do this. I'm strong enough."

Rhys had no doubt about it, but he didn't have to like it. "Of course you are. I just doona like him near you."

"I don't like being away from you."

"You keep saying things like that, and I willna let you out of this car."

She laughed softly, her eyes crinkling in the corners. "You've no idea how much better I feel knowing I'm not doing this on my own. No matter what happens, I want you to know that I appreciate your helping me."

He didn't bother arguing with her or telling her that all would be fine. Lily had been hurt too much, and the world had failed her too many times. Rhys would show her with actions. That's all that really mattered anyway.

"I'll see you in the morning," she said and turned to open the door.

Rhys pulled her back and claimed her lips. He wanted his taste seared on her tongue during the hours they were apart. He held her face in his hands and proceeded to kiss her senseless. When he pulled back, her lips were swollen and her eyes glazed with desire. He smiled in satisfaction, even as his cock ached to be buried inside her tight, wet sheath.

"That wasn't fair," she whispered.

"It was to tide me over until morning."

She caressed her fingers along his cheek before she slid her hands into his wet hair. "Be safe."

Rhys didn't stop her again when she opened the car door and stepped out, but it was a fight not to. He was able to remain in the car knowing that a Dragon King was watching over her.

He waited until Lily was inside her flat before he pulled away from the curb. As he drove slowly down the road, he spotted movement between two buildings and saw Darius. Rhys was so shocked at seeing the Dragon King who had been sleeping for the past five hundred years that he almost stopped the car.

Darius gave a subtle nod of his head of long blond hair toward Rhys. Rhys kept driving because he knew Lily was in safe hands with Darius.

There was a push against Rhys's mind with a voice he hadn't heard in a long time. He opened the link. *"Darius."*

"I'll keep her safe. Doona worry."

"I'm no'. When did you wake?"

After a long pause, Darius said, *"I never went back to sleep after Con woke all of us to join forces with the Warriors and Druids for their battle. I've just been . . . in my cave."*

So all those years of sleep hadn't helped him. Darius was a quiet one, a King who rarely spoke, but was lethal when riled. *"It's good to see you."*

Rhys was about to say more, but Darius shut him out. Rhys didn't mind. Darius was still acclimating to this time, and he would need his space. It was enough that he was willing to watch over Lily.

The thunderstorm was in full swing by the time Rhys parked the Jaguar in the garage on Dreagan. He shut off the car and got out. As he closed the car door behind him, he saw Kiril at the far doorway of the garage.

"I should kick your arse for no' telling me you finally gave in to Lily," Kiril said with a smile on his face.

Rhys chuckled and walked to Kiril, pausing to hang up his keys on the peg. "I didna plan it."

"Nay, you went to Ulrik first." The smile was gone from Kiril's face. "I should kick your arse for that as well."

"I needed answers."

"Did you get them?"

"You know I didna," he said and pushed past him to walk the short distance to the manor.

Kiril fell into step beside him, his wheat-colored hair pulled back in a neat queue at the base of his neck. "Ryder has hijacked a couple of satellites to search for Lily's brother, but so far nothing."

"Dennis must have put him somewhere. It's what I'd have done in his place."

They walked into the manor, and Rhys came to a halt when Con stood in his way, his arms crossed over his chest and his obsidian gaze hard as granite and directed at Rhys.

"I wanted to talk to Lily myself," Con said.

Rhys shrugged and strode past him, saying, "Guess you're going to have to wait."

CHAPTER TWENTY-EIGHT

Ulrik had showered and changed and was inspecting a first-edition Shakespeare when Mikkel came down the back hidden stairs with Abby. The space had been his alone for hundreds of years, and he was far from thrilled to be sharing it with his uncle and Abby for even the smallest amount of time.

He turned and looked at Abby who gazed once more adoringly up at Mikkel. There were similarities between him and Mikkel. Their coloring and height, but the main one was their drive to shape the world into what they wanted—or needed—it to be.

That's where the parallels stopped. Mikkel sported a hint of gray at his temples, and a few lines around his eyes making him appear older than Ulrik. It was obvious he wasn't happy about it by the way Mikkel kept looking in the mirror and unconsciously touching his gray hair.

"You should've joined us last night," Abby said as she stopped beside Ulrik and put her hand on his chest. "You rival your uncle in bed. I would like to have both of you at the same time."

Ulrik looked down at her hand, then to her face. She was pretty, her sexuality blatant. That's what originally caught his eye, but she'd proved she was more than competent as his assistant despite making a skirt and jacket sexy as hell.

To know that somehow she and Mikkel had deceived him for ten years was galling and thoroughly dampened any appeal she might have had.

"He never learned to share," Mikkel said as he turned away from the mirror and adjusted his suit jacket. "Besides, Abby dear, you barely survive your time in my bed. Do you really think you could live through having both of us?"

Abby smiled at Ulrik and slid her gaze to Mikkel. "I'd love to find out."

Ulrik dropped his gaze to her full breasts, accented by her clingy white sweater, to the indent of her waist, and then lower to the tan skirt that skimmed her body, only to have a four-inch flounce of material at the hem.

He'd found pleasure in her arms, but then again, he'd found pleasure in a great many women's arms. The one thing he couldn't abide was betrayal—in any form—and that's exactly what she had done to him.

How Ulrik hadn't been able to discover she actually worked for Mikkel in his extensive background checks throughout the years, he didn't know. But he wasn't happy about it. In fact, it infuriated him.

Abby willingly took part in the duplicity, making him appear the fool. One other woman had done the same thing, but Ulrik didn't get to dole out his justice before his so-called friends killed her.

In Ulrik's eyes, Abby could no longer be trusted. It irked him that she knew such intricate workings of his plans.

The only saving grace was his lack of confidence in any human, which is why he'd avoided including her in everything.

Mikkel thought he knew everything Ulrik was involved in, but Mikkel only touched the tip of the iceberg. Ulrik might have joined forces with his uncle, but he didn't trust him. Never had.

Never would.

Despite that, Mikkel was family. After Ulrik was banished from Dreagan, he'd wandered, lost and terrified. What he would've done to know he wasn't alone. If only Mikkel had made himself known then. Perhaps Con could've been taken down sooner.

That thought brought a hint of a smile to Ulrik. Seeing his once closest friend, the man he considered a brother, dead was what kept him going day after day.

"What do you say?" Abby asked in a low voice as she took a step closer to him.

Ulrik took her hand and removed it from his chest. "You chose who you wanted. I suggest you remember that."

Mikkel chuckled from his position against the divider wall that separated the back of the shop from the front. "Now you know why Ulrik was King."

Abby glared at Ulrik before she put a smile on her face and returned to Mikkel's side. "But you're King now."

"That I am," his uncle said and touched Abby's cheek. "Never forget that."

Ulrik returned to the book, noting how well the leather had been cared for and that there was only a hint of yellow on the pages. He would count the stars a thousand times if it kept him from listening to Mikkel and Abby.

"Put the book down. We have things to do." Mikkel walked past Ulrik and slapped him on the back.

Ulrik jerked his gaze to his uncle, but Mikkel was already halfway to the door. Abby followed, her hips swaying alluringly. Ulrik carefully returned the book to the plastic bag and secured it in a drawer of his desk.

He didn't bother to lock it. No one could get into his store without his knowledge, and his uncle could not care less about such a rare and expensive item.

Ulrik followed them outside and locked the door to the store. He turned around to see Mikkel and Abby crossing the street. Ulrik didn't like being kept in the dark. He'd agreed to join forces with his uncle for a few reasons.

He knew he could defeat Con on his own, but it was going to be pure brilliance for him to keep Con occupied while Mikkel swooped in and destroyed all that Con held dear. Then, Ulrik would kill Con.

Also there was the fact that Mikkel could come in handy in helping Ulrik achieve a few other . . . things he wanted.

All the while, he was going to have to keep a sharp eye on his uncle. If Mikkel hadn't already figured it out, he would as soon as Ulrik's full force of magic was returned. Mikkel could claim to be King of the Silvers all he wanted, but the right belonged to Ulrik.

In order for Mikkel to take the role as King, he was going to have to kill Ulrik before his magic was returned. Mikkel could do it now—or rather he could try.

Perhaps that's what he was about to do.

Ulrik trailed after the duo as Mikkel led them down one street after another. Ulrik was about to put a stop to it when he turned a corner and saw his uncle press Abby against the side of a building, kissing her passionately. Abby's moans of pleasure reached Ulrik. He was turning away when Abby's body jerked, her eyes flying open and astonishment filling her face as Mikkel ended the kiss.

Mikkel stepped back, and Ulrik saw the blade of a dagger covered in blood within his uncle's hand. Abby struggled to fill her lungs with air, her blue eyes silently begging Mikkel to save her. Without a word, Mikkel pivoted and continued down the street. Ulrik watched as Abby put her hands over the wound to try and staunch the flow of blood, but it gushed between her fingers, the stain of red growing on her white sweater.

Her legs buckled and she slid awkwardly to the ground. She looked at her wound, the hoarse sounds of her breathing coming loud and sparingly. Her gaze weakly looked around until she found him.

"Ulrik," she whispered, the healthy glow of her skin fading rapidly. "Help me."

He slowly walked to her. By the time he reached her, she was already dead. Ulrik squatted beside her and rubbed his thumb along his fingers. His dragon power was the ability to bring someone back from the dead. Con might be able to heal anything, but Ulrik was the only one who could give life to the lifeless.

Ulrik straightened and walked away. Just like everything he refused to think about, Abby and her betrayal were forgotten as soon as he put his back to her.

Rhys could've heard a pin drop; the room was so silent after he explained his plan. He looked around Con's spacious office to the Kings there.

Warrick, reclining in the chair with his arms crossed and his legs stretched out in front of him, said, "It's just ludicrous enough to work."

"It's fucking insane," Kiril stated and shot Rhys a smile. "I like it."

It was Kellan who sat forward in his chair and sighed. "If things go bad, that means Ulrik, through Dennis, could have the weapon. Because of that, I doona think we should even consider this."

"It might help if we knew what this weapon was," Laith said.

Con tossed the pen he'd been holding onto the desk. "I

willna divulge that information. There's a reason the King of Kings holds the secret alone."

"Except you doona," Rhys stated. "Kellan also knows."

"Because I'm the Keeper of History. Trust me, I wish I didna know," Kellan said and looked away.

Rhys frowned, a niggle of worry growing. "If only you and Con know, then there's no way Dennis will be able to find it."

Ryder rubbed his hand across his jaw and said, "If Ulrik has enough magic that he can do such damage to Rhys, we have to consider the fact that he has a way for Dennis to disappear once he's on Dreagan. That means either Ulrik or the Dark. We have methods in place to alert us if anyone crosses our borders. Thanks to Iona and her guarding the Campbell land and the hidden doorway onto Dreagan, we have that covered as well."

"No one has come onto Iona's land," Laith said. "No' since the last battle with the Dark."

Ryder nodded to Laith. "For the few who do cross our borders, we're able to find them quickly. But what happens if we can no'?"

"I refuse to believe someone can be on our land and we willna be able to find them," Con said with a brooding look.

Rhys itched to check in on Lily. It was all he could do to remain in his chair. "If Ulrik is able to stop me from shifting, I'd say anything is possible. No matter how much we want it no' to be."

"You could be right, Rhys," Kellan said. "Dreagan is made up of sixty thousand acres. It would take a mortal years to search every cave of every mountain, especially if he doesna know what he's looking for."

Kiril grimaced. "Have we considered that Dennis does know?"

"Impossible." Con shook his head and rose to walk to the sideboard and pour whisky in seven glasses. He began to hand them out. Once everyone had theirs, he turned to face the room. "The Dark tried in vain to get the information from Kellan, Tristan, and Kiril. Tristan and Kiril couldna tell what they didna know, but Kellan didna give up anything, even though they were torturing Denae in front of him. If Kellan didna tell them anything, and I've no', then nobody knows."

"For shits and giggles, let's assume Ulrik knows," Warrick said. "Now what?"

Kellan turned his glass in his hand. "Then we're screwed."

Rhys wasn't going to give up that easily. "Con, you've hidden this weapon on our land for eons. Each King of Kings before you hid it. It's never been used against us. Perhaps it's no' as deadly as everyone thinks."

"It is." Con drained his whisky in one swallow. "You doona want that weapon found, Rhys."

Laith threw up his hands in defeat. "Then our only course is to kill Dennis as soon as he comes onto Dreagan."

"What of our promise to protect the humans?" Warrick asked.

Kiril gave a loud snort. "He's coming onto our land with the intent to harm us. We need to protect ourselves."

Rhys wholeheartedly agreed, but he was also concerned with Lily. Rhys had given Lily his word that her family would be protected. For every minute that wasn't happening, there was the opportunity for Ulrik to harm them.

Rhys set aside his whisky on the table next to him and looked at Con. "You and Kellan are the only two who know where this weapon is hidden, and I understand and accept why you willna divulge the location or a description of the weapon to us. However, that leaves the two of you as the only ones capable of ensuring the weapon isna taken. I'm no' suggesting you go to the weapon," Rhys hurried to say when Con tried to talk. "I'm saying that you and Kellan focus your magic and attention on the weapon. If Dennis slips by us, as long as the two of you are keeping watch, he'll never succeed in getting his hands on it. Even if the fool does happen to find it."

Kellan and Con looked at each other. It was Kellan who shrugged and said, "That could work."

"I doona like leaving Dreagan two Kings short, despite it being a mortal we hunt," Con said.

Ryder cleared his throat, his face filled with guilt. "Well, actually we'll be down only one King. Darius has woken."

CHAPTER
TWENTY-NINE

Darius remained in the shadows, his senses bombarded with the lights and sounds of the humans. But his gaze wasn't on the village. It was on the mortal with red hair who watched Lily Ross. Dennis arrived minutes after Rhys drove off. The human's hate for Lily was apparent in the way he glared at the building.

Rhys's mate. Darius couldn't wrap his head around it. Of all of them, it was Rhys whom Darius had suspected would never succumb to a human female. A Light Fae, yes, but never a mortal. Apparently Darius had been asleep for too long for things to change so drastically. Over the past year he'd remained awake, but preferred to stay in his cave.

When he did leave his cave, he found the world turned upside down and some humans and the Dark Fae joining forces with Ulrik to take the Kings down. Darius wasn't surprised about Ulrik. He'd known the King of Silvers would one day come for them. But the Dark and humans?

Darius shook his head in confusion. No matter what, that wouldn't end well for the mortals.

But right now he was more focused on the man looking to hurt Lily. Darius might not have a mate of his own, but that didn't mean he wouldn't do everything to protect Lily while Rhys couldn't.

His target moved and was joined by a second human. He was younger, innocent by the way he shifted nervously while Dennis spoke.

Darius didn't care how many people he watched. One or a thousand, it didn't change his mission to protect Lily. At least none dared to enter her flat, but he was prepared in such an event. There were few things as important to a Dragon King as his mate.

Darius wasn't going to be the one to fail Rhys.

Lily's eyes opened as she lay in her bed. She turned her head and looked at the clock, shutting it off before the alarm sounded a minute later. She sat up and stretched, amazed to discover that she'd slept despite the debacle she was in. Rhys could be the reason she was able to rest. In fact, she knew it was. All night she'd dreamed of dragons. Small ones. Big ones. Giant ones.

Rhys promised to show her a dragon, and she was going to hold him to it. His conviction in his belief of the dragons was in every word, every syllable as he told her his story. Only a cruel, malicious person would've refused to even consider his words as truth.

It was a tale she would never repeat. Not just because people would put her in Bedlam quicker than she could blink, but because she wouldn't put Rhys or anyone at Dreagan in danger. Sometime in the night as she thought over Rhys's story and dreamed of dragons, she grasped that Dennis wasn't there to steal a piece of art. He was there to do something much, much worse.

Lily put her hand on her chest over her heart. She grew sick to her stomach as she thought of what might have happened had Rhys and the others not discovered she was the one being forced to help Dennis.

But Rhys had. There was a slim chance she could have him and her family. That wasn't going to stop her from killing Dennis, however. He was slime, a vile fiend who tainted everything around him with nastiness.

Lily grabbed her mobile phone from the bedside table, hoping there was a text from Rhys stating that her family was safe. Her heart kicked up a notch when she saw she did have a text from him. It didn't say anything about her family, but it did make her smile.

" 'I'm with you. Always,' " she read the text aloud.

She hugged the phone to her and closed her eyes. It wouldn't be too much longer now before Dennis was out of her life forever. She could remain at Dreagan and continue to work, and hopefully date Rhys.

After all the horror she'd endured—the fear, the agony, the scars—she might actually have some true happiness again. She couldn't wait to see her family again, to hug her parents, play video games with her brother, and spend all night talking with her sisters.

With a smile on her face, Lily got out of bed and walked into the bathroom. Fifteen minutes later she dried off from her shower and wrapped the towel around her as she turned on the blow dryer.

It had been so long since she'd styled her hair with the blow dryer that it took her a few tries to remember. With her hair so thick and long, it took a while to dry. As she was doing her hair, she was thinking over all her new clothes, trying to decide what to wear and what Rhys might enjoy.

Once her hair was done, Lily returned to her room and opened a drawer that held all her pretty new bras and underwear she had taken the time to put away the night before. She chose a light gray cotton set with a band of aqua lace around the waist of her underwear, and a matching band of aqua around the bottom of the bra that reminded her of Rhys's eyes.

She was about to put on her clothes when she remembered she'd also bought makeup. Lily hurried back into the bathroom and applied just enough to accentuate her eyes and cheeks. She looked in the mirror, pleased with the outcome and the fact her bruise was quickly fading.

Then she was standing before her small closet with her new clothes bursting out of the small space. Lily decided on a pair of black skinny jeans and an emerald green long-sleeved tee beneath a black sheer button-down. After putting on the same black boots as the day before, Lily checked her reflection.

As she walked from her room into the kitchen, she touched the diamonds still in her ears, thinking of her parents. Lily hadn't gotten two steps when she came to an abrupt halt. Her heart pounded with dread and her blood turned to ice as she looked at Dennis sitting in her living room. How she detested the smug look on his face.

She desperately wanted to tell him what she really thought, but she remembered at the last second that she needed to continue to play her part as the frightened and weak person he believed her to be.

"You look nice," Dennis said as he stood. "It seems that trip to Edinburgh did you good. I told Kyle you needed some time away to prepare to see your family again."

Lily frowned, wondering what Dennis was up to this time. She didn't have long to wait as the front door opened and Kyle walked inside. Lily took a step back; she was so shocked. Then she ran to him, throwing her arms around her brother and holding him tight.

"It's so good to see you," she whispered.

Kyle enveloped her in his strong arms and held her tightly. "It's good to see you, sis."

She blinked away her tears and leaned back. "Let me look at you. Goodness, you've filled out even more. I think you're taller than Dad for sure now."

"I am," Kyle said with a lopsided grin. His dark eyes were crinkled at the corners. "You look amazing."

Dennis came up beside her and wrapped an arm around her waist, pulling her away from Kyle. "Doesn't she? Your sister has always been quite the looker."

"I can't wait to catch up. It's been too long," Kyle said, glancing at Dennis. "How about breakfast?"

Lily fisted her hand as pain shot through her from Dennis pinching her waist. "I wish I'd have known you were coming. Unfortunately, I've got to leave for work. How about dinner?"

Kyle's smile was wide as he nodded. "Looking forward to it."

"I'm going to drive Lily to work. I won't be long," Dennis said as he shoved Lily toward the door.

Lily looked back at her brother with regret. She had no choice but to go with Dennis. It wasn't just Dennis that wanted her to go, it was Rhys as well. She climbed into the passenger seat of Dennis's BMW and stared straight ahead. He started the car and drove away from her flat and Kyle.

"That bruise is fading. Did you tell people how clumsy you were to fall and get such a mark?"

Lily looked for the strength she'd found in Edinburgh, the courage of the girl she'd once been, and held it within herself. She looked down at her arm and her tattoo covered by both her tee and the sheer shirt. "Of course," she replied meekly.

"You shouldn't have made me angry. You know how I hate to be angry."

She wanted to roll her eyes. How had she ever thought she loved Dennis? Dennis, however, had a golden tongue.

How else would he have convinced her that she loved him enough to ignore the warnings of her family?

"How are you going to get me onto Dreagan?" Dennis asked, breaking her out of her thoughts.

Lily took a deep breath. How she wished she and Rhys had gone over everything down to the last detail. Rhys trusted her enough to let her sort out her parts. She had to trust him to stop Dennis.

"There's a hedgerow behind the store that blocks any visitors from seeing the manor. I found an obscure entrance that will take you to the manor."

Dennis patted her leg. "I knew you'd come through for me. I've got my men watching your flat. If anything happens to me, Kyle will be taken immediately."

"What could I possibly do to you?" she asked, turning her head to him.

"Nothing, Lily. Absolutely nothing."

She looked out the windshield again and remained in that position as Dennis droned on about how easily she bent to his command, as if she were meant for it. All the while, Lily contemplated how she could find something to kill him. Preferably a gun, but she hadn't bought one yet. There had to be some sort of weapon around the store, and she would find it.

"We're here," Dennis said excitedly.

It was what Lily had been dreading. She yearned to see Rhys again, but now that they were at Dreagan, she wasn't ready. For any of it. So much could go wrong. And if Kyle was in Dennis's clutches, what if the rest of her family was as well?

Con watched Rhys vigilantly as they stood in the computer room. Rhys's restraint of the ire within him was new. His eyes blazed with fury, but the cool control with which he held himself in check was unusual. Con wasn't sure what that meant for any of them.

"What?" Rhys asked Warrick, who walked into the room, his voice low and deadly.

Warrick gave a shake of his head. "Lily's brother wasna with the rest of the family. We doona know where he is."

"No one does," Ryder said while continuing to punch letters on the keyboard. "We've searched everywhere. It's like Kyle disappeared."

Con shook his head. "He didna disappear. Ulrik has him somewhere."

Ryder shoved away from the row of computers. "I've exhausted all of my considerable resources. No satellites or facial recognition is picking Kyle up anywhere across the globe." He paused and looked at Rhys. "We have only one option left to us if we want to find Kyle soon."

"Broc," Rhys said.

The Warriors of MacLeod Castle had already been brought into this war against the Kings, and Con wasn't keen on asking them to help out again. With Rhys already marred by Ulrik, Con had to call the Warriors. As he was reaching for his mobile, Darius walked into the room.

Rhys's head snapped to Darius. "She's already left?"

"She's here," Darius said. He looked at Con before turning back to Rhys. "And her brother is sitting in her flat."

Con expected to have to have to detain Rhys, but once more Rhys surprised him.

A brutal look came over Rhys's face. "Dennis had him the entire time."

"Aye. I saw someone with Dennis late last night as they stood outside Lily's flat, but I didna know who the lad was until this morning."

"Is Kyle unharmed?" Rhys asked.

"Aye. Unbeknownst to the lad, Dennis set up men to watch him."

A muscle twitched in Rhys's jaw. "Or kill him should Lily fail."

Con caught Rhys's gaze. "Lily's family is being sent to safety, and we'll get Kyle."

"Will we?" Rhys asked, more to himself than anyone in the room. He paced the row of monitors, thinking.

Con turned to Warrick. "What did you say to get the Rosses to leave with you?"

"That Lily's life was in danger, and Dennis was part of it," Warrick replied with a smile. "I didna need to say more."

Con stepped in front of Rhys. "It's your plan, and it's a good one. Now put it into action."

CHAPTER
THIRTY

Rhys stalked from the manor to the store. All night while he and the other Kings hammered out details to his plan, his mind had been on Lily. There was no way he could have her so near to him now and not see her.

He slipped in the back entry and waited for her. Rhys saw her through the glass doors as she spoke with a man.

"Dennis," he growled.

When Lily finally unlocked the door and walked into the shop alone, he was able to breathe easier. He anxiously waited for her to put her purse down and turn on the lights. As soon as she walked into the hallway, he grabbed her by the waist and pulled her against him.

She clung to him, her head buried in his neck.

"I'm sorry," he said into her hair. "We have your family, but we couldna find Kyle until this morning. We're going to get him away from Dennis's men."

Lily lifted her head to look at him. Her black eyes were wide, hopeful. "So I don't have to cower to him anymore?"

"We need to see how much Ulrik knows. I know it's asking a lot."

"I can do it," she assured him. "I'm not scared of what Dennis can do to me. It was my family and everyone at Dreagan."

Rhys kissed her because she was brave and beautiful. And his. He ended it before he could succumb to his unquenchable hunger. "I'll be near."

She nodded and backed out of his arms. "Don't worry about me. Dennis has no reason to harm me."

"You look beautiful," Rhys said as she reached the doorway.

Lily paused and looked at him with a smile. She winked before she returned to the front.

Rhys leaned his head back against the wall. Lily's family was ensconced in a hunting lodge in Northern England protected by Henry, Banan, and Guy. Darius and Kellan were eliminating the men guarding Kyle.

That only left Lily. Since Dennis was more concerned with getting onto Dreagan, Rhys was counting on Dennis forgetting about her quickly enough.

Tristan and Kiril would be tracking Dennis from the sky while Hal and Laith would follow at a discreet distance. The mates were safely hidden deep within the mountain behind the manor. The rest of the Dragon Kings were patrolling the perimeter of their land in case Dennis was a diversion of some sort.

Every aspect had been covered.

Why then did Rhys have the unwavering feeling that something was going to go terribly wrong?

Rhys left the store, setting up watch at the manor. It went against everything for him to leave Lily alone. He wanted to be there with her, to protect her. But if anyone knew Dennis, it was Lily.

She'd survived so much already. He smiled as he thought about her trying to find the person she once was. Lily had no idea she had more valor and pluck than most people.

Dennis affected her on a deep level with fear and pain, and yet she faced Dennis valiantly.

Lily needed no one. She could take on a thousand Dennises and come out the victor. Her inner strength had gotten her through years of physical abuse. Dennis's verbal abuse was what made Lily question herself and her own ability to make decisions.

Already Rhys saw a difference in her. The change was slow enough that Rhys didn't really notice it until he was gone from Dreagan those few weeks. But her biggest transformation was in Edinburgh. Rhys worried if Dennis would see beyond the new clothes to the new Lily.

If Dennis did, there could be real problems. For one, Lily was still mortal. She was Rhys's mate, but they hadn't completed the ceremony. Which meant that Lily could be killed.

Rhys stopped himself from going down that road. Dennis wouldn't want to bring Lily with him in his search. He would move quickly and quietly. Lily would cause distractions.

With his mind at ease, Rhys made himself comfortable. There was no telling how long he would have to wait.

Darius stood behind Lily's flat, staring at one of the men left behind to watch Kyle. He didn't hesitate when he walked up behind the man and grabbed his head. With a quick twist, Darius broke the man's neck. Darius quietly lowered the man to the ground and moved to the next.

There were five mortals guarding Kyle outside. Darius and Kellan each took two. The third was closer to Darius, so he started toward him. The human turned and pointed a rifle at Darius who just smiled. The mortal never knew what hit him when Kellan came up from behind and snapped his neck.

"How many inside?" Kellan asked as he came to stand beside Darius.

"At least one. I didna wait around to see how many men Dennis brought in."

Kellan's lips thinned. "You mean Ulrik."

"Same difference," Darius said, looking around. "Any ideas?"

"Aye."

Darius turned to see Kellan smiling.

"Stay behind me," Kellan said as he moved to the back door of the flat.

Darius followed Kellan and flattened himself against the opposite side of the door. Kellan knocked, and a moment later a tall, muscular man with a shaved head opened the door.

"What?" the man demanded.

Kellan smiled and yanked the man outside, swinging him around so he smashed face-first into the brick building. "Just wanted to say hello."

Darius slipped inside the flat. He spotted Kyle coming from the living room, but then movement out of the corner of his eye made Darius pivot to the right.

A second mortal came out of Lily's bedroom firing a handgun twice, the silencer muffling the sound of the retort. The bullets slammed into Darius's chest. He looked down at the blood coating his white shirt, then looked up at the man.

The mortal's face was shell-shocked by Darius still standing. In two strides, Darius was standing before the man, all the while the human kept firing the weapon. Darius bared his teeth at the pain of each bullet slicing through his body. He grasped the mortal's hand holding the weapon, and turned the gun so that it was now aimed at the man's chest.

The human was so stunned at what was happening that he didn't realize he was shooting himself until it was too late. He slumped, and Darius let him fall to the floor, dead.

Darius turned around and found Kellan standing in the doorway staring at him. "What?"

"I didna think you'd wake so . . ."

"Unpleasant," Darius offered.

"Ready to fight," Kellan said.

Darius raised a brow. "Really? I heard how you woke."

"Perhaps we should finish this conversation another time," Kellan said and motioned with his head to Kyle.

Darius looked to the lad and let out a breath when he found Kyle pointing a gun at them. "We came to help you. No' to have a gun pointed at us."

"Dennis said someone might come for me," Kyle said.

Kellan leaned against the door frame and crossed his arms over his chest. "Did he now? I doona suppose Dennis told you how he beat and tortured your sister?"

"You're lying," Kyle said angrily. "I saw Lily myself this morning. She looks amazing."

"Because she left Dennis a year ago," Kellan said.

Darius let Kellan talk since he didn't know all the details about Lily. Not that he cared to know. It was enough that Rhys claimed her.

Kyle grunted, his face detailing exactly what he thought of Kellan's statement. "Dennis is the one who has been trying to bring Lily back to her family."

"Actually, Dennis is threatening no' just your family, lad, but yourself as well. He's using her to get onto Dreagan land without being detected," Kellan said.

"Dennis would never do that," Kyle argued. "He loves Lily."

Darius blew out a breath. "You're wasting your time, Kellan. The lad isna going to believe a word we say."

"You're right." Kellan pushed away from the door and walked to Kyle.

The lad shifted the gun to Kellan. "Stop right there."

"Or what? You'll shoot me?" Kellan chuckled and jerked his thumb to Darius. "You see how that worked out for Darius, aye? Besides, Kyle, you are no' a killer. No' yet at least. You stay in association with Dennis, and all of that will change."

Darius took a few steps to the side in case he needed to tackle Kyle. Kellan was able to easily take the gun away from Kyle and toss it aside.

"It's time you see Dennis for what he really is," Kellan said.

Lily was a nervous wreck. She was tired of waiting. She wanted it over with. Done. Finished.

Twenty minutes ago she'd sent Dennis a text telling him everyone was in a meeting, and that it was the perfect time to get him through the hedges undetected. She touched the knife she had up her left sleeve. It was the only weapon she'd been able to find in the store, and she wished it was a gun. Lily wasn't going to miss the opportunity to rid the world of Dennis if it came her way.

The door to the shop suddenly opened, causing Lily to jump. Dennis entered, looking around. His cocky smile, the one she used to think was charming, made her stomach roll.

"Look at this place," he said with a whistle. "I bet those bottles in the glass cases are worth quite a bit of money."

Lily moved to stand in front of him. "You didn't come to steal whisky."

Dennis's blue eyes narrowed. "I didn't, but that doesn't mean I won't take some."

"You have enough money to purchase a bottle if you want."

"Why would I do that?" he asked with a sneer. "I take what I want. You know that."

She swallowed, the old fear slowly returning when she saw that tic in the corner of Dennis's left eye. He always got it right before he hit her.

Lily fought to keep hold of her courage. She touched the still sensitive skin on her forearm, remembering the quote. "Do you want to stand in here? Or do you want me to get you onto the grounds?"

Dennis closed the distance between them and grasped her chin in his fingers, cruelly squeezing. "You don't tell me what to do."

"In this instance I do. I work here, remember. I'm to get you in unobserved."

He released her with a smirk. "So you are. Let's get moving."

"You'll need to go out the back. Thirty feet beyond is a row of hedges. If you go to the right about a hundred and fifty yards you'll come across the concealed entry."

Dennis chuckled and turned her so that she was standing beside him. He put his arm over her shoulders and started walking with her. "You're coming with me."

"I can't leave the store," she protested. "If any of them come back early they'll know I've helped you."

He paused and looked down at her. "Did you really think you would be able to stay here after all this was over? That's incredibly naïve." He started walking again, forcing her to go with him. "Did you really think I was going to take your word for everything?"

Lily knew Dennis would make her show him the entrance. If she'd appeared too eager, he would've questioned it. He was doing just as she'd expected. Dennis was nothing if not consistent.

She put in just enough resistance while they walked to continue making him believe she didn't want to go. In fact, she wanted to run to the hedgerow and show him the entrance.

Dennis shoved open the back door and pushed her through. Lily immediately looked up at the sky. It must have been all her dreams about dragons that made her search for a hint of yellow in the thick clouds.

"Where?" Dennis challenged as they reached the hedgerow.

Lily pointed to the right. "There."

"Take me."

She wondered where Rhys was. He was near. Of that she was certain. If only she knew his exact location. She wasn't the only one preoccupied. Dennis was so excited to get to the manor that he hadn't noticed there were no visitors at Dreagan.

Lily reached the secret entrance and stopped. "This is your way in. I've fulfilled my end."

"You think your part in this is over?" Dennis laughed and wrapped his fingers around her wrist to pull her through the opening. "It's just beginning, Lily."

CHAPTER
THIRTY-ONE

Rhys couldn't believe his eyes when he saw Dennis leading Lily from the hedgerow. "Nay," he whispered, shock and fear icing his veins.

Dennis was supposed to leave Lily behind. She was meant to be far from whatever was coming. She was supposed to be sitting safely with the other mates deep in the mountain where he knew she would be safe and he could focus on ridding the world of Dennis.

Rhys scrubbed a hand down his face, his mind rushing through every nuance of his plan. Every turn was danger for Lily. It made him break out into a sweat. He couldn't lose Lily. She was the only reason he could face each day. Without her . . . he was nothing. But mortals were so . . . fragile. Her life could be extinguished so quickly.

He started to follow Dennis and Lily, intending to do whatever was necessary to get Lily away, when he was roughly yanked back against the manor. He whirled around, a growl forming as he prepared to fight whoever dared to get between him and his mate. Then his gaze landed on Con's calm visage staring at him.

Rhys shook his head as he stared at Con in disbelief.

He glanced at Lily to make sure she was still close enough for him to get to. Once he saw her, he returned his focus to Con. "What are you doing here? You're supposed to be ready to guard the weapon. Doona tell me it's in the damn manor."

A blond brow rose as Con coolly stared at him. "Of course I'm no' dimwitted enough to keep the weapon at the manor."

"Then why are you here?"

Con's nostrils flared as he drew in a breath. "Because of you."

Rhys noticed Constantine wasn't in his usual suit. He wore a pair of jeans, a black tee, and boots. "You doona think I can protect Lily? You doona think I can keep my head when it comes to her?"

"That never entered my mind. I'm more concerned with you. Especially now that Dennis has decided to bring Lily with him."

Rhys ran a hand through his hair and briefly closed his eyes. "Lily knows about us."

"I assumed as much."

"You're no' angry?"

"Would it matter?"

Rhys held Con's gaze. "Nay."

"Then why ask?"

He didn't have a clue. Rhys took a deep breath and got control of the apprehension within him now that Lily was smack in the middle of everything. With her there, it changed how he needed to implement his plan. Before, he couldn't have cared less if Dennis was killed. In fact, he was counting on it. But now . . . now, his plan was for shit.

His heart pounded irregularly in his chest. Lily. The one woman who'd reached his heart without even trying. There were two main objectives now. Keep Lily safe, and stop Dennis from taking the weapon.

"You need to enact your plan," Con said.

Rhys cut him a look. "That would endanger Lily. Besides, Dennis could know what we are."

"Regardless, Dennis is a fool," Con said with distaste. "As you've always said, Dennis might know exactly where the weapon is."

Rhys began to smile as he realized where Con was going with the conversation. "Aye. Then he'll realize it's a trap if I lead him to the location I planned."

"True enough. However, we'll know then if Ulrik has discovered where the weapon is hidden."

"If that's the case, you're going to tell us," Rhys stated.

Con merely held his gaze, refusing to say anything.

Rhys turned and watched Lily and Dennis. He hated the way Dennis gripped her arm tightly, making her wince. It was time Dennis was out of her life—permanently.

"It seems things are going our way," Con said. "Kellan and Darius just arrived with Kyle."

Rhys swiveled his head back to Con. "I didna doubt those two would retrieve Kyle."

"I understand why you wanted Kyle here, but Guy will need to wipe his memories. There's no telling what he'll see."

"He needs to see the real Dennis. As far as his memories, I doona think Lily will be upset if we erase all traces of Dennis."

Con nodded his head once. "Go save your mate."

Rhys was vaguely aware that Con walked away, but his attention was on Lily. He purposefully hadn't told her the full extent of his plan so Dennis couldn't force it out of her.

"Hang on, Lily," Rhys whispered.

"You'll be able to see everything from here," Darius told Kyle as they led him into a vacant room on the third floor of the manor.

Kyle looked at them, a touch of fear in his eyes. "You want me to stay here? By myself?"

"We'll be about," Kellan assured him. "Dennis will never know you're here."

Kyle glanced out the window. "I'm not sure about any of this."

"Just stay here and you'll be fine," Darius said and shut the door behind him as he walked out. He paused in the hallway and looked at Kellan. "Should we lock it?"

Kellan started to shake his head, then frowned. "Kyle loves his sister, but he's friends with Dennis. Once he sees the man Dennis really is, he might want to go down and protect Lily."

"We can no' have him in the way. So, we lock it."

Kellan put a hand on his arm to stop him. He whispered, "He'll hear it and no' trust us. I'll stay behind and watch him. If he tries to leave, I'll stop him."

Darius looked at the door, thinking of the mortal within. He was young and foolish, and easily swayed. "I'll stay."

Kellan was at his heels as he walked away. "Why?"

"Why no'?" Darius asked over his shoulder.

"You've just woken."

"And you have a mate." Darius halted at the top of the stairs and Kellan came even with him. "Go to her."

Kellan blew out a breath. "Darius, you've only just woken—"

"I didna go back to sleep after we helped the Warriors. I remained in my cave. I'm back, Kellan, and I'm fine."

"Are you?" Kellan asked, his eyes intense.

Darius held Kellan's gaze. "I'm going to pretend you didna ask that. Get to your position. I'm going to hide here and see if Kyle remains in the room."

Several tense seconds passed before Kellan descended the stairs. Darius looked at his hands and slowly fisted them.

He wasn't all right. And he feared he never would be.

* * *

This was Lily's second trip past the hedgerow, and she was as taken aback by the glory of Dreagan as she had been the first time. If Dreagan was beautiful around the distillery, behind the hedges it was a heaven.

"What are you doing?" Dennis grumbled as he pulled her along.

Lily was looking at the sheep and cattle. She glanced at the manor, finding the dark gray structure intriguing and magnificent. But it was nothing compared to what lay around her.

The mountain behind the manor rose tall and sturdy, the craggy slopes sporting bright green grass between the rocks. On either side of the mountain were smaller slopes leading into a valley. Lily couldn't see onto the other side, but the valley she was in made her feel as if she were home.

There was a large pasture alongside the manor that was open, the grass thick. That's where she was, and Lily wanted to see more. Dennis was pulling her toward the sheep pens. They were empty now, the sheep dotting the hillsides. They passed a building that was obviously a work shed where they sheared the sheep.

Lily tried to see inside, imagining Rhys working there. It brought a smile to her face to think of him bending over and trimming the wool from the animals.

"What are you smiling about?" Dennis demanded.

Lily looked at him and made a face. "I was thinking about sheep."

He rolled his eyes and yanked her after him. Lily glanced around in hopes that she would see Rhys. She knew he was out there, as were the others. But where were they? What were they waiting for?

Dennis took her around the sheep pens and up a steep incline of one of the rolling hills. He stopped, his breathing heavy, as he looked around.

"Lost?" she asked hopefully.

He threw her a dark look. "No."

"You don't even know where you're going, do you?"

Dennis chuckled and spread his free arm wide. "Look around you, sweetheart. There are sixty thousand acres before us."

"You aren't seriously going to walk all of it?"

"Do I look that dumb?"

She had to bite the inside of her mouth not to answer.

"Of course not," Dennis said and made a sound at the back of his throat.

The longer Lily stood with him, the more anxious she became. It was almost as if he were waiting on someone, which surely couldn't be right.

"I saw you with him."

Lily slid her gaze to Dennis. She didn't have to ask who he was talking about. The night in Edinburgh was branded in her memories.

"I don't remember you ever being so . . . sensual with me," Dennis said with a sneer. "You certainly never let me hold you against a window naked so I could pound inside you."

Lily swallowed, but she didn't look away. "You were never man enough to make me want to do that."

"And he is?"

"He's a thousand times more of a man than you'll ever hope to be." As soon as the words were out of her mouth, she felt free. As if the chains around her suddenly fell away, chains she hadn't even known held her back.

"You may change your mind about your precious Rhys once you know who he really is."

Dennis said it so calmly, so coolly that her stomach dropped to her feet like lead. He knew what Rhys was.

Indifferent to her inner musings, Dennis continued. "I also saw him kissing you at the river. You best be careful,

Lily. It's not a good idea to fall for anyone from Dreagan. It could get you killed."

"Because you're going to kill them?" she asked, pretending she didn't have a clue what he was talking about. Her best bet was to play the innocent and let him think he was shocking her. "You said if I helped that you would leave them alone."

"I did say that, didn't I?" he asked with a smirk. "You should know you can't trust me."

"I've known it for a while."

"And yet you continue to do it. That should tell you that you have awful instincts."

She jerked her arm from his grasp and turned away. "You do love to hear yourself talk."

"I'm right, and you know it. You just don't want to admit it."

"As pretty as this view is, I need to get back to the store." She turned to leave, only to have him step in front of her. His menacing look made her draw up short. Her blood pounded in her ears.

Then she remembered where she was and who was watching over her. No matter what, she knew Rhys wouldn't let anything happen to her. She pushed the fear aside, holding onto an image of Rhys in her mind.

"You're not going anywhere."

Lily took a deep breath and crossed her arms over her chest. "What are you after, Dennis?"

"Something important. Something that'll change the world."

"You said I didn't know what Rhys is. Tell me then."

Dennis chuckled as he watched her, considering her words. "All right, though you won't believe me."

"Try me," she dared.

"They're dragons."

Lily's arms dropped weakly to her sides. So Dennis did

know. The secret Rhys and the other Dragon Kings had kept for countless centuries was being spread. What did that mean for those at Dreagan?

It must've been Ulrik who'd told Dennis so he would know who he was going up against. But how much did Dennis know? He couldn't possibly grasp that Rhys was immortal. "Dragons?" she asked skeptically.

"Dragons. Those here at Dreagan have been able to shift from human to dragon for eons. I'm helping to remove them from Earth."

"You're not afraid of fighting a dragon?"

Dennis's smile grew. "They won't be stupid enough to show themselves in dragon form in front of you."

"That's why you brought me?"

"That and in case your lover thought to free Kyle. As long as I have you, Rhys won't attack. They'll let me do exactly what I want to do."

"You're a fool." Lily started to say more, but gaped when she spotted a man walking toward them. She recognized the walk, the confidence and bearing of Rhys. That, along with the long strands of his dark brown hair hanging loose about his shoulders.

She wanted to run to him and throw her arms around him, to feel the strength and power of his muscles beneath her hands. Her flagging courage was boosted at seeing him. If only he knew what he did to her, how her body craved his touch and how she yearned to feel his skin next to hers.

Love. It's what she felt for him. She recognized the warm, calming emotion instantly for what it was. She smiled and relaxed. Everything was going to be all right now that Rhys was there.

Dennis turned to see where she was looking. "It's about to begin."

CHAPTER
THIRTY-TWO

Rhys didn't need to look up to the clouds to know his brethren were there, circling and watching. Every one of them knew that Lily was his, but the full weight of what could happen to her hung heavily on his shoulders.

The concern in Lily's eyes as he drew near gave him an idea that things were going badly. The plan was important. That's what Rhys kept telling himself, but as he approached Dennis, he was having a hard time remembering that when all he wanted to do was kill the bastard.

"Lily," Rhys said as he stopped before them. It was damned difficult to keep his distance from her and not pull her against him or let his caring shine through his gaze. "Visitors are no' allowed on this side of the hedgerow."

"I—" she started, but Dennis interrupted her.

"I won't be here too long." Dennis looked Rhys up and down. "Your pretense is good, I'll give you that."

Rhys cocked his head. "My pretense?"

"Of being human. We both know you're a dragon."

Rhys looked at Lily to see her furrowed brow. He slid his gaze back to Dennis and let his chest expand with a breath. He had anticipated this, so he wasn't surprised by the declaration. "A dragon. Interesting."

"I also know you won't chance shifting in front of Lily. You don't want your new lover to see you in your true form."

"You know an awful lot," Rhys said tightly, glaring at Dennis. "Since you've told Lily the truth, what do I care if she sees?"

"Because I have her, and if things went as I hope, you brought Kyle here."

That made Rhys hesitate, uncertainty tightening a hand around his chest. Why would Dennis want Kyle here? He quickly sent a warning through his mind to the other Kings. "What does Kyle have to do with this?"

"Kyle's watching, isn't he?" Dennis laughed. "So predictable, just as my boss said you would be. You want Kyle to see me act the monster. As long as he's watching, you'll never shift."

"My, my," Rhys said with a tsk. "You've certainly outthought us."

Dennis gloated with a half-smile. "I've been told that you'll go to great lengths to protect humans. If you don't want to see Lily dead, you'll take me to the weapon."

"What weapon?"

Dennis's face blotched red with fury. "The weapon I came to find!"

"You assume an awful lot."

"I knew one of you would come for her." Dennis smirked. "You'll be the one to lead me to the weapon, or I hurt her."

No longer did Rhys pretend he didn't care for Lily. He clenched his teeth and vowed, "If you harm one hair on her head, I'll rip you to shreds."

"Just show me the weapon."

Rhys glared at him for several moments. It irked him that Lily was put into such a position, but if anyone was strong enough to endure it, she was. Even with this new development, his plan was taking shape.

Dennis wrapped his fingers around Lily's arm and squeezed, causing her to gasp with pain. Rhys bit back a growl, his hands fisting as he imagined wrapping them around Dennis's skinny neck. He was going to draw out the time it took him to bring Dennis to the cottage, but Rhys didn't think he would be able to hold back his rage and not kill Dennis if he hurt Lily again.

It was only Lily's slight nod of her head, indicating that she was all right that allowed him to breathe easier. Slightly. He was still going to enjoy killing Dennis.

Rhys finally pointed to the right. "It's that way."

"Lead the way," Dennis ordered.

He walked past Lily and grazed her fingers with his. Rhys didn't like her being in danger, but as long as Dennis needed her as leverage, she was safe. He would feel infinitely better if she were with the rest of the mates, however.

With another glance at Lily, Rhys led them to the cottage that had been prepared for the trap. Dennis thought he had everything in order, but he was too cocky and too sure of Ulrik's intel.

"Why didn't your boss come himself?" Rhys asked.

Dennis made a noise of annoyance. "He's the leader. He doesn't do the dirty work. That's what I'm for. And I'm good at it."

"So you've been working for him for a while?"

"Since I was twelve."

Rhys helped Lily down a set of rocks that served as steps. He looked at Dennis and glowered. "You're nothing more than a pawn."

"We all have our talents."

Rhys deftly navigated the rocks to move ahead of Lily and guide her.

"Lily was another mission," Dennis said.

Rhys struggled to keep his anger in check. "You've had this planned that long?"

"No, mate," Dennis said with a laugh. "I was asked to pick a girl from an aristocratic family and see if I could make her fall in love with me. By the by, Lily, you were way too easy."

Rhys glanced at her to see her jaw clenched and hatred shining in her eyes.

"I told your father you were a bet," Dennis continued. "I knew for sure he would tell you, but neither of your parents did. He assured me that you would see me for what I really was. Too bad he was wrong."

Lily jerked her head to him. "My sisters hated you."

Dennis shrugged. "Yep. Either way, I not only got you to fall in love with me, but you moved in with me against your family's wishes."

"Did you no' want her family's money?" Rhys asked before Lily could say anything else. Her black eyes skated to him, and Rhys wished like hell he could fly her far away. Perhaps back to the hotel in Edinburgh where he could make love to her for days, only allowing her to get up from the bed to eat and for them to soak in the large tub together.

"I have plenty of money. I didn't need hers then, and certainly not now," Dennis said.

Lily halted and faced him. "And the beatings? The scars you've given me?"

Dennis's smile was pure evil. "I've always had a need to hurt things. I like it, in fact. It's not my fault you were too stupid to leave."

Lily launched herself at Dennis. Rhys deftly grabbed Lily around the waist and pulled her back. He turned her away from Dennis and held her tightly against him. "Just a little longer," he whispered in her ear.

She sighed loudly. "Only for you."

He knew what it was costing her to be near Dennis, and it killed him to put her through it. But he was going to make it up to her when all of it was finished. He was going to show her only happiness and pleasure and laughter.

"Quite protective, aren't you?" Dennis asked Rhys as he came to stand beside them. "Lead on, Dragon."

Reluctantly, Rhys released Lily, but kept ahold of her hand. He had to touch her somehow, and even that little bit was enough to calm the storm within him.

"What is this weapon?" Lily asked into the silence that followed.

Dennis kicked a loose rock as they reached the bottom of the hill. "It's none of your concern."

"He doesna know," Rhys stated as he proceeded up the next rise.

"I know," Dennis declared arrogantly. "It's a weapon to be used against the Dragon Kings."

Rhys felt Lily's startled gaze on him. He ignored it and asked, "Did your boss tell you what the weapon looked like?"

"I'll know it when I see it."

Since Rhys himself had no idea what the weapon was, he was glad that Dennis didn't either. The fact the weapon had been kept secret from the rest of the Kings for so long was amazing. The question was: how did Ulrik discover it?

Rhys was on his way down the second rise when Dennis said, "Where are we going?"

"To that building," Rhys said, pointing to the structure set atop a hillock in the distance.

Dennis snorted contemptuously. "The great Dragon Kings hiding a weapon powerful enough to kill them in a cottage? How ridiculous."

"Perhaps." Rhys didn't bother to say more.

Dennis, however, wasn't finished. "Why Earth? Why choose our planet to invade?"

Rhys might have been furious with the humans for their slaughter of the dragons, but his species wasn't completely innocent in the war. Now, however, he found himself hating one particular human with such enormity that, for a moment, he forgot the mission, forgot Lily, forgot everything but the life that was taken from him.

His steps slowed, and he readied to turn and happily rip Dennis's throat out.

Then a soft hand slid into his. A silky, gentle voice whispered his name. Rhys turned his head and looked down into Lily's beautiful face. He lost himself in her endless midnight eyes. A strand of her jet-black hair touched his arm before the wind lifted it higher, allowing the lock to caress his cheek.

Rhys brought himself back under control and lengthened his strides. "We were here first."

"Piss off," Dennis scoffed. "I know the history of humans. The only thing here before us were dinosaurs."

"Believe what you will."

"I do, I just don't appreciate being lied to."

Rhys glanced at Dennis over his shoulder. "Did it ever occur to you that I'm not the one lying?"

"It doesn't matter," Dennis said. He pulled Lily back to walk with him. "We're going to make you leave once and for all."

Rhys fought not to look to the skies. He kept a good pace to hurry and reach the cottage. There was only so much control, and he was fast losing his being near Dennis.

Darius sat in a small cubby hidden in the ceiling. It was constructed when the manor was built as another exit for the Kings to get to the mountain.

He used it now as a hiding spot to watch over Kyle. Perhaps it was his misgivings about everyone that led him to believe Kyle wouldn't stay put in the room. So he wasn't surprised when he heard the soft click of the door opening.

The shadows hid Darius, and Kyle didn't bother to look up as he glanced around to see if anyone was about. The mortal didn't tarry. He made his way down the stairs in quick order. Quick enough to make Darius suspicious.

Darius jumped from his spot, landing quietly. He looked over the railing as Kyle reached the bottom and disappeared out of sight. The only place Kyle would go was after his sister, in a vain attempt to rescue her.

"Stupid human," Darius mumbled as he hurriedly followed.

Darius exited the manor and slid to a stop when he saw Con leaning against the side of the manor. "You didna stop Kyle?"

"He was gone before I got here. We can no' stop him now without Dennis seeing us."

Darius glanced into the distance. All Dennis had to do was look back and he would be able to see Kyle—or them if they tried to bring the lad back. "Shite."

"That's certainly one word for it."

"It's just one mortal. What can he do?"

The King of Kings slowly turned his head of wavy blond hair, his soulless black eyes pinning Darius. "Did you forget the part where we said Ulrik was leading him? You've been holed up in your cave, so you've missed Kellan and Denae being taken by the Dark. You also missed Tristan having to venture into the Dark world to get back his mate, Sammi. You avoided the worry when Kiril went to Ireland as a spy and was captured. You escaped the many battles we've had with the Dark, including one on the Campbell property that borders ours when the Dark located the hidden doorway onto Dreagan."

Each word was spoken with silent fury, stony irritation. Callous disdain.

Darius took immediate offense. "Every King takes to his cave at some point."

"No' all," Con said and pushed off the stones to face him. "Some of us remain awake dealing with all the senseless stupidity of this realm along with whatever torments we have in our past."

"We can no' all be you, can we?"

Con's chest expanded as he took a deep breath. "You were awake. You heard the calls I put out, you knew Rhys was in pain and dying."

"It's why I'm here."

"Weeks later. Where were you before? You knew all that was going on, Darius, and you chose to ignore it."

Darius snorted. "If you were so worried, why no' send someone to wake up the ones who sleep?"

"Because it's a choice I've always given each of the Kings," Con stated tightly. "I allow you to choose whether to help your brethren or no'."

"Some of us have . . . torments . . . that shouldna be brought into the world again."

Con sighed and shook his head. "Doona believe you're the only one who has suffered. Every damn one of us has. Including me."

CHAPTER
THIRTY-THREE

Lily was having a difficult time managing the rocky hillside in her heeled boots, but she wasn't going to ask Rhys to slow down. She knew his hurry. And she welcomed it.

Dennis's eyes were on her as she let Rhys get ahead of her. She looked at his blue eyes and noticed how . . . pallid and colorless they were compared to Rhys's magnificent blue.

"What?" Dennis demanded angrily.

Lily shrugged. "Nothing. I'm just realizing how very unattractive you are."

"Lily," Rhys warned.

She knew she shouldn't bait Dennis, but she was so weary of it all. The fear, the anxiety. The pain.

"It's all right, sweetheart." Dennis reached out and gripped her arm again, his fingers biting into her flesh. "Keep trying to hurt me with your words."

He dragged her along cruelly, causing her to twist her ankle. She glanced up and saw Rhys watching her, his eyes filled with concern and a hint of fury tightly leashed.

Lily touched the knife hidden up her sleeve. She could use it right now. She could plunge it deep into Dennis's heart and it would all be over. That would be the easy thing to do. However, she knew Rhys and the others had a plan, and she needed to consider that before she did something to ruin it. As much as it infuriated her to wait.

A look back at Dreagan Manor in the hopes of seeing dragons, instead, she saw someone running toward them. He moved low and fast, as if he were hiding from something. She didn't point him out since it could be another King trying to sneak up on Dennis.

She did turn her gaze to the sky. For just a moment there was a break in the thick gray clouds to show a spot of sky. That's when she caught sight of burnt orange scales. Her breath hitched and she stumbled again since she hadn't been looking where she was going. Dennis let her fall to her hands and knees, and it was Rhys who rushed to her.

With her chest heaving, she looked at him in wonder. She hadn't believed his story at first. Then she'd listened to him and heard the certainty in his voice that made her consider it. Somewhere along the way she began to deem his tale truth.

Believing and seeing were two different things however.

There were dragons flying above her. One for sure, but she had an inkling that there were more. Whatever fear she had vanished. She was on Dreagan, surrounded by dragons who promised to protect her.

Lily's smile was slow, but it grew. Rhys's befuddled look dissolved as he returned her grin.

"What are you two smiling about?" Dennis asked angrily. "Get on your feet, and let's get moving."

Once Lily was up, Dennis grabbed her arm again and waited for Rhys to take the lead. They walked in silence, the hills growing steeper and higher with each one. At the next rise, Dennis stopped.

"We're no' there," Rhys said.

Dennis laughed. "We have someone approaching."

Rhys stiffened slightly and turned to look. Lily was hoping to recognize the face, but she was aghast to see it was none other than her brother.

"Kyle," she said and tried to run to him. Dennis held her in check and withdrew a gun from his coat.

Dennis waved Kyle closer with the gun. "Come join us."

Lily couldn't rein in her shock. She waited until Kyle was close before she asked him, "What are you doing here?"

"Those from Dreagan wanted me to see what a monster Dennis was," Kyle said, anger tinting his voice.

Lily couldn't believe this was happening. "Why didn't you stay with them? Why didn't you stay where you weren't in danger?"

Kyle's face suddenly broke out into a grin. "Then I wouldn't have been able to join in the fun."

Lily watched, horrified, as Dennis tossed the gun to Kyle. They shared a laugh as she stared, speechless. When Rhys tried to go to her, Kyle stopped him by pointing the gun at him.

"I saw the other dragon get shot multiple times. He barely flinched," Kyle said. He rubbed his chin with his free hand. "We've been told you're hard to kill."

"The word was 'impossible,' actually," Dennis said.

Kyle's dark eyes were hard as granite when they looked at Dennis. "Nothing is impossible to kill. There's a weapon here that will do it, but I think there's another way."

"Kyle, please," Lily begged. She couldn't believe this was her sweet brother who used to beg her to play games with him. What happened? Where was the kind boy who loved to laugh?

His cold look froze her heart. "Did you really fall for my act? You've not seen me in four years, and you thought I was the same young kid as before. Naïve and stupid."

"You were never stupid. Naïve, yes, but we're all that way. You were innocent and sweet."

"Until Dennis showed me the world." Kyle sneered at her. "I'm the one who sought out Dennis six months after you left. It was to see you, but he took me on a few jobs with him. Then I joined in the ranks."

"No." Lily didn't want to hear any more. She couldn't. "Stop talking. It's all lies."

Kyle stormed to her and peered down at her. "The lies are what you've been telling yourself. Had you bothered to talk to our parents, you would've learned I haven't been home in three years."

Lily felt sick to her stomach. "So you were part of the plan."

"Of course," Kyle said with a mocking laugh. "This was all my idea. I knew you would do anything for the family."

Dennis smiled and looked on approvingly. "He's a quick learner, your brother. I've known few who took to a gun the way he has. It's a gift. He hits anything he aims at."

"How nice for him," Lily said, letting the contempt lace her voice.

"Careful," Kyle said and waved the gun in her face.

She stepped back and spread her arms. "Kill me. If you're such a big man, then pull the trigger."

"Finally got that spine back, huh?" Kyle asked. "About time. Let's get to the weapon. It's taken too long already. I don't like this place."

"You'll never get off Dreagan," Rhys said.

Kyle slowly turned his head to him. "For a minute, I'd forgotten you."

"I'm still here."

Kyle's contemptuous gaze locked on Rhys as he asked Dennis, "Do you know where the weapon is?"

"At the cottage," Dennis answered.

"Are you sure?"

"The dragon's worried I'll kill Lily. He didn't lie."

Kyle's lip turned up in a sneer. "He's a dragon. They all lie."

"Do you want to stand around and argue about it?" Lily asked. "I wonder how much time it would take to have you surrounded by dragons."

Kyle gazed at her silently. "So you believe?"

"Does it really matter?"

"Have you seen them? Have you watched your new lover shift into a dragon?" he pressed.

Lily turned her eyes to Rhys. She was amazed that neither Dennis nor Kyle realized the predator they had near them. Did they not sense Rhys's tightly leashed savagery?

She was aware of the violence building, saw the wildness escalating. Recognized the fury swelling.

Whether Rhys could shift or not, he was the ultimate warrior. She might not have touched his scales herself, but she saw him in her dreams. She rode through the clouds with him, felt the wind upon her face.

"Yes," she finally answered.

There was the faintest flicker in Rhys's eyes. His presence reminded her of what was at stake. A hidden world of Dragon Kings who protected the world. Dragons. And to think she had a dragon of her own.

"Don't you realize what they are?" Kyle asked in shock. "You've sullied yourself."

Lily jerked her head to her brother. "Sullied myself? Did you really just say that? Are you so screwed up that you think it's all right to kill someone, but not for me to share my bed with Rhys?"

"I'm not the one screwed up. Your head has everything backward, and you don't even know it."

"You've always been obstinate, Kyle, but even you have to see the flaw in your rationale."

Kyle gave a loud snort of contempt. "There's no flaw. This is our world, and there's no place for dragons on it."

"What about the Dark Fae?"

"Fae?" Kyle asked with a bark of laughter. "You believe there's Fae?"

Lily glanced at Rhys to see him give a barely discernible shake of his head, warning her not to say more.

"That's rich, Lily. Crazy, but rich."

It was Dennis who stood stiff. "Actually, Kyle, there are."

"I've had enough. Move!" Kyle shouted and shoved Rhys.

Lily was once more relegated to remain by Dennis while Kyle walked with Rhys. Her anger and shock mixed together, leaving her weak with denial. Never in her wildest dreams did she imagine Kyle working with Dennis. The sweet boy she knew had vanished sometime in the four years she'd been gone. If only she hadn't left. If only she'd remained and listened to her family.

But it didn't do any good to look back at what couldn't be changed. She had to look ahead, to look at the present and what she could do to help. No longer was she going to be the cowardly female. She'd gone looking for the girl she'd once been, and Lily had found her. But she'd found something else as well.

She found Rhys.

He'd helped her find the ability to see her worth, to realize what she was capable of. Which was much more than she'd ever thought possible.

The closer they came to the cottage, the tighter Rhys's muscles bunched. He all but snarled at Kyle when her brother shoved him to get him moving faster.

"Why doesn't he know about the Fae?" Lily asked Dennis.

Dennis shrugged and ran a hand through his short red hair. "He didn't need to know. He has a mission."

"You don't ever intend to show him the Dark Fae."

Dennis didn't answer, but that in itself was the answer. There was only one reason to keep information from soldiers, and that was because the men in charge didn't intend for them to stick around long.

"You're going to kill him," Lily whispered in dismay.

Dennis tsked. "You always think the worst."

"If he was as valuable as you keep saying, Kyle would know as much as you."

Dennis laughed softly. "You've always had such a sharp mind. It's really too bad I couldn't turn you as I did Kyle."

"What's going to happen to my brother?"

"He's to get the weapon."

Lily glared at Dennis. "What? Not brave enough to get it yourself?"

"I'm needed elsewhere," he said.

Lily started to call out to Kyle when Dennis grabbed the wrist he'd broken years ago and squeezed.

He jerked Lily close and whispered in her ear, "Don't even try it. He won't believe you for one, but if you attempt to change his mind, I'll kill him myself."

"That might be better. At least he would be out of your clutches."

"Don't be so sure."

Lily realized they had reached the cottage. It looked like a vacant building waiting for occupants. Innocuous, safe. Plain.

How looks could be deceiving.

"We're here," Kyle said, awe lacing his voice. "We can finally have what we need to end the rule of the dragons."

Lily watched in slow motion as Kyle pointed the gun at Rhys's head, a malevolent smile upon his lips.

"Live through this," Kyle said and pulled the trigger.

Lily screamed, the retort of the gun drowning it out. Rhys's body jerked and then he fell, blood pouring from the wound at his temple.

She waited, expecting him to rise. Yet, Rhys lay unmoving. Lily tried to go to him, but Dennis held her in place with an arm about her waist. She stretched out her arm, desperately trying to touch Rhys.

Tears fell freely down her face as she called Rhys's name over and over again. He was a Dragon King. He'd said only another Dragon King could kill him, but the seconds ticked by without him so much as twitching a finger.

"Dragons can die," Kyle said with a laugh. He held up his revolver. "With a little magic added in."

"No!" Lily screamed.

CHAPTER
THIRTY-FOUR

Rhi looked down at her newly painted nails on her hands and feet. She wiggled her toes and sighed. A pedicure was the perfect thing to take her mind off of her troubles.

"Great job, Jesse," Rhi told her nail technician.

Jesse smiled and handed her back the three bottles of polish. "You let me do whatever I want. You're my favorite client."

Rhi chuckled as Jesse went off to tend to her next customer. While Rhi waited for her toes to dry, she looked again at the mix of blues and silver on her nails. The stripes, done at angles with silver, called It's Frosty Outside, setting off the bright blue—Suzi Says Feng Shui—and dark blue—Unfor-Greta-bly Blue.

It had been a long time since she'd worn blue on her nails. It wasn't that Rhi didn't like the color. There were few colors that she didn't like. It just seemed that blue made her feel, well . . . blue. This time, however, she felt serene instead of sad. Which was a really good sign. Of course it didn't hurt that the colors were going to go great with her blue dress.

Rhi checked her toes. Once she was sure they were dry,

she wiggled her feet back into her sandals, something she
was able to wear in the Austin warmth.

She waved to Jesse and walked from the salon. Rhi
got into her Lamborghini and drove off. She was turning
a corner, heading back to the garage to park her car when
Rhys's voice sounded in her head. All he said was her
name.

But it was the pain she heard in his voice that had her
speeding to the garage and drifting the car around corners
until she skidded the vehicle to a halt in the garage. Rhi
hit the button to shut the garage door and immediately teleported to Dreagan.

She appeared next to Rhys veiled. Rhi saw the two men
and Lily walk into the cottage as Lily looked back at Rhys,
tears coursing down her face.

Rhi knelt beside Rhys, but remained veiled since she
knew Con and the other Kings would be watching. "Rhys.
I'm here."

"Lily," he managed to say.

She looked at the wound in his head and felt the dragon
magic around it. This couldn't happen. Not to Rhys. It had
been so long since a King had died that Rhi had almost
begun to think they never would again.

"Li . . . Lily," he murmured again.

Rhi looked at the cottage. "I'll get her, Rhys."

She rose and walked to the cottage, only to run into an
invisible wall. Rhi tried to teleport in, but each time she
was thrown out. It wasn't until she approached the door
and looked at its frame that she saw a small design etched
into the wood.

Rhi stepped back, numb. There were few who knew that
symbol. The Kings didn't even know it. She looked up and
saw the dragons flying through the clouds instead of above
them. Whatever was going on had been set up by the Kings,
but it had gone horribly wrong.

Rhi returned to Rhys to see his skin turning gray. "Rhys?"

His hand twitched, but he didn't open his eyes. "Lily?"

"I'm sorry." She ducked her head, hating to fail in any way, but especially to a friend. "They've blocked me from the cottage. I can't get in."

Rhys struggled to open his eye. His breathing was labored as he fought to stay alive. He wasn't going to give up so easily. His mate was in trouble.

"Where's Con?" Rhi asked as she looked around. "Call to him, Rhys. Get him here to save you."

Rhys dug his fingers in the grass. It took too many words for him to tell Rhi that Con was protecting the weapon. "Nay."

"Then I'll get him."

Rhys said Rhi's name again, but she didn't answer. He bellowed in frustration, but the sound didn't make it past his lips. He couldn't die, not when Lily was still in danger.

The Kings allowed themselves to become too confident that the humans couldn't hurt them. Rhys wouldn't die from this wound, but the injury—with just enough dragon magic in it to cause problems—was preventing him from healing properly.

Hatred grew within Rhys. Ulrik was responsible yet again. He'd targeted Rhys for a reason, and Rhys was going to ensure that he repaid Ulrik in kind.

But first there was Lily.

The fact Rhi couldn't get into the cottage was surprising. What had the humans used to keep her out? As far as he knew, nothing short of magic could prevent a Fae from going wherever they wanted.

Rhys rose up on an elbow even as his body spit out the bullet. The damage was already done since the magic was around the slug itself. His magic was battling against another's inside him.

He looked at the cottage and smiled as he heard Kyle's yells as they searched the place. It infuriated him that the Dragon Kings had fallen neatly into the trap Dennis and Kyle had laid for them. Had they taken a little more time and investigated Kyle, they might have learned he wasn't the innocent Lily thought him to be.

Lily. Rhys's chest ached for what she was going through. He would never forget the sight of her face crumpling with disbelief and shock when she learned her brother was in league with Dennis. After the initial blow, Lily turned to her anger. Rhys loved the way her dark eyes sparkled when she was furious.

He managed to get to his hands and knees. It was time Kyle and Dennis learned what they had walked into.

A whoosh of air went by him. Rhys looked up in time to see amber scales. "*No' yet, Tristan. Lily is still in there.*"

The door to the cottage was flung open. Kyle filled the entrance. A flicker of unease passed across his face when he saw Rhys. "You're supposed to be dead."

"We're hard to kill."

"Where is it? Where's the weapon?" he demanded.

Rhys smiled. "What? You can no' find it?"

"Don't fuck with me!" Kyle yelled and pointed the gun at Rhys again.

Rhys sat back on his haunches, his hands resting on his thighs. "Shoot me again."

"Oh, I won't shoot you." Kyle's hand reached out and yanked Lily to him. "I don't like being played the fool."

The cold edge of fear sliced through Rhys. He was reminded—yet again—of humans' fragility. If he and Lily were mated, she couldn't be killed. But they weren't, which meant she could die. By the look of malice and evil in

Kyle's eyes, he had no problem committing murder, even on his own sister.

Dread filled Rhys, along with anxiety and worry. All for Lily. "Doona do anything you'll regret."

"You mean like this?" Kyle asked and aimed the gun at Lily's stomach a second before he pulled the trigger.

Rhys was stunned, his heart stopping when he saw the dark stain of blood spread through Lily's shirt. She looked from Rhys down to her stomach, her eyes wide with shock. Her fingers touched the blood. She looked skeptically at the red on her fingertips, then to Rhys.

Something fell into her hand from her sleeve. She palmed the knife and jammed it into Kyle's leg. He bellowed from the pain, but Rhys couldn't take his eyes off Lily. Everything had happened so quickly, and he was taken unawares.

The he watched her collapse and lie unmoving.

A new kind of rage built within him. He'd been provoked, riled to the point of no return. He became maddened, incensed.

Enraged.

The dragon inside him thundered for retribution, bellowed for justice at having his mate torn from him.

And he was going to exact his brand of reckoning.

The ground shook as dragon after dragon landed around him, but Rhys only saw the humans, the two mortal men who dared to take something so precious, so treasured from the world.

Lily. She was the only thing he'd had to hold onto, the only one who'd found a way into his soul. Without even knowing she did it, the mere thought of her had pulled him from the darkness when Ulrik cursed him. She alone had brought him back.

Rhys shook, not from his wound, but from his wrath.

He climbed to his feet while Dennis and Kyle looked for an escape. But there was no escape.

Not now.

Not ever.

Rhys flung out his arms, his heart shattered beyond repair, and threw back his head as he roared. He started running toward the cottage, not realizing until he busted through the door and stood protectively over Lily's body that he was in dragon form.

His brethren fanned out, encircling the cottage on the ground and in the air, blocking the two mortals. Rhys looked down at Lily. She had a hand on his front leg, touching his yellow scales.

Their gazes met as the last breath left her body.

Something inside Rhys snapped. He recognized the anguish and grief, but it didn't touch him. How could it when he was now dead inside?

Rhys briefly thought about roasting Kyle and Dennis alive. There was nothing hotter, nothing that killed as quickly as dragon fire, but it would be too swift. He wanted something that lasted, something that would torture them as long as he wanted.

He spread his wings, knocking the rest of the cottage to the ground. Then he called the shadows

Dennis and Kyle glanced around in panic when they heard the first whispers of the shadows approaching. Dennis, the fool, tried to run when he caught sight of the black mass, but the shadows ensnared him quickly enough.

Rhys didn't look away until the screams of both men echoed around them. Then Rhys lowered his head to gaze upon Lily once more. His attention was pulled when he heard someone walking through the rubble. Somehow he wasn't surprised to see Rhi. The Light Fae's horrified expression showed what he didn't dare.

She walked beneath him to kneel beside Lily. After Rhi touched Lily's neck she looked up at Rhys. "I'm sorry. She's gone."

Rhys knew it, but hearing it spoken aloud broke his heart all over again. He needed to hold her, to bury his face in her hair. Uncaring if he lived or died, Rhys shifted back into human form.

He snorted. Fate always mocked him. When he didn't want to die, he was on the brink. Now that he didn't care, the curse was broken. And he lived.

"How fucking marvelous," he muttered contemptuously.

Rhi backed away, stumbling over debris. "Rhys? I didn't think you could shift."

He ignored her and gently, tenderly lifted Lily in his arms. Rhys was going to carry her away from the screams of her brother and ex-lover, but as soon as he had her in his arms, he fell to his knees.

Rhys rocked her, the pain of losing her so thick and overwhelming he couldn't breathe. He clutched her tightly. "You can no' be gone," he whispered. "Lily, wake up. I need you. I love you. Come back to me."

"She's gone, Rhys."

He stilled at the sound of Con's voice. Rhys lifted his face, uncaring that he had tears falling down his cheek and neck.

Con shook his head sadly. "I'm sorry I wasna here to save her."

Rhys wearily got to his feet and adjusted Lily in his arms. "It was my duty to protect her. I let her down."

"You couldna have known her brother would shoot her." Con blew out a breath and looked beyond Rhys's shoulder. "How long are you going to make them suffer?"

"It's only been a few minutes."

Con's gaze softened when he looked at Lily. "It's been hours, Rhys. We've been waiting."

"We?" For the first time Rhys took notice of his surroundings. All of his brethren on the ground and in the sky remained in dragon form holding vigil.

Only Con was in human form, and since he was as naked as Rhys, he'd flown there as a dragon. Then Rhys's gaze landed on Rhi. She stood off to the side silently waiting.

The screams of Kyle and Dennis increased. Rhys glanced at them over his shoulders. "I wanted Dennis to feel as much pain as he put Lily through. I wanted Kyle to know what it meant to have everything stripped from him."

"Then we'll see it done," Con said in a low tone.

Rhys nodded and called back the shadows. Dennis and Kyle had had their clothes ripped, flesh shredded. They were lying on the ground, barely moving. But they were alive.

In the next instant, Con leapt into the air, shifting into a gold dragon. Rhys didn't wait to see what the Kings would do to the mortals. It was enough that they would die.

He started walking when Rhi fell into step beside him. As he left, the terror-filled screams of Dennis and Kyle reached him.

The smile on Rhys's face held not a shred of happiness.

CHAPTER
THIRTY-FIVE

Ulrik swirled the whisky in his glass as he sat on the sofa in his uncle's office. Ulrik had no illusions that this was Mikkel's only home. His uncle was too cautious to show Ulrik where he lived.

The light reflected off the amber liquid in the crystal cup. Mikkel poured it from a decanter, but after one taste, Ulrik knew it was Dreagan. He wondered if his uncle would admit he bought Dreagan whisky.

"Do you intend to continue to make the whisky once you take over?" Ulrik asked.

Mikkel looked up from his papers. "Of course not. There won't be humans to drink it, and we'll be in dragon form. Why do you care?"

"It's fine whisky," Ulrik said before taking a drink.

Mikkel studied Ulrik for a moment. "Whisky is whisky."

"Is that what you tell yourself when you pour Dreagan out of the bottle into your decanter? Hate them or no', the Kings know how to make excellent Scotch."

Mikkel tossed down his pen as one of his phones rang. "I demand the best of everything. I have no idea what my staff buys."

"Liar," Ulrik whispered and took another swallow.

He watched as Mikkel chose one of the six mobile phones lined up neatly on his desk. Six. Why six? What was the need for so many?

The few hours Ulrik had been with Mikkel, each of those phones had rung at least once. Mikkel wasn't keen on Ulrik hearing any of the conversations, so he would walk out onto his patio to take the call.

As if that stopped Ulrik from hearing. Mikkel might have been a Dragon King for all of a few minutes, but even he should know the heightened senses it gave them in human form. Then again, Mikkel was entirely too confident of his abilities.

Ulrik finished his whisky and rose to pour himself more. He waited until Mikkel ended the call and was once more seated at his desk before he said, "I'd consider the fact your two men failed in retrieving the weapon from Dreagan a great disappointment."

Mikkel's gold eyes narrowed into slits. "Eavesdropping now?"

"If you didna want me to hear the conversations, then you shouldna have asked me to remain." It would take more than a pane of glass to prevent Ulrik from hearing, but his uncle didn't need to know that.

Mikkel leaned back in his chair and slowly replaced the mobile phone with the others. "I was going to tell you anyway."

"Were you?" Ulrik put the stopper in the decanter and picked up his glass. "So your big move was to go after the weapon. You thought two humans on sixty *thousand* acres could find it when the Dark couldna? I also doona think the Dark Ones will be happy when they find out you made a play for the weapon yourself."

Mikkel waved away his words. "I've already explained to them why I was going after it. They believe me."

"Ah. But does Balladyn?"

"That cretin?" Mikkel asked, scorn lacing his words. "I don't know what Taraeth sees in him."

"Balladyn is a great warrior. You shouldna provoke him."

"He provokes me."

Ulrik sat back down and lay one arm along the back of the sofa. "Balladyn will rule after Taraeth. You might want to consider that."

"So. Abby was right," Mikkel said with a smile. "You are watching the Dark Fae."

He was doing much more than watching. "I observe everyone."

"Except me." Mikkel chuckled, his smug look directed at Ulrik. "With all your watching of the players, you missed me. If you missed me, what else have you overlooked?"

Ulrik wasn't interested in talking about himself. "The Kings will be coming for me now that they think I'm running things."

"Yes, they will."

"I've taken care of them in the past. I'll do it again."

The slight frown on Mikkel's face was the only hint Ulrik had that something was off before his uncle said, "Actually, I believe Rhys will come to kill you."

"Con willna let him. Con wants that pleasure himself."

"Ah, well there's the rub of it." Mikkel sat up and gave Ulrik an innocent look. "You see, one of my men killed Rhys's mate."

Ulrik paused with his glass at his lips. He lowered it slowly at the news. Rhys. With a mate? Now that was surprising. "If she's Rhys's mate, she can no' die."

"She can if they haven't performed the ceremony."

Ulrik knew what it felt like to have a mate killed. The

Kings had killed his. Though they'd had their reasons, it didn't make Ulrik's suffering any easier.

There were few Dragon Kings who knew what it felt like to have their mates killed before the ceremony. Rhys would be crazed with the need for vengeance, just as Ulrik had been. And nothing would be able to stop him.

Ulrik leaned forward and set his drink on the glass coffee table. "You knew they would kill the woman."

"Of course. Although I had no idea she was Rhys's mate."

"Did you know she was seeing someone at Dreagan?"

"That's why I chose her." Mikkel smiled and spun his pen on the desk. "One of my men was her ex-lover. The one who killed her is her brother."

Ulrik stood and started toward the door. "I must go and prepare for Rhys's arrival."

"Not quite yet."

The last time Ulrik had been so commanded he'd been just an adolescent dragon, and it had been his father. He hadn't liked it then. He hated it now.

Ulrik slowly turned to face Mikkel. "And why no'?"

"Because I need your power."

"For?"

His uncle rose and braced his hands on his desk. "The Kings killed my men. I want you to bring them back from the dead."

"Let me see if I've got this straight," Ulrik said in a quiet voice belying his irritation. "You want me to waltz onto Dreagan and revive two men who were killed by the Kings for what they did to a mate?"

"That's right. And I can get you to Dreagan."

Ulrik had schemes of his own, and he wasn't ready to give them up because Mikkel didn't have the forethought to tell his men not to kill the woman. Ulrik wouldn't stop until he had Con. In order to do that, he had to continue making his uncle think he was running things. But damn, it was difficult.

"All right, but not before you answer me something."

"Fine," Mikkel said. "What do you want to know?"

"How are you getting all this information about what's happening on Dreagan?"

Mikkel's secretive smile was in place as he walked around the desk. "I have someone there watching things."

"You expect me to believe you turned a King?"

"No."

Ulrik thought a moment. "Surely no' a Dark using glamour."

"Nope."

Ulrik shook his head as he thought of the only option left. "A human."

"Who else?" Mikkel said with a laugh.

Ulrik had never attempted to turn someone from Dreagan. Now that Mikkel had done it, Ulrik was going to get his own information from the informant.

Mikkel snapped his fingers and a Dark Fae appeared next to Ulrik. As soon as the Dark touched his arm, they were gone, appearing at the Dreagan border a millisecond later. Ulrik stepped away from the Dark and looked around to determine where he was.

"You have an hour. I'll meet you back here," the Dark said before he disappeared.

Ulrik walked out of the forest and saw the decimated cottage in the distance. The landscape was barren of any trees, which meant Ulrik would have to chance being seen. He started running to what was left of the cottage. When he finally reached it, he saw the two men. One was completely ripped apart, the savagery, vicious and brutal.

"He beat her."

Ulrik jerked at the sound of Rhi's voice. He sighed and turned his head to her. "How did you know I was here?"

"I knew someone would come for them. Are these your men?"

"Would you believe me if I said nay?"

She regarded him a moment before she shrugged. "What are you doing here?"

"I wanted to see what happened. Tell me of the men."

Rhi pointed to the dismembered one with red hair. "That's Dennis. He physically abused Lily. Her scars are . . . substantial."

"How do you know of her scars?"

"I saw them."

Interesting. Ulrik walked around the parts of Dennis he could find. "Is that why Rhys tore him apart?" When Rhi didn't answer, Ulrik looked at her. Understanding dawned. "Ah. Rhys didna do this."

"Con did."

Now that surprised Ulrik. "Constantine? The King of Kings? The one who doesna want any of the Kings to find mates?"

"Yes," Rhi answered and looked away.

Ulrik stopped next to the second man. He was young. In his early twenties if Ulrik had to guess. Though he wasn't dismembered, there were claw marks all over his body, as well as evidence that Rhys's shadows had had a go at him.

"Who is this?" Ulrik asked.

"Kyle Ross. He was Lily's brother."

He looked up at Rhi who stood stoically off to the side. "You're shocked at this?"

"What kind of monster kills their own family?"

Ulrik pointed to Kyle. "This kind. And you wonder why I abhor humans."

"You make use of them," she retorted cheekily.

He shrugged and turned back to Kyle. "That I do."

"As well as the Fae."

Now that surprised Ulrik enough that he wrenched his head around to her.

"Don't act surprised," she said with a sassy smile. "I know all about your dalliances, stud."

Ulrik reached behind him and covertly touched Kyle's shoulder. "Do you follow me, Rhi? Is it my bed you want to share?"

"No. I've had my fill of Dragon Kings."

"Then why are you here?"

She lifted her chin and turned away. "Because I consider a few of them friends."

Ulrik glanced to see Kyle's fingers contract. The human would live, but he wasn't going to be around when Kyle woke. Ulrik stood and walked to stand beside Rhi.

"I can help Rhys's mate."

It was Rhi's turn to be shocked. "You did all of this! Why do you want to help?"

"I never wanted her to die. I know how it feels to have a mate killed," he said and looked into her eyes. "And you owe me."

Rhi's lips parted as if she were about to argue, then she thought better of it. "I don't know why you've targeted Rhys. He didn't deserve the curse. That alone about did him in. Then you let his mate be killed."

"I didna."

The Light Fae's silver eyes that reminded Ulrik so much of his dragons swung away from him. "Why? Why do you want to bring her back?"

"Because no one else can."

Rhi shook her head, tucking the long strands of black hair behind her ears as the wind picked up. "I'm crazy for even thinking about doing this. If Con catches us, we're both dead."

"Con willna catch us."

She rolled her eyes and looked at him. "I'm not doing this because I owe you for taking me out of Balladyn's fortress. I'm doing this for Rhys."

"Whatever makes you sleep at night, darlin'."

She huffed and faced him. "She's in the mountain."

Ulrik smiled. "I'll meet you there."

CHAPTER
THIRTY-SIX

Lily stood still as her mind tried to wrap around why she was suddenly standing in a forest. Except it wasn't like any forest she had ever seen. Everything was gloomy and dark. The trees, the leaves, the sky. All varying shades of gray. As if not a single stitch of color existed.

She glanced down at her stomach to her wound, but there was nothing there. Not even a spot of blood. Lily listened for birds or even the rustle of leaves from the wind, but it was still as death.

Death.

Her knees went weak and she grew dizzy as she realized she was dead. It seemed . . . impossible. Yet she recalled everything. Rhys getting shot—in the head—by Kyle, Dennis holding her so she couldn't go to Rhys, their tearing the cottage apart looking for a weapon, Kyle holding a gun to her as she saw Rhys sitting up, and then her brother shooting her.

The pain of the bullet tearing through her was excruciating. All she'd thought about was Rhys and how she would have to leave him. As she struggled to draw in breath, a beautiful dragon with yellow scales appeared.

The dragon—Rhys—looked at her with the most vivid orange eyes. He had a series of tendrils extended from the back of his head, and his long tail had a bladelike extension on the end. His wings, leathery and huge, were folded against his sides.

Rhys was enormous, bigger than she ever thought possible. He was fierce looking, primal and savage. Terrifying even.

Until he looked at her.

The last thing Lily saw was Rhys's orange dragon eyes filled with remorse.

Then she ended up . . . here.

Lily shivered. Where exactly was she? Heaven? Hell? In between?

In the distance she heard someone's terror-filled scream, the sound echoing around the bleak woods. She wrapped her arms around herself and turned in a circle.

She blew out a shaky breath. Then she chose a direction and started walking. Since she heard a scream, she knew she wasn't alone. But . . . she wasn't alone. Something was out there hurting others. Animal or person, it appeared there was a chance she wouldn't come away from this unscathed either.

"Wasn't it enough that I got shot?" she asked herself. "By my brother?"

She still couldn't get her mind around the fact that Kyle had fallen in with Dennis so easily. Hadn't her parents seen what was going on?

"It's not like I can ask them now. Being dead and all," she said sarcastically.

So much for a happy life with a husband and children with Rhys. She snorted. For all she knew, Rhys would never marry, and it wasn't like any of the women at Dreagan had children or were even pregnant.

How did it work between a mortal and a Dragon King

anyway? Did the Kings simply watch their mates grow old and die before moving on to someone else? If they had been around since the beginning of time, then they had to have had several mates. Which meant Lily was just one of many.

She had known that when she'd thought Rhys was mortal, but his being immortal changed things drastically. It wasn't just years, it was centuries, millennia of him dating woman after woman. How could she even compare to that?

But she had wanted to try. More than anything else, she wanted Rhys.

"Do you know where you are?"

She whirled around at the male voice behind her. Lily looked at the handsome man with his long black hair and gold eyes. "No."

"Do you want to know?"

"Yes, but first: where did you come from?"

He leaned back against a tree and hooked a thumb in the front pocket of his jeans. "That doesna matter. You're in between worlds. Your soul is waiting to go either up," he said with a finger pointing to the sky. Then his finger turned to the ground. "Or down."

"How long will I be here?"

The man shrugged, the black T-shirt pulling at his shoulders. "It depends. Sometimes people never leave."

"Who are you?" she asked, taking a step back.

His smile was kind, but held a hint of cruelty. "Right now, I'm the only friend you have."

"Why do you want to help me?"

"For several reasons, none of which matter." He pushed away from the tree. "I can take you out of here. I can bring you back to life."

She frowned, unsure of what to believe or if she should trust him. Yet the idea of returning held appeal. "Back? Is that what you do? Pick and choose who you want to give a second chance to?"

"Nay." He chuckled softly and glanced at the ground. "In truth, I've no' done this in a verra, verra long time."

Did he have a Scottish accent because she loved Rhys's so much? Is that what her mind was doing? Crafting someone that sounded like him if he couldn't look like Rhys? "Why now then?"

"As I said. I have my reasons."

She dropped her arms. "I need a reason to trust you."

"Trust? Lass, you have two choices. Stay here or leave with me."

"It could be a trick to take me to Hell."

This made him laugh. "Have you heard the screams yet?"

Lily nodded.

"Those are the poor souls that are being taken to Hell."

"So nothing can hurt me here?"

"I didna say that," he said with brows raised. "Dennis and Kyle are roaming around somewhere, and I doona think you want them to find you."

Lily recalled the knife in her sleeve. She checked, but it was gone. Then she remembered plunging it into her brother's leg.

"Do you have the strength to kill someone with your bare hands?" the man asked.

She scoffed at him. "I'm already dead. What can happen here?"

"A lot actually. Your body is gone, but you have your soul. Souls can be killed. It ensures the soul never returns reborn. I know this, because I've killed a soul."

Lily looked into his golden eyes and shuddered. "Will I ever be safe?"

"You're mortal. Since the moment you drew your first breath, you've been dying."

"And you haven't?"

He lifted a shoulder and gave her a half-smile. "I never said I was mortal."

"Are you some kind of angel?"

His smile grew as he shook his head at her. "Now I understand what drew Rhys to you."

"You know Rhys?" She was surprised by the news, but elated that someone knew Rhys.

"Once. Long ago. He loves you, you know?"

Lily sat on a thick root protruding from the ground at the base of an oak tree. "How do you know that?"

"Take my word for it. Do you return his love?"

She clasped her hands together and recalled how he'd lovingly touched her scars, how he'd brought her exquisite pleasure, and how he'd held her so tenderly. For weeks she had watched him, dreaming of being his.

Then it finally happened.

Lily knew how gorgeous Rhys looked with his hair rumpled from sleep and his dark blue eyes watching her drowsily.

She knew the feel of his calloused hands over her body, the touch of his warm lips.

She felt the strength of his body as he thrust inside her, the sway of his masculinity.

She'd glimpsed his pain and heartache, experienced his tenderness and passion, and witnessed his power and command.

"I see that you do," the man said in a soft voice.

Lily swallowed and bent forward to rest her forehead on her knees. "I didn't believe him at first when he told me he was a dragon."

"What changed your mind?"

"His eyes. His voice." Lily lifted her head. "He believed what he was saying. The conviction I saw and heard made me stop and consider the possibility."

"Without seeing a dragon yourself?" the man asked with a snort.

Lily straightened. "Rhys told me he would show me a dragon."

"You still believed him without seeing one?"

"I had some doubts, but I'd been around Dreagan for a while. I knew the people. I knew them to be kind and decent. So, I did what he asked. I trusted him."

The man moved to sit beside her. "You saw the dragons."

She nodded woodenly. "I don't know what I was expecting, but it wasn't . . . that. They're colossal."

"You believed him without seeing anything, but now that you've seen, you're scared?"

"Wouldn't you be?" she asked as she looked at him.

He considered her words as he took in a deep breath. "Any beings with power are going to be fierce. They're also going to have many enemies."

"So even if you brought me back, I could die again?"

He simply returned her look, refusing to answer.

"I see."

"As I've said, you have two choices. I need your decision. Now."

She frowned at him. "Why the rush?"

The man motioned to the left with his head. Lily turned her gaze to see Dennis and Kyle step around a tree into her line of sight.

Her brother's malicious smile when he spotted her made her blood run cold. Kyle only got two steps toward her before he simply vanished.

Lily swung her head back to the man. "Where did he go?"

"Your decision," he pressed.

She glanced back to see Dennis still walking toward her with murder in his eyes. "I don't want to stay."

"Then take my hand," the man urged.

Lily looked down to see his large hand held out to her. She put her palm in his and everything vanished to darkness.

"Hurry," Rhi pressed Ulrik.

She couldn't believe she had actually told him where Lily was. If any of the Dragon Kings discovered what she'd done, she would never be welcome again. But it was worth the cost. Rhys and Lily were meant to be together. She was his mate, and he her match in every way.

Death might have attempted to sever the link between them, but Rhi was going to give them a second chance. One she'd never had.

Or ever would.

She tried not to look around the mountain with the dragons—large and small—etched into the walls of rock. It was a reminder of the first time she and her lover were together. Even now, thousands of years later, her stomach fluttered at the memory of his kisses, of his skill to make her writhe and beg for more.

Rhi's body tingled just thinking of his expert hands and mouth. But then he'd turned his back on her and their love. He let her go.

She blinked and focused her attention back on Ulrik who stood beside Lily's body. "Today might be good," she murmured.

Ulrik lifted his head to look at her over Lily's body. "Have you ever brought someone back from the dead?"

"No," she replied icily.

"Then doona question what I'm doing."

Rhi walked beside the slab of rock where Lily lay. "You're taking forever. Rhys will be back soon."

"It's done."

She looked Lily over. "She's not waking."

"It's no' instantaneous, Rhi. Give it some time," he said and turned on his heel.

Rhi hurried to follow Ulrik. "Where are you going?"

"Worried I might do something crazy like kill Con?"

"I know it's coming, but you wouldn't do it now."

He glanced at her. "That's right. It'll happen on my terms."

She halted and watched him disappear around a corner. There was no need for her to stay. Rhys would have Lily once more. Rhi let her gaze wander the walls and the dragons on the walls. Every time she left Dreagan, a part of her heart remained.

"Rhi?" Henry called as he came around the corner.

She needed something to stop her heart from shattering. She strode to the human and cupped his face a second before she planted her lips on his and kissed him. His arms wound around her, holding her against him as he deepened the kiss.

CHAPTER
THIRTY-SEVEN

Rhys wanted to take Lily to his mountain where he could be with her always. Then he remembered her parents and sisters. They would want the body to bury as humans did.

He left Lily only long enough to put on clothes appropriate to face her parents. Rhys would hand over their daughter, but he wasn't going to destroy them by telling them it was Kyle who had killed her. Con disagreed, but Rhys didn't care. He knew how much Lily's family meant to her.

Rhys adjusted his suit jacket and turned the corner of the tunnels in the mountain, only to come to a halt when he saw Rhi and Henry kissing, their hands roaming over each other's body. Any minute now, their clothes would be coming off.

Rhi was a valued friend, but she was a Fae. Henry, on the other hand, was a mortal who would never be able to break the hold of a Fae once he had a taste of her. He wasn't the only one who'd warned Henry away from Rhi, but there were few mortals who could refuse a Fae. The only ones Rhys knew were the women who were first with a Dragon King.

Rhys was sure that was why Denae and Sammi had been able to rebuff the Dark. Both of the women went on to become mates to a Dragon King. As positive as he was that the love that bound a mortal and a King was the answer, he wasn't ready to test it.

Rhys had to clear his throat twice before Henry looked up from the kiss. As soon as he saw Rhys, he smiled. It was Rhi who hesitated before she faced Rhys. She met his gaze, waiting to see what he would say. Both were adults, and Henry had been warned. Perhaps they were meant to be together. Maybe Rhi could finally find some happiness and let go of the love her King withheld.

"This isn't the place for such things," Rhi said as she glanced at the doorway leading to where Lily was held.

Rhys sighed as a fresh wave of pain enveloped him. How was he ever going to face another day without Lily? He no longer cared about Ulrik or the war that was coming. Nothing mattered anymore. Lily had taken the light from his life when she left.

He turned away from the doorway and braced a hand on the wall of the tunnel. The warmth was gone from Lily's body. She was growing cold.

Rhi walked to him and put an arm around him. "The hurt won't ever go away. It might lessen, but it'll always be there."

"I was meant to protect her," he ground out, feeling more powerless than he had since Ulrik's curse.

"You couldn't know her brother would shoot her," Henry said.

Rhys slammed a fist into the wall, the force causing a carved bit of a dragon's wing to break off. "Ulrik won. Or at least he thinks he has. His men got onto Dreagan, they shot me, and they killed my mate."

"But they didn't get the weapon," Henry reminded him.

Rhi leaned back against the wall to look at Rhys. "In

case you've forgotten, handsome, you broke the spell Ulrik used. You shifted without dying."

"How does that even matter now?" Rhys asked as he met her gaze.

Henry stepped toward them. "It means you can kill the asshole."

Rhys pushed away from the wall. "That I already planned to do."

"Con will stop you," Rhi said.

"He can try."

Rhys was tired of talking about all of it. He needed to take Lily's body to her family and explain as best he could. Then he was going to track down Ulrik. He spun away from Rhi and Henry and strode into the small chamber, only to draw up short. Lily's body was gone. He stared in shocked confusion as the last shred of his control snapped.

"Where is she?" Rhys bellowed. He pivoted and found Rhi blocking his way. "Who was here? Who took Lily?"

"Took her?" Rhi asked, her brow furrowed. She leaned to the side and looked around Rhys. "How is she gone?"

He gently pushed Rhi out of the way and walked out. Whoever took her couldn't have gone far. Since Rhi was there, he knew she hadn't taken Lily. But whoever did was going to be beaten to a pulp.

Rhys was so distraught, he almost missed the movement in the shadows of the tip of a black boot. He slowed and then stopped. He knew those boots. Slowly he turned and faced the shadow. "Lily?"

With his heart pounding in his chest, Rhys anxiously waited for a response. He stumbled backward when she stepped out of the shadows.

"How?" he asked hoarsely.

If it was a trick, it was the cruelest form. His vision blurred as tears gathered along with hope that she might truly have returned to him. Could she have some Fae blood that brought her back?

"I'm going to get Lily some clean clothes," Rhi said and vanished.

Lily's eyes widened.

Henry chuckled as he walked to Lily. "I'm fairly certain that was my reaction the first time I saw Rhi as well. She's a Fae, a Light Fae, that is. I'm Henry North, just a common mortal."

Rhys had never been so jealous of Henry as he was when Lily shook his hand. She had yet to come to Rhys, and he couldn't fathom why she'd left the chamber instead of calling his name. He was right outside. She had to have heard his conversation, she had to know how broken he was.

Henry glanced at Rhys and lightly placed an arm on Lily's back to return her to the chamber. "I didn't get the chance to meet you earlier, Lady Lily, but it's a pleasure."

Rhys watched them, unable to move. He was ecstatic that Lily was alive, but concerned with how she was. And he was hurt because it appeared as if she were running from him. Him. Of all people.

Did she blame him for her death? Was she angry that he had failed her? She couldn't possibly hold more contempt for him than he did himself. He'd promised her she would be safe, and yet she died.

Ever since Ireland, his life had been unraveling. Lily was the only thing that kept him together. He'd taken it for granted that he could win her. His plan to stop Ulrik had failed spectacularly, and it was the one person he cared for above all others that got hurt.

The one who wasn't even supposed to have been there.

"I should've thought of it," he said.

Rhys should've taken the time to think through every possible scenario. He thought he knew Dennis and Ulrik.

He assumed their methods would be repeated from the past, but he had been wrong.

So very wrong.

Con often called him reckless and rash. He'd proven that day that he was both of those things, even with his mate.

He looked up when Rhi appeared in front of him. Her face was lined with regret. "She's done changing if you want to talk to her."

Rhys lifted his gaze to the doorway. He went to Lily as Rhi and Henry walked away. Rhys stopped at the door. Lily was leaning against the slab she'd previously lain dead on. She looked at her hands, which held a string in her fingers that she twirled.

"I've never been so happy as I am to see you alive."

Lily lifted her head, and for the first time he noticed the bruise completely gone from her cheek. Would the wound from the bullet be as well?

"Me too."

He tried to catch her gaze, but her eyes went anywhere but him. It was like a dagger to his heart that she wouldn't look at him. "I was about to take your body to your family."

"I'd like to see them."

"Of course."

"Can we leave now?"

Rhys nodded, unable to find any words his throat was so swollen with emotions. The fact she was so anxious to leave wasn't a good sign. "Lily, please," he begged when she turned her head away. "I thought I'd lost you forever. Talk to me, please. How are you here?"

She blew out a breath. "I was dead. I was shot by my brother and died."

It was like being stabbed with each word she spoke. But Rhys would gladly listen to anything she had to say because she was talking to him.

"I ended up in a place I can only describe as purgatory. That's when he came to me."

That got Rhys's attention. "He?"

"Yes." Lily looked back down at her hands. "He offered to bring me back."

"In exchange for what?"

She shrugged. "He never asked for anything."

"Who was this man?"

"I don't know, and it doesn't matter. He gave me a second chance at life."

Rhys shrugged out of his suit jacket and tossed it aside. He'd worn it for Lily and her family, but it felt too restrictive now. "For that, I'll be eternally grateful to him, but I've learned with such gifts there are consequences."

Finally she lifted her gaze to his. He stared into her bottomless black eyes. "Kyle and Dennis were coming for me. I saw them. The man told me how a soul could be killed and never return in another life."

"In all of my endless years of life, I've never been as happy as I am to be talking with you."

She didn't return his smile.

Rhys rubbed his jaw and felt all of his hope and happiness slipping through his fingers like the sands of time. "You must know I never expected Dennis to keep you with him. We brought Kyle here so we could break whatever hold Dennis had over him."

Lily held up her hand to stop him. "You couldn't think of everything, Rhys. I don't blame you for what happened with Kyle. That lies with me. Had I spoken with my parents, I might have guessed he'd changed."

"You were supposed to be safe on Dreagan."

"Is anyone really safe here?" she asked softly. "You have many enemies. This won't be the last time something happens when it involves the Dragon Kings."

Rhys dropped his chin to his chest. "It's too much for you, is it no'?"

"I died!"

It was her first real show of emotion, and it made him cringe. He lifted his gaze to her and winced when he saw the despair on her face.

"I was dead," she repeated in a hard tone. "All I wanted was to finally be happy. I thought I'd found that with you, but you're immortal, for the love of God. You're a Dragon King. And I'm just a mortal."

He'd had all he could take. Rhys took the three steps separating them and grasped her arms. It felt so good to feel her warmth again that it nearly brought him to his knees.

"You knew what kind of man I was from the beginning," he told her. "You saw everything bad about me. Then you showed me a part of yourself you kept secret. You let me in when I didna want it."

Rhys swallowed and licked his lips. "You scare me. You always have. From the moment you arrived at Dreagan all I've done is think of you. You fill my thoughts constantly. It was you I turned to in my darkest hours after Ireland. It was the verra thought of you that pulled me through it all."

Her eyes filled with tears, but he wasn't going to stop.

"I knew in Edinburgh that I was wholly under your spell. It wasna when we made love, but before when you smiled at me. I quit pretending you didna affect me. And I admitted then what I knew to be truth—you're meant to be mine."

"Stop. Please," she said, freely crying now. "I can't be what you need."

Rhys cupped her face. "Ah, sweetheart. You're what I need just standing there. I love you. I've never spoken those words to another woman before, and I'll never speak them to anyone else. I love you, Lily Ross. Whether you remain with me or leave, I will always love you."

She ducked her head, her shoulders shaking.

"I'll never give up on you. Never," he whispered as he kissed the top of her head. He tilted her face up to his. "One day I'll convince you that we're meant to be together. One day I'll make you fall in love with me."

She shook her head.

He held her gaze, sinking into the dark depths. "Aye. I'll prove I can be a good man. I'll prove that you can depend on me and that I'll keep you safe. I doona care how many years it takes. I'll show you my love, and then perhaps you'll love me."

She sniffed. "It's too late."

Rhys parted his lips, but he no longer knew what to say. She couldn't be lost to him.

"I already love you."

For the second time that day, his heart stopped. Rhys searched her eyes and sighed when he saw the truth in them. "Doona leave me, Lily."

"I can't," she said and sniffed again. "I tried. But I'm scared of all of this, Rhys. It terrifies me."

He softly kissed her lips. "Let me protect you. Be mine, Lily. Be my mate and stay with me for eternity."

"Eternity is a very long time."

"It's no' nearly long enough, lass." He caressed her cheek. "Say you'll stay. Say you willna leave me."

"I could never refuse you," she murmured before wrapping her arms around his neck.

CHAPTER
THIRTY-EIGHT

Ulrik didn't knock as he walked into Mikkel's house near St. Andrews. He strolled into his uncle's office and poured himself some whisky even as the Dark Fae who had teleported him to Dreagan was arguing with Mikkel.

"Where the hell have you been?" Mikkel demanded of Ulrik.

Ulrik turned and raised his glass to his uncle. "I'm recently back from Dreagan."

"Why didn't you return to the designated place?"

"That would've been difficult seeing as how there were Kings everywhere. I choose no' to be seen rather than return to you quicker."

The Dark made a sound of contempt before he vanished. Ulrik cut his eyes to his uncle who sat behind his desk with his elbows resting on the arms of the chair and his fingers steepled.

"The Dark found Kyle wandering the village outside Dreagan and brought him here. Where is Dennis?"

Ulrik lifted one shoulder in a shrug. "I was barely able

to bring Kyle back. Dennis was in pieces. It would've taken me much, much longer."

It was an outright lie, but since no one else could bring back the dead, they had no idea if what he said was true or not.

"Damn," Mikkel said and slammed a hand on his desk. "Dennis was one of my best men here in Britain. Can't you find his soul without touching him?"

Ulrik shook his head.

"Bloody hell."

He finished his whisky and set the glass down before he started walking out.

"Where are you going?" Mikkel demanded.

"To Perth. I'll be getting a visit soon," Ulrik said over his shoulder.

He didn't wait on Mikkel's response. Ulrik was happy he'd driven his own car. He got behind the wheel and quickly drove off. Ulrik knew Rhys would come to Perth, and he was sure Rhys wouldn't be alone.

It was a half-hour later as he drove down the road that Rhi appeared in his passenger seat. He did a double take and flattened his lips in irritation. "That would've been awkward had someone been there."

"Perhaps," she said flippantly. "I want to know why you really brought Lily back."

Ulrik sighed heavily. "I'm fairly certain we've already been over this."

"You glossed over it with your pretty words. I want the truth."

"I told you the truth," he said and glanced at her.

She snorted. "You gave me enough bullshit that I believed you."

"What does it matter what I say? You willna believe it anyway."

"I have a theory," Rhi said as she crossed her arms over her chest.

Ulrik smiled and motioned for her to talk. "By all means, tell me."

Rhi shifted in the seat so she was half-facing him to better see his face. She hadn't been able to stop thinking about Ulrik's reasons since she'd agreed to help him. And she wanted her answers. "I think you felt bad for Lily dying. I think you know all too well what it feels like to lose the love of your life."

His hands tightened briefly on the steering wheel. "You know how it feels to have love betray you."

"We're not talking about me, Ulrik. This is about you. Why would you send your men to Dreagan and kill Lily only to bring her back?"

That's the part that kept confusing Rhi.

"Tell me you're not working alone. Tell me someone else had Lily killed."

"You think too much."

"And you wiped every shred of emotion from your face," she said with a smile.

He threw her a dark look. "And that means what?"

"That you're trying to be careful about what you say or do. I know you want to kill Con. I know you want your vengeance. What I could never understand is why you would target Rhys or anyone other than Con. If you wanted one of the Kings to suffer the inability to shift, that would've been directed straight at Con."

The tires squealed on the McLaren as Ulrik slammed on the brakes and jerked the wheel so the car pulled to the side of the road. He looked at Rhi with fury in his gold eyes. "Enough!"

"Because I'm right?"

"No' even close. What do you want, Rhi?"

She refused to look away from him. "I want to know if someone can do bad things and still be decent."

His anger faded, replaced with unease. "You broke free of the Chains of Mordare. You held out against Balladyn turning you Dark."

"Did I?" she asked in a soft voice. "I'm not so sure."

Ulrik put the car in park and ran a hand through his hair. "I'm no' a good man. I have no' been for a verra long time, and I've accepted that."

"You saved Lily. That was good."

"It was for my own interests. I knew Rhys would come for me, as well as the others. I know I'll die, but I refuse to do it until I take Con out."

Rhi scoffed at him. "Are you telling me you brought Lily back from the dead to save your own ass?"

"I am."

It was a valid reason, but she still believed there was more. "And?"

"And?" he repeated with a frown. "There is nothing else."

Rhi looked out the windshield to the dark blue waters of the North Sea. "I can spot a liar easily, Ulrik."

"I've told you the truth."

"You told me part of it."

"That's all there is."

She turned her head to him, and was surprised when he suddenly leaned over and kissed her. When he pulled back, she asked, "What was that for?"

"I've always wanted to know if your kiss would taste as spirited as your words, or as sweet as your walk."

"And?" she asked, unable to keep her curiosity at bay.

He licked his lips. "It's a wee bit of both."

"That's all you'll ever know," she said and teleported out.

Rhi returned to Dreagan in the hopes of discovering that Rhys and Lily had worked everything out. And because it wasn't a good day unless she irritated Con, she popped into his office and leaned casually against the wall.

His black gaze immediately went to her. "Rhys told me you were unable to get into the cottage to save Lily. Is that true?"

"It is," she answered snippily.

"So it was warded," Constantine said with a grin. "I'll need to learn what was used to ward the manor—my office especially—against you."

Rhi was taken aback by the fury that rose so quickly within her. It was the darkness. It always answered swiftly. She turned her face away so Con wouldn't see the anger—or her fear of it.

"This is a private place," Con said, unaware of her turmoil. "I doona appreciate you coming in whenever you damned well feel like it."

The more he talked, the more her temper grew. She had to get away from him and calm down before she did something stupid.

"You've always overstepped our boundaries," Con continued.

Rhi whirled around, only belatedly realizing that she'd begun to glow. "Do you ever shut up?"

Before he could answer, the door opened and a man walked in.

She gaped. It couldn't be Darius.

All of her anger vanished in an instant.

He started to say something to Con, but he paused and turned his head to her. "Rhi."

She was too shocked to even speak. No one had told her Darius had woken. Rhi lifted her chin and pulled her gaze away from Darius. That's when she saw a hint of a frown on Con's face as he regarded her.

A moment later, Henry walked into Con's office. His face brightened when he saw her. "Rhi," he said in a whisper.

It was too much. All of it. She really did need to stay away from Dreagan from now on.

Without a word to anyone, Rhi teleported away.

Henry was more than a little disappointed when Rhi disappeared yet again. He was falling hard for the Light Fae, and the more the Kings warned him away from her, the more he wanted her. Their kiss in the mountain had been breathtaking. It had ended way too soon, but he hoped it wouldn't be the last. Rhi was too amazing a find for him not to pursue her.

"I know that look," Con said to him. "You do understand what the Fae do with humans, right?"

Henry nodded, scratching his chin. "Banan has explained it multiple times, but that's the Dark. The Light only sleep with a human once."

"That's all it takes," Darius said as he sank into one of the two chairs before Con's desk.

Con nodded. "One time with a Light, and you'll never find satisfaction with a mortal female again."

"Who would want to after someone like Rhi?"

Darius leaned back in the chair. "All Fae are forbidden from a relationship with a human. There's nothing that can come of this infatuation with Rhi."

"He's right, Henry. I know she's beautiful, but all Fae are that stunning. If you continue to sleep with a Fae, you'll die."

Henry didn't want to talk about Rhi and their doomed relationship any longer. He cleared his throat and said, "I'm heading into London to track down which of the ten were responsible for betraying me to Ulrik."

"Is there anything we can do to help?" Con asked.

"I'll let you know if there is."

"Please do. We owe you for all that you've done for us."

Henry was taken aback by the King of Kings' declaration. From all he'd learned in his time with the Kings, Con wasn't one to so blithely say such words. "It shouldn't take me long. I'll check in with Banan."

Con waited until Henry left before he shifted his gaze to Darius. "Something on your mind?"

"So Rhi comes and goes as she wants?"

Con closed the file he had been reading and leaned back in his chair. "She's as she's always been."

"I see."

"Our conversation earlier has brought to my attention that I've been lax."

Darius snorted. "You? Lax? I doubt it. What are you going to do? Wake every King who is sleeping?"

"Aye."

Darius sat up, his face a mask of confusion. "Are you serious?"

"I am. I'd like you to begin waking them. Tap whoever else you want to aid you, but make sure everyone wakes. We're going to need them in this war."

CHAPTER
THIRTY-NINE

Lily couldn't look away from the three colossal silver dragons sleeping so peacefully within the cage deep underground in the mountain she had stared at so often from the store.

"This is what I promised to show," Rhys said from beside her.

"I saw you instead." She glanced at him. "Can I touch them?"

"Of course."

Lily recalled how warm Rhys's scales had been. She gently rested her hand upon the head of the closest Silver. Once more the scales were warm.

"You're right, you know," Rhys said. "We do have many enemies. There's a war brewing, Lily. You saw just the tip of what is coming."

Ever since she'd been brought back from the dead, she was slowly forgetting what the place she had been in was like. All the fear she'd felt within that place was also leaving her. To think that fear had almost made her walk away from Rhys. Had he not pressed her, had he not spoken such sweet words, she might have walked away.

"Do you want me to leave?"

Rhys grasped her face in his hands and stared deeply into her eyes. "Never. I want you as mine for always, but you need to know what you'll be getting."

She pulled her hand away from the Silver and faced Rhys as he dropped his arms. "Then tell me."

"The Kings doona marry. We have a ceremony that bonds us to our mates and vice versa."

"All right," she said with a nod. "That sounds simple enough."

He looked down for a moment. "You'll be marked with a tattoo of a dragon eye on your arm, and you'll become immortal. The only way you die is if I die."

Lily raised both brows. "Wow."

"That's the upside. There's a down."

"Of course," she mumbled. Lily took a deep breath and waited for him to explain.

"There are no children."

Her disappointment was intense. She had always dreamed of children. "At all?"

"It takes a lot for a mortal to become pregnant with our children. Worse than that is that most times there is a miscarriage within a few weeks. In the verra rare instances that a mortal doesna miscarry, the child is stillborn."

This certainly was a downside. No wonder Lily never saw any of the women pregnant around Dreagan.

"That's no' all," Rhys continued. He turned his face to the side to look at the Silvers. "Your family can no' know of us. Even if our secret is kept, they'll begin to notice you doona age."

"Which means I'll need to sever all ties with them?"

Rhys nodded slowly. "Cassie, Elena, Jane, Denae, Sammi, and Iona had no family to speak of. Shara does, but they're Dark and already know of us. Your situation is one we've no' encountered before."

For four years all Lily thought about was returning to her family. How could she sever ties with them for good, especially now that Kyle was dead? It was Henry who had informed them that Kyle was killed in an accident, his body burned beyond recognition. There would be a funeral to attend as well.

"I know it's a lot to ask. I willna willingly let you leave, but it is your family," Rhys said. "I'll continue to fight for you and our love."

Lily thought about walking away from Rhys, and she knew she would never bear it. Nor could she lie to her family over and over. "I'm not ready to say good-bye to my family, but I also can't leave you."

"I understand your need to be with your family after how you left four years ago. I need you to also understand that we need our secret to remain that way. Guy can wipe your memories of everything you know about Dreagan as well as anything about Dennis from your mind. That should keep Ulrik from you."

"So I'll forget about you," she said slowly. "Will you have your memories wiped?"

Rhys shook his head.

"I didn't lie earlier. All of this frightens me tremendously. I don't know how I would fit into this world, but I don't want to leave it. I love you, Rhys. I look into your eyes and I see our future there."

"Then be my mate, Lily. We'll figure out about your family along the way. I willna lie. Ulrik is out for blood, and he'll stop at nothing to bring us all down. If you're mated to me, you'll be hunted just like I will."

Lily lifted her chin. "Then let them come. I'll have my Dragon King beside me. Children or not, my family or not, my place is beside you on Dreagan."

Rhys seized her mouth in a fiery kiss. She clung to him, her body a mass of need.

Suddenly Rhys lifted his head. "In one day I lost you, and then got you back. You mean everything to me, Lily. You are my soul, my breath. My heart."

"And you are my soul, my breath, my heart. And my dragon."

Lily glanced at the Silvers and walked with Rhys from the cavern. Whatever came tomorrow, she knew her place—right beside her Dragon King.

EPILOGUE

A week later...

Rhys stood in the mountain staring at the tunnel that Lily would walk through at any moment. He'd wanted to give her more time before the mating ceremony, but Lily had been insistent on doing it sooner rather than later.

He certainly wasn't going to complain. As soon as they were mated, she would be immortal. After a bit of questioning, Rhys discovered it was Ulrik who had brought Lily back to life. Rhys still didn't know why Ulrik did it, but he wanted to know. The few instances he'd thought of going to Perth, he only had to look at Lily and feel their love.

Whatever curse Ulrik gave him was broken, and Lily was alive. Rhys wasn't about to forgive or forget what Ulrik had done, but love had a way of putting things into perspective—like spending hours making love to Lily instead of planning Ulrik's death.

As much as he hated it, the other females talked to Lily extensively about what it meant to be bound to a King. Rhys worried for all of a minute that she would change her mind. Then he looked into her eyes and saw the love there.

Rhys smiled as soon as he saw her. His breath locked in his chest as he took in the vision that was his woman. The gown was a soft yellow with a band of intricate crystals showing off her tiny waist. The sleeves draped off her shoulders in soft pleats and were held in place by a single strap of yellow. The neck of the dress crisscrossed to show just a hint of her breasts. With her long black hair gathered in a messy updo, Rhys was held mesmerized.

"You're a vision," he said when she reached him.

Her dark eyes were glowing with excitement. "And you look handsome as ever in your kilt."

Rhys adjusted his tux jacket and smiled when he saw how her dress exposed the scars she'd hidden for so long. She had come a long way from the timid woman who'd first arrived at Dreagan.

He took her hands and felt something against his finger. When he looked down he noted the five-carat cushion-cut yellow sapphire set in a thin band of platinum. Rhys gave Con a nod of appreciation. None of the Kings knew what gift Con would give the mates, but Con always managed to get just the right thing for each of them.

"Ready?" Rhys asked Lily.

Her smile widened. "Try and stop me."

They faced Con together as the ceremony began.

Warrick stood at the very back. It wasn't that he didn't appreciate or approve of Rhys and Lily's union, it was just that he chafed at being around so many. None of the Kings understood why he felt this way, and he didn't bother to tell them.

He waited to witness Rhys and Lily share a kiss and the dragon mark to appear on her upper arm before Warrick turned on his heel and walked out of the cavern. There would be celebrating all night long in the manor. It made him itch just thinking about it.

Warrick began to shed his clothes when he came to the entrance of the mountain. With a thought, he shifted into dragon form and took to the skies. It was the only place he felt truly at home—and at peace.

He was alone with only his thoughts and the moon and stars. It also gave him a chance to look in on the humans, who fascinated him to no end. Other Kings despised them, but Warrick found them intriguing. Not that he would ever tell the others that.

The one thing he never had to worry about was Con sending him on any kind of mission with other Kings. The short one he willingly went on with Rhys had been enough to prove he was much better off by himself.

As it had always been.

As it should be.

Rhi wandered the ruins of Pompeii. She had long been fascinated by how beautifully the city had been preserved by the ash of the volcano. It was a pity that none survived. She remembered Pompeii before the volcano. It had been a vibrant, beautiful city laid to waste in a matter of hours.

Which would be what happened soon to the entire realm. Perhaps she should go to Usaeil and convince the queen to have all Light Fae leave the realm for good. That meant she would leave behind her lover and any last shred of hope of rekindling their love.

"Perhaps that's for the best," she told a bird who'd landed on a stone near her.

The bird flew away, and that's when she spotted Balladyn. He stood at the far end of the road watching her. His long black and silver hair was free of any braids. He wore black pants and a dark gray shirt.

Rhi was tired of running from him, tired of running from the darkness within her. What had it gained her? She was welcomed by only a few at Dreagan, and her lover still didn't want her.

Balladyn held out his hand and simply waited.

Rhi turned away, trying to fight against his pull. After several minutes, she gave up. Rhi walked to Balladyn and stopped just short of his outstretched hand. She looked into his red eyes, then placed her hand in his.

Read on for an excerpt from the next book by
Donna Grant

SOUL SCORCHED

**Coming soon from
St. Martin's Paperbacks**

Darcy jumped at the sound that came from the conservatory. She got to her feet, her heart pumping wildly. Then a tall form came into sight.

"Warrick," she whispered.

Her smiled died before it got going when she let her gaze run over him. Blood splattered his shirt, or what was left of his shirt. It was torn and ripped so that it barely hung on his shoulders.

His gaze was direct, unblinking as he stared at her as if he hadn't just been in a battle with the Dark Fae.

Without thinking, she ran to him looking for injuries. She gently moved aside his still wet shirt in case there was a wound beneath, but all she saw was skin and the black and red ink of the tat.

Then she recalled what he was and his immortality.

Darcy dropped her arms and met his cobalt gaze as he remembered the fear that had consumed her not that long ago. "They surrounded you, and then I couldn't see you."

"The fight wouldna have lasted that long had I been in dragon form," he said matter of factly.

"I was scared out of my mind, and you make a joke?"

"It isna a jest. In my real form, I could do much more damage."

She shuddered, remembering Ulrik's memories she saw and the sheer size of some of the dragons. She turned away, embarrassed to let her emotions get the better of her. "Of course. I forgot."

"Where you worried for me, lass?"

She halted and looked over her shoulder at his softly spoken words. He actually sounded surprised. "Yes."

After everything she said to him, he returned to the shop, to her. There was no anger in his visage or his voice, as if her harsh words never happened.

He risked his own life for her. Though he was immortal, there was no doubt the Dark could do damage to the Kings.

"I'll get you out of Edinburgh if that's what you want," Warrick said. "Damn Con and what he has planned for you."

Darcy was so taken aback that, for a moment, she couldn't find any words. "I thought Con wanted information."

"If you give it, then Con will have it. But I willna keep you here with this many Dark just so Con can have some tidbit on Ulrik."

"Even if that tidbit might be the difference in Con winning over Ulrik?"

Warrick rubbed his hand on the back of his neck and sighed.

Just as Darcy thought. "Ulrik is gaining in this war, isn't he? You need information to win."

"There's a chance that even if I get you to Skye, the Dark will attack you there."

She snorted. "They could try."

"You've never faced the Fae, Darcy. You doona know what it means to fight them. As powerful as Skye magic is, it isna enough to keep the Dark out."

Could Darcy bring such repulsive terrors to Skye? To her family? Just to save her own ass? No, she couldn't. Regardless of how scared she was, this fiasco couldn't reach Skye.

"Can the Dark hurt you?"

Warrick made a face, confusion marring his features. "They can no' kill us."

"But they can hurt you?"

"Aye."

It felt like someone kicked her in the stomach. "You were injured out there, weren't you?"

"I'm fine."

But he wasn't before. All she had to do was look at his clothes to see how vicious the battle had been. He stood alone against the Dark while being bombarded with their magic.

How many wounds had he sustained that healed before he came to see her? She inwardly cringed just thinking about it. And she was the one who sent him out because of her anger.

"So their magic can harm you?" she asked.

"It can weaken us, and they can also make it where we can no' shift into dragon form for a while."

"What else?" She didn't know how she knew there was more, but she did.

Warrick blew out a harsh breath. "During the Fae Wars, they captured two Kings. Both lost their minds. We had to kill them."

Darcy's legs grew weak. She grabbed hold of the edge of her desk to keep standing. The thought of Warrick being captured and tortured by the Dark made her sick to her stomach. That couldn't happen to such a proud, powerful man. "I don't want that to happen to you."

"It willna."

She stared at him aghast. "I'm sure the two Kings they captured thought the same thing."

Warrick shrugged, as if it happened every day. "It's part of being who we are."

"You and Thorn should leave before neither of you can."

It was his turn to look at her as if she'd sprouted wings. "You can no' be serious."

"I am. I'm not going to bring this," she said, gesturing to the front where the Dark were, "to Skye. I'm also not going to be responsible for the Dark taking you or Thorn."

"Remaining here is mine and Thorn's decision. No' yours."

Darcy shook her head in dismay. "You have no idea how it felt to watch them surround you as you stood out there alone against them. I thought you were gone!"

Her words hung in the air for long moments as they stared at each other. Warrick's cobalt eyes were bright, his gaze intense.

All Darcy could think about was his kisses. The rest—Con, Ulrik, the Dark, the elders on Skye, and even her family—faded away.

"I promised I would keep you safe. I'll no' leave until you are."

Darcy rushed to him, throwing her arms around his neck as she planted her lips against his. He enfolded her in his embrace, holding her tight as he tilted his head and parted his lips.

A low, deep moan rumbled his chest as they kissed. She slid her hands into his wet hair and sank into the kiss until she was living, breathing him.

It didn't take long for the flames of desire to overtake them. Darcy was teased by the bits of his skin she felt against her from his torn shirt. She reached between them while they kissed and ripped his shirt in half. There was a smile on his lips as he let it fall to the floor.

Their kisses became heated, frantic as they sought to get closer to the other. With a flick of his hand, he unbuttoned her jeans and had them unzipped. Then his hand was down her pants cupping her sex.

Darcy gasped for breath as he kissed across her jaw and down her throat as his fingers began to lightly stroke her through her panties.

She clung to him, her breath locked in her lungs at the force of desire that tightened low in her belly. His tongue was hot against her skin, his lips soft.

In the next instant, his hand was gone, leaving her squeezing her legs together to hold back the tide of need that enveloped her.

Her shirt was pulled over her head so quickly she had no idea what he was about. There was a ripping noise as her bra followed. Then he jerked her against his chest, skin to skin.

She looked into his eyes and recognized the same longing, the same yearning she felt within herself.

He bent, grabbing her bottom, and then stood. With her legs now wrapped around him, he claimed her mouth in a wild, fiery kiss.

Darcy didn't have long to wonder where he was going as he began to walk. He leaned over, holding her firmly with one hand as he gave one swipe of her desk with the other, clearing it of everything.

He pressed her against the top of the desk, his thick arousal rubbing against her already swollen sex. He rocked against her several times before he pulled back, ending the kiss.

"I need you, lass," he whispered in her ear.

Darcy opened her eyes to find him over her. "How fast can you get out of those clothes?"

A grin started right before he straightened and kicked off his boots while pulling down his pants. Darcy wasn't having as much luck with her own attire. She only got one boot off in the time it took him to get undressed.

He yanked off her other boot. Then he grabbed her jeans and pulled. For him, they slid right off, leaving her in nothing but her black silk panties.

His gaze wandered over her, beginning at her feet and working upward. As soon as his eyes landed on her breasts, her nipples hardened. He smiled in anticipation as he stepped between her legs once more.